VETERINARY SURGEON

By the Author

Veterinary Partner

Veterinary Technician

Veterinary Surgeon

VETERINARY SURGEON

by
Nancy Wheelton

2021

VETERINARY SURGEON

© 2021 By Nancy Wheelton. All Rights Reserved.

ISBN 13: 978-1-63679-043-5

This Trade Paperback Original Is Published By
Bold Strokes Books, Inc.
P.O. Box 249
Valley Falls, NY 12185

First Edition: October 2021

CREDITS

EDITORS: VICTORIA VILLASEÑOR AND CINDY CRESAP
PRODUCTION DESIGN: SUSAN RAMUNDO
COVER DESIGN BY TAMMY SEIDICK

CHAPTER ONE

W ho leaves a dog whelping and does nothing? It's neglect. It's criminal," Kay said as she rolled her stiff, aching shoulders with annoyance.

Dr. Lauren Cornish shook her head. "It's not neglect. She was a stray. The Palmers have been feeding her for a couple of weeks, but she wouldn't let them touch her. She didn't show up for dinner last night, so they went looking for her and found her whelping. They're good people and they brought Casey here."

"Casey? Isn't she a stray?"

"They said she looked like a Casey." Lauren shrugged. "So, they named her. You're really upset. I've never seen you like this."

Kay adjusted the hot water bottles so one was along Casey's back and one was against her chest. "I can't stand to see animals hurting, but I'm glad somebody cares about her."

"They're going to adopt her and pay the bill."

"X-rays are ready," Val said as she entered the treatment room.

Kay tapped some buttons on the keyboard to pull up the X-rays. "Sorry, I get it. It's just—"

"Oh, the poor puppy." Val stared at the X-rays in horror.

Valerie Connor looked like she might cry, but as head veterinary technician at Prairie Veterinary Services, or PVS, Kay figured she'd seen worse. But then, Val had a big heart and a soft spot for anything on four legs.

Kay inspected the black cockapoo lying on the exam table and ran a gentle hand over Casey's head. She studied Casey's X-rays displayed on the thirty-two-inch monitor. "Two puppies? Did she have any already?"

Lauren shook her head. "Nope. No other puppies."

Val pointed to the image on the computer screen. "They're huge pups."

Casey was cold and lethargic and in poor shape. Kay jammed her hands into the pockets of her lab coat and took deep breaths until her pulse lowered and she could speak without screaming in frustration. "Casey needs emergency surgery to remove the puppies." She petted Casey. "I'm surprised she's still conscious."

"She's a tough dog. After all, she survived a Saskatchewan winter outside." Lauren rested her hand on Kay's shoulder. "I told the Palmers that Casey was in good hands with our new expert surgeon, Dr. Kay Gallant. I know you can do this." Lauren pocketed her stethoscope and turned to leave. "Well, I'd better carry on with appointments or they'll stack up. Call me if you need any help. Good luck."

"Thanks. Val and I've got this." PVS was busy with enough small animal clients that the receptionists booked Lauren all morning doing vaccinations and medical appointments and Kay had a full day of scheduled surgeries. It would be a longer day with Casey to look after, but Casey was her responsibility now. "Let's get this done."

Kay opened the drug cupboard and started to mix up her premedication mixture of ketamine and other drugs. It would knock Casey out so they could intubate her and put her on a gas anesthetic. "Val, we're on our last bottle of ketamine."

"Really?" Val peered over Kay's shoulder. "But we had three last week."

Kay laughed. "Now that you're at university two days a week you forget how busy we are. Lots of surgery these days. Can you hold Casey while I give her the injection?"

"Three bottles. I'm sure of it," Val muttered. "I'll put in an order right away."

"Thanks. Okay, Casey, time to feel better. Good girl," Kay said as she administered the premedication. In the surgery log under Casey's name, she recorded the amount of each drug she used, along with Casey's name, weight, and her owner and then got to work.

At seven p.m., Kay yawned and stretched her shoulders yet again as her horrifically busy day ended. Casey's surgery had gone well and then she and Val spent hours taking care of her after-surgery needs and checking on the new puppies.

Kay leaned against the counter and wrote notes in the medical record. She glanced at Casey, who slept peacefully in her kennel. "You're a tough dog, Casey. Good girl." She checked the IV fluids and antibiotics. Her plan had been to sleep in the clinic and keep an eye on Casey, but the two veterinary technicians, Val and Minnie, volunteered to take turns checking on patients throughout the night. Kay planned to be back at six a.m.

Kay focused on the gray schnauzer in the kennel next to Casey. "You're a tough dog too, Jackson." Jackson had arrived at PVS with a broken leg. She'd immobilized the fracture and treated him for shock. No point in rushing him to surgery until he was stable. Minnie and Val would have their hands full tonight. Val had left earlier, so Kay sent her a quick text with updates on the two dogs.

Ian Wilson, her boss, hadn't scheduled Kay to work the next day, but now she had Jackson's surgery and she wanted to see Casey in the morning. It would take her an hour and a quarter to drive from Thresherton to her apartment in Saskatoon and the same again to return. She hated all the driving but didn't have the money for a motel. If she cleaned off the back seat of her car, could she sleep there?

Lauren stepped into the treatment room. "I'm headed home now. Want to stay over at Poplarcreek tonight? I heard you tell Val and Minnie you're operating on Jackson tomorrow."

"You could operate on Jackson, but since I'm here, I can do it."

Lauren shrugged. "I could, but you're a trained surgeon and I'm just a country vet. Nope, Jackson is better off with you. Anyway, come to Poplarcreek. We have lots of room."

Kay fiddled with her notebook. She'd only been part-time at PVS for two weeks and was curious to see how Lauren lived and to meet Callie Anderson. Callie dropped into PVS occasionally, but the one time Kay had been there at the same time, she'd been too busy with a complicated surgery to say hi. But tonight, she'd meet Callie. She couldn't possibly be as beautiful as everyone said. "Thanks, I appreciate it."

"Want to follow me?"

"No, thanks. Give me your address, please. My phone has GPS. I'll only be another ten minutes or so, but I don't want to hold you up." Lauren dictated her address and Kay entered it into her phone.

"See you later," Lauren said and left.

Kay did a final check of all the cages, talking to the animals as though they understood her, and then verified that all the doors were locked and turned off the lights, except a small light left on for the dogs. She loved this peaceful time of day when the only sounds were an IV machine and snoring dogs. She rolled her shoulders and found the ache was gone. Her surgeries were done for the day and her patients were doing well.

With a final glance to ensure the treatment room was tidy, she collected her shoulder bag and computer and locked up. Her GPS led her to Poplarcreek, and she parked beside Lauren's silver four-door pickup truck which dwarfed her rusty two-door sedan. Her first purchase when she had the money would be a decent car. Not the reject from the demolition derby she currently drove.

Stiff and sore from a busy day, Kay gave her poor knee a second to stretch as she exited her car. She glanced around the property and took in the several barns and a huge house. At work, Lauren told her that Callie raised crops, horses, and purebred Charolais cattle. She pictured the family enjoying the balmy June weather while sitting in the comfortable chairs on the porch. It wasn't her life plan, but she could tell it suited Lauren.

She sighed and listened to the peaceful evening at Poplarcreek. Only the buzzing insects and the quiet noise of Callie's animals broke the stillness of the air. She'd trade the noise of the city for the peace of the country too as long as she wasn't too far from the action. Kay grinned. But Lauren didn't live at Poplarcreek for the property. She hefted her bags, walked up the porch stairs, and knocked on the door.

"Hi, Kay, welcome to Poplarcreek. I'm Callie."

Kay put her bags down as she accepted the proffered handshake. Tall, with blond hair and model-perfect features, Callie Anderson towered over her. Her tank top showed off tanned, finely muscled arms as if she lifted weights every day. She was just as stunning as everyone said.

"Sorry, to rush you, but dinner's ready." Callie grabbed Kay's bags and carried them both in one hand, as if they weighed nothing. "I'll show you to your room and we'll have dinner."

Kay kicked off her shoes in the mudroom and hurried after Callie.

"This is my farm office," Callie said. "I only have a fold-out couch in here. It's not new, but the springs have bounce, and I purchased the mattress last year. Next door is a full bathroom. Will this suit you? I understand you prefer to avoid stairs."

"Thanks. Climbing upstairs isn't the problem, but coming down is painful." Kay rubbed her left knee to ease the pain. Her knee always hurt a little, but tonight after a full day of running around at work it was hot and puffy and screamed for rest.

"Kay?"

"Pardon?" Kay's mind had wandered, and she shook her head to refocus on Callie.

"I put fresh towels in the bathroom. Can I get you anything else?"

"I'm good, thanks."

"Great. I'll leave you to it. Lauren's gone upstairs to shower and change. Dinner as soon as you're ready." Callie tossed the last sentence over her shoulder as she strode from the room.

Kay looked around Callie's farm office. She examined several books and discovered the shelves were full of old account ledgers and books on animal husbandry, some over fifty years old. Modern books and recent farming magazines were within an easy reach of the desk and laptop computer. Callie kept a nice mix of the traditional and modern.

Kay unzipped her overnight bag. She needed to curb her curiosity and stop her bad habit of snooping because dinner was ready. She quickly washed and changed her clothes. When she entered the kitchen, she barely held back a gasp. Overflowing dishes of food covered the table. "Can I do anything to help?" She asked out of politeness, but in no way did Callie need her help.

Callie pointed to a chair. "Sit. Relax. I've got this." Callie placed several more dishes of food on the table.

Kay dropped into a chair and pressed her hands against her stomach to smother the growl that announced lunch was seven hours ago. Lauren came downstairs into the kitchen and sidled up behind Callie. She rested her hands on Callie's hips and kissed her on the nape. Lauren's tracksuit was tight through the middle accentuating her significant baby bump that she disguised at the clinic under a loose lab coat.

Lauren grinned and rubbed her abdomen. "You're staring."

Kay dipped her head. "Sorry."

"Callie and I've been for several ultrasounds. No sign of twins. I'm just big."

"Twins?" A girl bounced into the room and hugged Lauren around the waist. "Are we having twins?"

"No twins, honey," Callie said. "We were joking because Lauren is big already."

"Okay, Mom."

Lauren lived with Callie and Callie's ten-year-old daughter, but Becky looked nothing like Callie, except in the height department. Becky was almost as tall as Kay's five feet four. Val's daughter, Gwen, followed Becky in and hugged Lauren. Kay grinned. Gwen Connor with her red hair and blue eyes looked identical to Val.

"Girls," Lauren said. "Meet Dr. Gallant. She just started at PVS."

Kay shook hands with Becky and Gwen. "Just call me Kay. I recognize both of you from the photos your moms show everyone who comes in." She only had a few pictures of her brothers and their families on her phone. How long had it been since she'd been home? Kay pushed away an unexpected longing for family and shook her head to refocus.

"Thanks for putting me up tonight," Kay said.

Callie sat down. "I'm just glad you're here and that Lauren can stop doing surgery."

"We're not sure if anesthetics would harm the baby. It's better with the new machines and scavenging systems, but we're not taking any chances," Lauren said.

Callie kissed Lauren's cheek. "We've got lots of room and you have an open invitation to stay anytime you want."

"Thanks." Kay smiled into Callie's genuine warm blue eyes and could tell she meant every word she said. When was the last time she'd sat down to a family dinner with her parents and brothers? Had it really been over two years ago? Becky and Gwen joked around like sisters, just like her brothers used to, but without all the punching her brothers did at that age. A wave of loneliness washed thorough her. She missed her brothers and that shocked her. These days, the people in her life were clients, colleagues, and casual hookups. And that suited her. She was too busy with her career for family, but maybe in a year or two she'd go home for Christmas.

CHAPTER TWO

Dinner was a noisy affair. Gwen and Becky talked and seldom required input from the adults. That suited Kay because she didn't have much to say. It had been a long day, and she was worried about Casey and Jackson. Her phone vibrated in her pocket and she checked for an update from Val. Kay sighed with relief as she read the text telling her the patients were well. Jackson was young and healthy, but Casey was in rough shape, even after a successful surgery.

"Sorry, did you say something?" Kay's brain resurfaced to find the other four staring at her. Her mind had wandered again.

"I told Gwen about the orthopedic surgery you're doing tomorrow on Jackson. I told her it's a tricky one." Lauren squeezed Gwen's shoulder. "Gwen's going to be a veterinarian, and if she didn't have school tomorrow, she'd ask to watch."

"A veterinarian? Aren't you too young to be making that decision?" Kay asked.

Gwen sat back and peered anxiously at Lauren. Lauren patted her hand. "Don't worry. I chose a career at your age or younger. Sometimes you know what's right for you and sometimes you need time to examine your options."

"Sorry," Kay said. "I just meant the world is full of wonderful opportunities." She'd let herself be steered into a career in the military, which nearly killed her. "Stick to your dreams, if you can."

"What would you be if you weren't a vet?" Lauren asked.

Kay tapped her lip and pretended to think. "A kept woman or a lottery winner."

Callie and Lauren laughed, but Gwen and Becky looked confused.

Becky shrugged. "I haven't decided what I'm going to do. I love art, but I also like farming and basketball."

"You have plenty of time to decide, honey." Callie draped her arm around Becky's shoulders and kissed her cheek.

While Callie and Becky looked at each other, a wave of envy flowed through Kay. She caught the love and easy understanding between mother and daughter. She'd been so close to her parents growing up, but they'd drifted apart. She felt no pull to visit and had left them in Charlottetown, Prince Edward Island, more than two thousand miles away. Unfortunately, her brothers lived near their parents, and it was an expensive plane ticket to go home for a visit.

"What is it?" Callie asked.

Callie and Becky, heads both tilted to one side, looked at Kay. Kay smiled. They were undoubtedly mother and daughter regardless of whether they shared genetic material. "Sorry, I didn't mean to stare."

"You think I don't look like my mom," Becky said. "My other mom, Liz Anderson, had me. She was an RCMP officer and died on the job when I was four."

"Oh wow. How terrible for you." She was surprised at how easily Becky shared the information and wasn't sure how to respond.

"Knock knock," a deep voice called from the mudroom.

"Mitch!" Becky jumped to her feet and ran to the door, with Gwen on her heels. Callie rose and followed at a more sedate pace. Kay caught Lauren's subtle eye roll. Whoever this Mitch was, Lauren didn't like him.

Becky and Gwen entered the kitchen with a tall RCMP officer. "Kay, meet our friend Mitch. Officer Mitchell."

Kay's stomach flipped and her senses kicked into overdrive. Mitch was a gorgeous, tall woman in an RCMP uniform with short brown hair cut in an almost military style. She had bold, hazel eyes that took in the room with one glance.

"Hi, Kay, pleased to meet you."

Mitch stepped around the table to Kay's chair and stuck out her hand. She clasped it and watched Mitch's hand engulf her much smaller one. "Nice to meet you, but have we met before? I feel like..." Kay gave her flirtiest smile.

Mitch shook her head. "I'd remember you."

"I just heard myself." Kay laughed. "That sounded like a bad pickup line." It was a bad pickup line, but still intentional. No way would Officer Gorgeous get away without her making some attempt to indicate her interest.

"No problem."

Callie returned with cutlery, a glass, and a plate and set them across from Kay. Mitch excused herself to use the bathroom. When she reappeared, she dropped into her chair. "Sorry to barge in on you at dinner."

"Isn't a free dinner the point?" Lauren mumbled.

Callie gave Lauren a sharp look.

Kay smirked down at her plate. Mitch must have done something serious to annoy Lauren. She got along with everyone.

"How're you doing, Lauren?" Mitch asked.

Kay sensed the slight stiffening in Lauren's posture as if she waited for a blow.

"Fine, thanks, Mitch. How are you?" Lauren replied in clipped tones.

"I'm good. You look amazing. Pregnancy agrees with you."

Kay grinned. She enjoyed watching Lauren and Mitch interact, and so did Callie who smiled down at her plate as Lauren blinked, clearly stunned at the compliment.

Dinner picked up where it left off, except now Becky and Gwen were quizzing Mitch about her job. She liked Mitch's warm ready smile and the relaxed, easy way she joked with the kids while still imparting serious advice about staying out of trouble. She had a natural way with children and was probably one of those women who wanted a houseful of kids. How did a successful career woman have the time for that?

After dinner, Gwen and Becky ran upstairs to play. "You two are on kitchen duty tonight," Callie called after them.

"Yes, Mom."

"Yes, Callie."

"I can help," Kay said.

Callie shook her head. "You've had a long day. I'll call them when we're done in the kitchen and they can bang the dishes around all they want. It's good for them to do chores and help out around the house and the farm."

Kay sipped her milk. The others looked as if they planned to linger at the table, which was good because she wasn't ready to go yet. She'd stay if she could stare at Mitch. "Are there many lesbians in Thresherton?" It wasn't exactly smooth, but she tended to speak her mind and think later.

Callie waved her hands. "Thresherton is a real hotbed. As far as we know, the gay community is us, Sonny Bishop, she's a CFIA veterinarian, and Val and Ronnie."

"Ronnie? Minnie mentioned Ronnie the other day. I assumed Ronnie was a man."

Lauren gave a comical shudder. "Whew. Better not let Val hear you say that. Because she wears makeup and feminine clothing, some people, including other lesbians, mistake her for straight."

Kay grimaced. "I get that."

Callie leaned toward Kay. "Ronnie is Sharon Yakimoto. She teaches English at the Thresherton Public School. Val and Ronnie fell in love last year after Val saved Ronnie's dog."

"Bromadiolone poisoning," Lauren said. "Val told me Dover was in rough shape when Ronnie brought him to the clinic, but he survived."

"I'm glad," Kay said. "So, are all of you from Thresherton?"

Callie squeezed Lauren's hand. "Lauren is from Ontario, Ronnie Manitoba, Sonny Alberta and I grew up in British Columbia. Mitch is from Saskatchewan but grew up in Regina. Thresherton is Val's hometown, and you'll soon see what that means."

Kay nodded. "I have already. She knows everybody and they all know her."

Callie laughed. "When they go for a stroll after dinner, Ronnie says people stop them all the time to talk to Val."

"You're from Prince Edward Island, right?" Mitch asked.

Kay smiled. She wasn't surprised to find they'd been talking about her. "I grew up in PEI."

"It's a beautiful province," Mitch said. "Where did you go to school?"

She anticipated Mitch's next two questions and answered those too. "I went to vet school at the Atlantic Veterinary College in Charlottetown, and interned at OVC, the Ontario Veterinary College in Guelph, Ontario. I'm in my third and final year of the small animal surgical residency at the Western College of Veterinary Medicine in Saskatoon and when I'm done, I'm headed to the US. I'm hoping to land a job at Davis or Cornell."

"Davis or Cornell? Where's that?"

"UC Davis is in California. Cornell University is in New York State. I have lots of options, but those two are my top choices."

"Were you in vet school at the same time Lauren was?" Mitch asked.

"Lauren was years ahead of me. I'm a little younger and didn't start university until I was twenty-four."

"Where were you before university?" Mitch looked contemplative, as if she were working on a puzzle.

Kay searched Mitch's expression. "I was in the military for a few years, but it was too structured. Too much yes sir, no ma'am for me. You must get that, being a cop?"

"I do, but it doesn't bother me. Our detachment commander is a good leader."

Kay waggled her eyebrows. "So, no family in Thresherton? Are you all alone?" She wasn't trying to be subtle, but if Mitch were taken, she'd back off.

Mitch smiled warmly at Callie. "Not alone. Not with such good friends at Poplarcreek. This is my family."

Kay was about to make a joke but bit back the comment. Genuine affection passed between Callie and Mitch, and even Lauren added in a smile. She didn't have any friends at the college. There were lots of work colleagues she hung out with on the job, but she'd turned down every invitation to meet their families until nobody asked anymore. Friends, family, and love would hold her back. And distract her from her job and her goals.

"Kay?"

"Sorry." Kay looked up and was struck again by Mitch's eyes that seemed to miss nothing. Kay wasn't up for love, but lovers was another option. She leaned closer across the table and smiled. "I was just thinking about some patients." Kay rested her chin in her palm. "When do I get your life story?"

"What do you want to know?"

"Do you have a girlfriend?" Mitch hadn't answered that question. Now it was time to be direct.

"No. You?"

Kay smirked and shook her head slowly. This had possibilities. Staying at Poplarcreek had been a good idea.

"Callie forgot Thomas and Marcus. They run this amazing upscale restaurant twenty minutes east of here. They moved from Vancouver for the quiet and are only open four days a week."

"I'll keep that in mind, but I don't eat out much. I'm still a student and my budget is tight. My version of eating out is having a packed lunch in the park." She waited. Had mentioning the restaurant been a segue to something more?

Callie squeezed Lauren's hand. "We eat at Thomas and Marcus's restaurant twice a year, if we're lucky. After last year, I'm also watching my money. I had an expensive calving season and I'm still paying the vet bill."

Kay's head spun with conversation and new information. She never spent three hours chatting with a group of lesbians. At a bar or club, there was minimal conversation until she found a woman to take home. She didn't have steady girlfriends or close friends because they got in the way of her plans. She only needed sex and surgery.

A job at PVS would give her excellent experience and help her find a surgical position at a university in the USA. A position at Davis had the added benefit of California girls, but Saskatchewan had women too. It was clear from the dinnertime conversation that Sonny and Mitch were single lesbians, and local. Her time here was temporary, and she'd move on like she always did. But that didn't mean she couldn't have a little fun in the meantime. Life in Thresherton had become a little more interesting.

CHAPTER THREE

When they finished dinner, Kay stood. "Thanks for a wonderful dinner, but I'm exhausted. I can hardly keep my eyes open. Night, everyone."

Mitch searched for some topic of conversation to keep Kay at the table, but her mind drew a blank. Maybe she'd chased her off? Kay had steered the conversation away from family. Maybe she wasn't that close to hers.

"Night, Kay," Lauren and Callie said in unison.

Mitch rose when Kay did. "I should probably go too. Callie, can I borrow your old binoculars? I dropped mine and they're in for repairs."

"Sure. They're in my office. Kay's staying there."

"I can get them another time." She didn't want to intrude.

"Get them now." Kay headed toward the office and looked over her shoulder. "Or later, if you want to tuck me in."

Mitch shrugged, attempting a look of nonchalance, and followed Kay. "Thanks, I'll be quick."

She followed Kay into the office and with a glance took in the fold-out couch and the clothes in a heap on the bed. She scanned Callie's desk and bookshelf and scrambled for something to say. "Have you ever been to the Rainbow Club? It's our local queer club. I could show it to you." Mitch forgot what she was looking for when Kay laughed softly. Kay stood leaning against the desk so close Mitch caught the scent of fresh soap.

"Oh, I've *found* the Rainbow Club. Not sure I like the gay cowboy decor, but it's a nice place to meet women interested in a little fun."

"That's what you go there for? A little fun?"

"Don't you?"

"Do you dance?" Mitch wanted to slap her forehead. She loathed dancing because she was about as elegant as a drunken polar bear. What was she doing? Inviting Kay to go dancing?

"My moves aren't impressive so I dance as little as possible." Kay smiled and pointed to the top bookshelf. "There, maybe?"

Mitch turned and grimaced as she spotted the binoculars. They were in plain sight, yet she missed them because she'd been thinking about Kay and not paying attention to her task. "Yup, that's them." Thankful that she rarely blushed, she grabbed the binoculars. "Thanks, and…well, thanks." She stood rooted to the spot. Had she invited Kay out? She wasn't sure, so how could Kay be?

Kay tilted her head and winked. "Is that all, or did you want something else?"

Mitch blinked and backed up until her back hit the doorjamb. "Have a good sleep." She headed toward the kitchen as Kay's soft laughter followed her. *Have a good sleep?* She shook her head. *So lame.*

Callie was washing the milk glasses. Becky and Gwen had already returned to do the bulk of dishes and gone to bed while the adults lingered and chatted.

"I should go. Everyone's gone to bed."

Callie wiped her hands on a towel. "I'm headed out for a final check on my animals. I'll walk you out."

Mitch followed Callie outside and dropped onto the porch bench beside her when Callie sat.

"Interesting meal, tonight," Callie said.

Mitch shrugged.

Callie playfully punched Mitch in the shoulder. "Kay's eyes bugged out when she saw you and yours did the same."

"Matchmaking again?"

"You know I'm right. Let me help. I pushed Val and Ronnie together last year and look at them."

"At the club, they're plastered together on the dance floor like some two-headed body."

"They're head over heels in love. Now, what about you?"

"Not having the greatest luck. It's safer on my own."

"Marion was a jerk. Don't let one failed relationship ruin you for life. Everybody has to keep trying."

"I know. I shouldn't have let her move in, but she needed help. She seemed so scared and unsure of herself."

"That's the rescuer in you." Callie held up her hands. "It's not a criticism. You were a big help to Becky and me when we first moved to Thresherton. You're a generous person and can't stand by when a friend is in need."

"I didn't expect to support Marion forever, just to help her for a while, but I don't think she worked more than six months the whole three years she lived with me."

Callie rubbed Mitch's shoulder. "You'll be more careful next time. Enough about Marion. Have you been on any dates lately or do you need help?"

"You'll have an uphill battle to find anyone for me."

"You're very loveable. I want you to find somebody to wipe the loneliness from your eyes." She brushed the hair off Mitch's forehead as she spoke.

Mitch fidgeted and looked away. "You see too much."

"I see my best friend. A kind, honest, loving woman who doesn't want to be alone and who would make a great wife."

"Wife? Not so fast." Mitch snorted but she secretly liked the idea. She longed for what Lauren and Callie had.

"What about Kay? You think she's beautiful. I can tell."

"Have to be dead not to. All those blond curls and perfect features. And her eyes, blue like yours, but more..."

"More?"

"Wary. She makes jokes, but she's tough. I'm not sure how I know that. It's just a feeling." Mitch tipped her head from side to side. "I can't explain it." A wounded person was hiding behind all the flirting and talk of casual sex. Kay was avoiding something.

"Well, Kay's not rich, but one day she'll have money. And she's independent. You won't have to support her."

"Maybe." Mitch stood. "I should get going." She walked to her cruiser with Callie following. She leaned against her cruiser and Callie leaned beside her.

"Well, you don't have to wonder if she's a lesbian," Callie said.

"No, you took care of that."

Callie chuckled. "Yes, I did. Good for me. So, ask her out."

Mitch yawned. "Maybe. Thanks again for dinner."

Callie handed her a plastic bag. "Leftovers, and I'm about out of plastic containers. When are you planning to bring mine back?"

Mitch raised her hand. "They're washed and waiting. Sorry."

"Well, come for dinner Sunday night and bring my containers back if you want me to fill them again."

Mitch hugged Callie and smiled at the kiss on her cheek. "You're a good friend."

"And you are too, Suzanne."

"Callie." Mitch didn't hide the whine in her voice. "Only my mother and sister call me Suzanne and that's usually followed by a criticism or a demand for money, which I usually end up giving them."

"That's the rescuer in you again. Sorry your family is such a problem."

"You're my family. You, Becky, and now Lauren and the baby."

"Yes, we are." Callie pointed at her. "So, Lauren's family?"

Mitch grinned and rolled her eyes. "She is if she wants to be. I'm trying to be friends."

"Give her time. You were a little overprotective of me when she and I first met, and she's not forgiven you for trying to run her off."

"I promise to play nice. It's true I wouldn't have picked Lauren for you, but nobody suits you better. I'm happy for you both."

"Ah, thank you, sweetie." Callie kissed her cheek. "I should get to my cattle and get to bed. Sunday, dinner."

"Thanks, Callie. Night." Mitch watched her sprint to the barn. Callie was anxious to get to bed where love waited for her. Mitch sighed and slipped into the cruiser. A cold dark house waited for her.

As she drove back to Thresherton, she brought up the image of Kay. She was beautiful, but something lurked in her eyes, behind the flirting and jokes. Challenges didn't scare her, and Kay was interesting and hot in a petite, fit way. She was curious to know more about the intriguing Dr. Kay Gallant, but women who had secrets and hid behind walls weren't her type. Not anymore. They led to drama and complications she didn't need. Maybe she should ask Callie to fix her up with somebody else.

CHAPTER FOUR

Lauren tipped her head toward the bar. "Can I buy you a drink, Kay?"

"No, thanks." It surprised Kay to find herself at the Rainbow Club in Saskatoon with the Thresherton crew. After the dinner at Poplarcreek on Wednesday, Mitch had suggested going to the club, and now they were all there together for women's night.

Kay seldom danced, and the pounding noise made her jumpy. Often, she came to the club to find a lover for the night, and it never took long, which meant she could avoid the noise and crowd for the most part. Tonight, as part of a group, she needed to socialize, for a little while at least, before finding company. It was Saturday night, but she had to be at the college the next day and needed her sleep.

Kay rubbed her left knee and straightened the feminine, flowing slacks that disguised the wrap on her knee. She straightened and scanned the crowd of attractive women for one who might be interested in a little fun for the night. She smiled encouragingly at Mitch when she looked her way.

Mitch walked over and slipped into the chair beside her. "Are you having fun?"

Kay shrugged. "It's a good crowd."

"Would you like to dance?"

"I'm not a big dancer unless you have steel-toed boots on." The vision of being held against Mitch's body made her shiver and reconsider dancing. Maybe she'd take Mitch home with her.

"You're a people-watcher?"

"Sometimes. Who's that woman talking to Callie and Lauren?" Kay asked.

"That's Rachel Popper. She and Callie met in Saskatoon a few years ago when they were taking some computer courses together. Do you think she's beautiful?"

"Callie could be a model, no problem."

"I meant Rachel."

Kay laughed as she scanned the tall, curvy brunette from head to toe. "Who wouldn't? You and she date?"

"Callie?"

"No, Rachel. Lesbians, eh? Got to watch the pronouns."

"Rachel isn't interested in me, not for anything serious. She's more into fun, no strings kind of stuff."

Was this Mitch telling her she wasn't into hookups? That would be too bad, but there was Rachel. Kay grinned and studied Rachel as she hugged Callie. "I like fun." If Mitch didn't work out, she'd get Callie to introduce her to Rachel.

"So, I'm not clear. Would you like to dance? I don't fast dance. I move like a robot whose joints haven't been oiled in ten years, but the next song is a slow one. Oh, and I don't do the fancy steps like Callie and Lauren. I'm just a clutch-and-sway slow dancer."

Kay laughed at the description and the wry smile on Mitch's face. Callie and Lauren flowed around the dance floor appearing almost glued together. They never stepped on each other's feet. "How do you know it'll be slow?"

"The club's pattern is eight fast and two slow."

Rachel headed to the dance floor with another woman. Kay shrugged. "Okay then, thanks."

Mitch rose with the next slow song and Kay followed. She looked up at Mitch. "How tall are you?"

"Five ten."

Kay rested her head against Mitch's shoulder and enjoyed the hardness of the muscles flexing under her cheek. She warmed under the heat of Mitch's large hand against the bare skin of her back. Kay's short top showed off her midriff and defined abdominal muscles.

She'd not set out to build a six-pack, but she started exercising as part of the physiotherapy program for her knee and had kept going. After the first song, Kay saw an attractive twentysomething moving toward them. Was she going to cut in? Did people still do that? And more importantly, who was she after?

Mitch whispered. "Don't go. Please."

Kay peered up at Mitch before resting her head against Mitch's shoulder again. The girl waved when Mitch glanced at her, but Mitch drew Kay in tight and turned her back. When the second slow song finished, Mitch followed Kay to their table.

"You don't have to stay with me. That young thing is hovering. I'm all right on my own," Kay said.

Mitch grinned. "Please, let me stay. Protect me."

Kay winked. "Do you need protecting? I left my Ninja skills in my other suit."

"Yes, please. She's cute, but only twenty-two and has no conversational skills. She's done nothing, seen nothing, and experienced nothing. Plus, she's incapable of putting her phone down for five minutes. She texts her girlfriends in the middle of a meal." She cleared her throat and tossed her head dramatically. "I have to answer this. Kylee is having a problem with her boyfriend and I'm helping her." Mitch reverted to her own voice and groaned. "Then I get the play-by-play of Kylee's relationship woes."

"You're too hard on her. She's just young. How about I buy her a drink and sacrifice myself to save you?"

"Stay, please."

Kay laughed, a little intrigued by Mitch's desire to pass up company to stay with her. "Well, she's leaving you alone now."

"They know I only dance slow dances."

"They?"

"Her and her friends."

Kay smiled and leaned toward Mitch. "Do you have many admirers?"

"Sonny calls them my groupies." Her expression a little sheepish, Mitch fidgeted. "I'm here most weekends when I'm not working. Sometimes my luck holds, and those girls don't find me in the crowd."

"You're like chum in the water being circled by sharks." Kay patted Mitch's hand. "I'll protect you. I've got your back." The chagrined expression on Mitch's face was adorable and Kay had the urge to caress her soft cheek. She didn't care if Mitch had a hundred girlfriends. But sleeping with much younger women could be fun, and usually meant nothing serious would come of it.

"Hey, Mitch."

Kay scanned the tall blonde as she dropped into a chair across from them, a bottle of beer in her hand. The newcomer was no kid.

"Hey, Sonny, meet Kay Gallant, the new veterinarian at PVS." Mitch turned to Kay. "Kay, this is Sonny Bishop. Sonny is a CFIA vet at the Thresherton District Office."

Kay studied Sonny as they shook hands. So, Sonny worked for the Canadian Food Inspection Agency. And, she was attractive and single. Kay liked Sonny's short blond hair, intelligent blue eyes, and square jaw. "Hi, Sonny. Nice to meet you."

Sonny wore a dark blue suit jacket and Mitch a charcoal gray one. They were both tall and fit and could be US Secret Service protecting the president. Kay grinned as she imagined these two protecting her, all night. When her mind slid further into sexual fantasy mode, she straightened and focused on Sonny. "Lauren speaks highly of you and planned to introduce us." Kay sensed Mitch stiffen beside her. *Interesting.*

"Lauren's a good friend." Sonny slouched over her beer. "Are you enjoying the club?"

"The music's a little loud for me and I don't dance. How about you?"

"I'm here to meet friends." Sonny glanced at Mitch and leaned back.

Kay glimpsed a ghost of a possessive expression on Mitch's face before it melted away. *Promising.* "Sonny, are you at the veterinary conference next week?"

"I registered for the regulatory medicine lectures on Thursday morning, but after lunch I'll sneak into the equine medicine and surgery ones."

"I'm speaking Thursday afternoon in the small animal surgery stream. We should have dinner afterward."

Sonny glanced from Mitch to Kay and back again. Kay's bullshit meter shot through the roof when she caught Mitch's slight nod to Sonny, as though giving permission.

Mitch said, "Sounds cool."

"I'll look forward to it." Sonny stood. "Lauren's got my phone number. Text me and we'll set it up. Anyway, folks, I need to talk to an old friend. Have a good night."

"Bye, Sonny. Next Thursday then."

Sonny approached a woman in her late thirties who hugged Sonny and kissed her on the cheek. Another woman joined them, shook Sonny's hand, and slid her arm around the first woman's waist. It was a small community indeed.

Kay looked at Mitch and considered addressing the fleeting proprietary look on her face, but before she could, Mitch rose and held out her hand. "Will you join me in the lounge for a drink?"

Did Mitch think she needed help to get up or was it Mitch's old-fashioned manners?

"Kay?" Mitch waited.

Kay smiled. A quiet chat could lead to more. She gave Mitch her hand and stood. "Thank you."

Mitch held Kay's hand as she led her to a table in the lounge, where the music faded to a light thump beyond the doors. Mitch tipped her head toward the bar. "What can I get you?"

"Just soda please. I don't drink."

"Be right back."

Kay fiddled with her hair as Mitch walked away. Had jeans ever fit a woman better? She scanned the couches and tables of the half-full lounge for familiar faces and hoped to find none of her old hookups. The calmness of the room attracted people who wanted to relax and talk quietly. She'd done some serious flirting and more in the dark corners of this room during the first three years of her residency.

Mitch returned with two cans of diet soda and set one in front of Kay, along with a glass half-full of ice.

Kay poured her soda into the glass. "You're welcome to drink alcohol around me. I'm not an alcoholic or anything. After I got home from Afghanistan, I was drinking too much and decided to stop before it became a problem. I haven't had a drink in years and don't miss it."

"Afghanistan? I heard it was rough."

"I've had more fun." No way was she going to get dragged into a conversation about her tours in Afghanistan. She leaned toward Mitch and turned on her flirtiest smile. "Are you into fun?"

"Not tonight. I have to drive home, so I'm done. I can take or leave alcohol, but I might be addicted to chocolate." Mitch laughed.

She played along with the joke and patted her flat stomach. "Mine will be sugar if Val brings any more baking to the clinic. She brought eight kinds of cookies last week."

"Callie brought us cookies too. She works part-time at the RCMP detachment office. Apparently, Val, Callie, Becky, and Gwen made cookies for a bake sale and got carried away."

"What rank are you in the RCMP?" she asked.

"A corporal for the last five years."

"Five years?" Kay couldn't imagine not moving up the ladder more quickly. She'd go crazy.

"I know what you're thinking. The RCMP isn't like the military. People don't move up the ranks quickly in the RCMP. I started as a constable twelve years ago. My detachment commander is a staff sergeant. That's typical."

"And Callie works with you?"

"She does administrative and reception jobs. It began as a way to get off the farm, but now it's helping pay the bills."

Kay frowned. "She mentioned her huge vet bill from last year."

"And now she has eight horses as well."

"Lauren helps with those, though, right? After all, she adopted them after Val and Ronnie rescued them from that burning barn." Being part of a couple meant sharing the expenses and responsibility. At least, that's what she figured. She wouldn't know.

"Callie's also saving to put a new roof on her house, and eight horses are an expensive hobby, especially as she doesn't ride."

"Ronnie's going to teach Callie and Lauren to ride after the baby is born. Do you ride?"

"Nope. Born and raised in the city. I know nothing about farming or animals, except what I've learned at Poplarcreek." Mitch leaned forward. "Is it safe to confess to a veterinarian I have no real interest in farm animals?" She grinned and spoke softly, like it was their secret.

Kay laughed. "I can't believe I'm even talking to you." She scanned Mitch's strong physique. "So, what's fun for you, besides the gym?"

"I bought a broken-down motorcycle. I took it apart and rebuilt it into a working bike. I like to travel and explore new places in my spare time."

"So, you're good with your hands?" Kay winked.

Mitch shrugged. "I just like to fix things and keep busy."

Mitch had dodged the opportunity to flirt back. *Disappointing.*

"What do you do for fun?" Mitch asked.

"Besides women?" Kay paused hoping Mitch would bite and then sighed. "I like kayaking. It requires upper-body strength and is easier with my crappy knee. The river through Saskatoon is wide and smooth, perfect for kayaking."

"I've seen the kayakers there, moving fast. What color is your boat? Let me guess. Is it red or yellow?"

Kay shook her head. Most of the kayaks around there were red or yellow. "My brother bought me a camouflage-colored one. He thinks it's hilarious."

Kay spent another half an hour talking and trying to get Mitch to flirt until Lauren found them.

"We're heading home now," Lauren said. "Somebody has to take Val and Ronnie. They'll stay or leave, depending on who they can get a ride with. It's our decision."

Mitch opened her mouth, but Kay covered Mitch's hand with hers. "I'm starving, and Mitch invited me to a twenty-four-hour breakfast place. I crave French toast."

"Okay with you and Callie?" Mitch asked, not missing a beat.

"Sure, no problem. We'll pour Val and Ronnie into the SUV and drop them at home. Have a good evening. See you next week, Kay." Lauren waved as she left.

Mitch shifted to look at Kay, a little half grin on her lips. "There's no twenty-four-hour breakfast place unless you mean the truck stop on the highway."

"I make excellent French toast."

Mitch leaned back. "It's a deal."

Kay sipped her drink and anticipated a satisfying end to the evening with company after all. She glanced up and watched Lauren, Callie, Val, and Ronnie collect their coats and leave the club. She waited two more minutes and stood. Mitch followed her to the coat check and waited for Mitch to collect their coats. Success at last. Mitch was coming home with her. Some women wanted a lot more than casual sex, but she needed the time and interest. Work and school were her priority right now and the rest could wait until later, much later. Or not at all.

CHAPTER FIVE

When they arrived at her apartment building, Kay said, "Park down at the end in the overnight parking for visitors."

"I'm not staying the night," Mitch said.

Kay shrugged. "Well, then for however long you stay." *Perfect.* Some company for a few hours suited her, but then she needed to be left alone so she could sleep.

"I'm just seeing you home."

"You're kidding." Kay stared at Mitch. "Well, okay. Thanks for the lift." She stepped from the truck and walked to her apartment. How could she have misread Mitch so badly? Had it just been wishful thinking? She turned to close the door just as Mitch appeared. "I thought you were dropping me off?" She tilted her head. "In case I wasn't clear, the offer of French toast was really an invitation to join me in bed."

Mitch hovered by the front door. "I didn't expect French toast. Or bed. But maybe a chat?"

Kay sighed and stepped aside. "All I want to do at one a.m. is chat. Why not?"

Mitch removed her coat and shoes and settled on the couch a foot from Kay. "I want to get to know you better before making love."

"Making love?" Kay laughed. "You were serious? I want to have sex. Simple physical fucking. Nothing fancy. I thought you were interested, but I guess not." She'd just wasted a whole evening flirting with Mitch.

"So, all you want to do is fuck?" Mitch stood and in one fluid motion she scooped Kay up in her arms and carried her into the bedroom. Mitch's eyes flared with annoyance, not desire.

"Put me down. You're not into this," Kay said.

"You've been pushing for this all night."

"Put me down!" She twisted Mitch's ear as far as possible until Mitch dropped her on the bed. She bounced on the mattress and scooted out of Mitch's reach.

Mitch glared at Kay while she rubbed her ear. "Ouch. *Shit* that hurt."

"Serves you right. This isn't some stupid bodice ripper novel where I'll swoon and spread my legs because you're so powerful." Kay laughed but it sounded false to her own ears.

"Sorry if I hurt you."

"I'm not hurt, but I am a little pissed. I don't appreciate being carted around like a sack of potatoes."

"I'm sorry. I guess I hoped you might see me as more than a fuck toy."

Kay winced. "I like you. And fucking is fun. Why is that a problem?"

"It's not. Sorry."

"Well, Corporal, don't do it again." Kay struggled to contain her smile. She couldn't be annoyed at Mitch anymore. She looked so sweet and vulnerable, which was interesting given the macho vibe she gave off.

"What rank were you in the military when you left?" Mitch asked, sitting on the bed next to her.

"Private."

"Too bad. I hoped you were an officer."

"Were you hoping I was an officer and outranked you? Do you want me to dominate you or something? Let's be clear, I'm not interested in BDSM. Each to his own and consenting adults and all that, but not for me."

Mitch chuckled. "You have an air of authority and I wondered where it came from. That's all."

"I'm a surgeon. Authority is what we do."

"And your job in the military?"

Kay examined her hands resting in her lap. "I don't want to talk about it."

"Bad, eh?" Mitch said in a soothing tone.

Kay grimaced. "No, boring. I was a quartermaster's assistant."

Mitch looked confused. "What's that?"

Kay sighed yet again. She really hated talking about her past. "I ordered the food, cooked it, served it, and cleaned up after. I only held a rifle in basic training."

"Food is important too. I enjoy eating."

"Are we back to French toast?"

Mitch shrugged. "Maybe."

Kay stomped to the kitchen, but she had to admit to enjoying the strange way the night was turning out. "Very sneaky, Mitchell." Twenty minutes later, she set a plate of French toast and a bottle of maple syrup in front of Mitch.

"Awesome," Mitch said around a huge mouthful. "Thanks."

Kay sipped her milk. She wasn't hungry for food, but she enjoyed watching Mitch eat.

Later, Mitch swallowed the last bite and scraped her plate before pushing it away. "Delicious. Thanks."

Kay put the dishes in the sink. "Coffee? Milk?"

"Milk, please."

Kay fetched the glass of milk. She set it on the table and sank into a chair across from Mitch. "Do you want to hear about Afghanistan?" She had no idea what made her ask, since she didn't want to talk about it. But there was something about Mitch that made talking easy.

"If you want to tell me."

"I was posted to Afghanistan at the start of the Canadian buildup. I'd been in the military three years and I'd taken food service courses at the local college. Along with many others, I believed in the mission and volunteered for Afghanistan." Kay grimaced. "Leaving for war seemed important."

Kay stared into her glass. "They sent us on seven-month tours, but lots of us did back-to-back tours. In my eleventh month, we left the compound in a convoy to recover misplaced supplies." She put air quotes around the word misplaced. "My right foot was up on the seat beside me." She demonstrated by resting her right foot on the chair beside her backside. "An IED exploded under our vehicle and trashed my left knee. I was lucky my right foot wasn't on the floor." She shook her head. "My sergeant died. He was only twenty-nine. What a shitty waste."

Kay focused on Mitch when she gasped. Mitch had remained otherwise silent, but her mouth was stretched in a fierce line.

Kay walked to her couch. She curled into the corner and clutched a throw pillow against her chest. She kept talking, but concentrated on her memory, and no longer looked at Mitch. "The Taliban captured us, the three survivors."

"Shit. What happened?"

"They stuck me and two guys in a cave with a heavy carpet hanging over the entrance. I was the only one with serious wounds. I remember little after the infection and fever set in. The guys did their best, but they weren't medics and had no medical supplies."

Mitch sat on the couch beside Kay. "What happened?" Mitch asked.

"After two days without supplies, the guys grew thirsty enough to stick their head out of our cave when it went silent, and we couldn't hear anything out there anymore. The Taliban had just abandoned us, which was weird and something we've never understood. There was no movie-worthy rescue."

"But you were rescued."

Kay nodded and shifted to face Mitch. "The guys I was with carried me until they found another Canadian unit. My knee was a mess and all I remember is the heat and the pain. At some point I passed out. Later, I woke in the hospital and discovered the explosion had actually shattered my left knee."

Mitch swallowed hard several times and set her glass of milk on the table.

"Are you all right?" Kay asked. "You going to be sick?"

Mitch had turned pale and a light sheen of sweat coated her forehead.

"I'll live."

Kay considered fetching her the mop bucket but went ahead. "The surgeons cobbled the bones of my knee together, and for that I'm thankful. They saved my leg. They said my knee would never bend properly and it would never support my weight again. I'm happy to report that they were wrong."

"But it still hurts?"

"Some." Kay grimaced. "After the surgery, I was ill for weeks with infection and septicemia. When they sent me back to Canada, I weighed ninety-eight pounds."

"How horrible. What happened next?"

Kay shrugged. "After finishing the first round of physiotherapy, the military shipped me home to Charlottetown. I took my medical discharge and thus ended my rewarding career in the military." Kay laughed.

"Can I give you a hug?"

"You think I need one?" Kay tried to joke, but she ached to be held by Mitch. It wasn't as a prelude to sex, but just for comfort. She could allow herself that, this one time.

"Maybe I do. If I wrap my arms around you, will you bite me?" Mitch whispered.

"You wish."

Mitch slowly slid her arm around Kay's shoulders.

Kay grinned. Mitch moved as if she expected to be bitten. She searched her earnest hazel eyes and found them full of compassion. She shifted to sit in Mitch's lap and rested her head against Mitch's shoulder. She laid her hands on Mitch's strong arms where they encircled her waist.

"This is nice," Mitch said.

"Hmm." She'd just rest for a minute, where she felt safe and warm. Talking about Afghanistan and tamping down memories of the fear and horror often left her exhausted.

Hands gripped her, smoke squeezed the air from her lungs, and pain made her vomit. Screams and shots, gunfire...

Kay woke with a start and rolled off Mitch's lap onto the floor. She scuttled backward until her back hit the wall and she stared at Mitch in horror, trying to blink away the terror and focus on where she really was.

Mitch tilted her head up and pinched her nose to keep the blood from dripping onto the carpet as she stood and stumbled to the bathroom.

The desert smoke faded and Kay crawled up the wall until she could walk to the kitchen. She splashed cold water on her face, fetched an ice pack and brought it to the bathroom. "Sorry."

"You *punched* me." Mitch spoke through a pinched nose, sounding more surprised than angry. She accepted the ice pack and placed it on her nose. "Too cold."

"Try this." Kay took the ice pack from Mitch's hand, wrapped it in an old towel, and handed it back. "You've dripped on your shirt. Take it off and let me sponge out the blood before it dries."

Mitch grinned and then groaned as the movement hurt her face. "Still trying to get me naked?"

"If it didn't work before I punched you, I doubt it will now. Give me your shirt."

Mitch attempted to undo her buttons with one hand while holding the ice against her nose with the other.

Impatient with Mitch's progress, Kay did it for her. She'd yearned to undress Mitch, but the nightmare had chased away the sexy, until Mitch's strong body was uncovered. Kay shook her head to clear away the resurfacing sexual thoughts and carted the white shirt to the kitchen, leaving Mitch standing there in a sports bra. She ran the blood spots under cold water and briefly considered sticking her head under the cold spray to cool off. Mitch was fit and her sculped body deserved attention. With effort, she focused on the task. She sponged the blood away and draped the shirt over a kitchen chair to dry.

When she returned, she discovered Mitch on the couch with her suit coat on and buttoned and still holding the ice against her nose.

"That's a sexy look," Kay said. Sexier without the jacket, but she would get back to that very soon.

"What? A broken nose?"

"No, the bra and suit jacket, and I didn't break your nose. Don't be a baby. I tapped you and I'm sorry. I wasn't myself."

"You had a nightmare. You yelled and punched me. Did telling me your story about Afghanistan bring it on?"

"Probably." She shrugged. There was no point in denying it.

"I'm sorry." Mitch yawned and gingerly touched her swollen nose. "Well, this has been a riot, but I should go before I'm too tired to drive."

"You're yawning and already too tired. Stay the night."

"Can I borrow your couch?"

"No." Kay tried to stuff her libido to the back of her brain. Nothing was going to happen tonight. Mitch had been clear, and their misunderstanding was her fault because she'd refused to pick up on Mitch's words and signals.

"Pardon?"

"You'll sleep in my bed."

Mitch winced. "I will?"

"I'm shorter and will fit on the couch." Kay hooked a blanket and one of her pillows off the bed and set them in the living room. She gave Mitch a towel, but had no clothes large enough for her to sleep in. She curled under her blanket and imagined Mitch naked in her bed. Were there boxers to match that sports bra? Kay pressed the pillow against her face. What a waste.

Kay woke early in the morning and tiptoed through her apartment. She'd revealed a great deal to Mitch the night before. More than she had to anyone in a long time. Having feelings and displaying weakness made her feel humiliated and weak. She wrote a note and slipped it into the pocket of Mitch's shirt.

Work to do. Gone to school.

Kay dressed in clean clothes, grabbed her shoulder bag and computer, and headed outside. As she drove to the veterinary college, she rewrote the note in her head searching for better words. The note was a poor way to start a day, but fitting. It hadn't been a date because a date wouldn't end with her punching a woman in the nose.

She sat at her computer and found it hard to focus on the video of the surgery scheduled for Monday. It appeared simple and failed to distract her from picturing Mitch naked. It didn't matter. She'd scared her away with war stories and a well-timed nightmare. But it wasn't like she'd been interested in more, either. Making love? No thanks.

Kay shrugged. Thursday night she had a date with Sonny Bishop. She wouldn't wait on Mitch to change her mind, because it didn't matter. If their plans didn't match, she'd find another woman, one on the same path. Mitch was just a bump in the road. Kay frowned. If Mitch was no big deal, then why was she so disappointed?

Chapter Six

As Kay drove from Saskatoon to Thresherton she mulled over her misunderstanding with Mitch on Saturday. How had something so promising turned into a farce? Did she want to see Mitch again? She couldn't easily avoid her, but she wouldn't actively seek her out. It was clear Mitch didn't want to hook up, and Kay didn't want anything more. No messy relationships or draining emotions. She'd worked too hard to get where she was, and nothing was getting in the way. But it was too bad to miss out on the sex.

Kay shook her head. It was Tuesday morning, and she had a busy day. She'd wasted enough energy thinking about Mitch on the drive in. It was time to concentrate on her work. She hung up her coat and bag in her locker at PVS and headed into the treatment room to greet Val, just as Callie and Lauren arrived.

"Hello there. I have a delivery for you." Callie entered holding onto Lauren's arm.

"Hey, Callie," Kay said. "Lauren, what happened to you?"

Lauren limped in using a cane and sat on a stool in the treatment room. "A little accident."

"She moved one of my cows to a calving pen to deliver a calf." Callie shook her head. "I could've told her that one kicked. Some of my girls are full of attitude. When I got back from the field, Max greeted me barking his head off, so I followed Lassie into the barn." Callie cocked her thumb toward Lauren. "Where I found this one, on her ass, squished in the corner of the calving pen, and my big old cow staring at her as if she was dinner."

Lauren grimaced. "It wasn't as bad as that. I was resting and waiting for a chance to escape."

"You could've been seriously hurt. What about the baby?" Val said.

"Thank you," Callie said and frowned at Lauren.

Kay watched Lauren squirm as Callie and Val, one tall and one short, scrutinized her with arms crossed over their chests. Callie was joking but couldn't hide the love and real worry for Lauren. Had anyone looked at her like that? Maybe right after Afghanistan, but she didn't need it now. But there'd been a hint of it in Mitch's eyes after her nightmare.

Lauren raised her hands. "I surrender. Never again."

Callie pointed at Lauren. "If you're not doing large animal work for PVS you're not doing it for me. I'll call Fiona or Ian, and before you argue, I don't care about the cost. You and our baby are more important than avoiding one more vet bill."

"What happened to the calf?" Kay asked.

"It had one leg bent back. I straightened the leg and delivered the calf." Callie winked at Kay. "I had an excellent teacher and a ton of practice last year."

Val pointed to Lauren's leg. "How bad is it?"

"A bad bruise, but hopefully not more. I dragged her to the hospital, but she refused X-rays because of the baby. If it doesn't improve in two days, I'll toss her over my shoulder and cart her back. She's allowed to walk on it but shouldn't stand for long periods."

"Hello, I'm still here," Lauren said. "I'll be careful. I promise. But I have to walk to do my job."

"Callie, I have a busy morning, but I'll call you when the dust settles and you can collect Lauren," Kay said as she joined Callie and Val to stare at Lauren.

"Will you three stop it, please? You look as if you're posing for the next Charlie's Angels movie." Lauren laughed. "It's a sexy image. Anybody have a camera? Callie, you be Cameron Diaz."

Callie dropped her arms and frowned. "She's hallucinating and thinks getting stomped is funny now. Thanks, Kay. Call me when you're done with Super Vet and I'll come back, or should I return with lunch and collect her then?"

"Lunch?" Kay said.

Val squirmed with joy. "Please, pretty please."

Callie smiled. "I might have something going by then. Time for me to go be a farmer." She bent and kissed Lauren. "You take it easy." Callie straightened. "Bye, everyone."

Lauren hobbled to her office and Val disappeared into the cat room. Kay leaned against the doorjamb and watched Callie stop at the front counter to speak with Ian. Ian and Fiona Wilson were the father and daughter team who owned PVS and they were familiar with Poplarcreek. Callie gestured toward the treatment room while she talked to Ian. Judging by the smiling and head shaking, he sided with Callie.

Kay lifted a shoulder in a half-shrug. Callie and Lauren appeared to be deeply in love. Lucky them. They were the nesting type, but commitment wasn't for her. Relationships took too much time and energy. She spent fourteen hours a day on her career and had no time for anything more, except a little sex. Fun, exciting sex like she'd planned to have with Mitch, but that was a no-go. She returned to the treatment room where the surgeries of the day captured her attention.

After Kay finished her last surgery of the morning, she discarded her scrubs, got dressed, and entered the treatment room just as Val slid a hot water bottle into a kennel beside a sleeping dog.

"You doing an order soon?" Kay asked.

"Not planning on it. What're we missing?"

"Down to a half bottle of ketamine," Kay said.

"I saw that, but we can't be. I just ordered it."

"We must have used it." Kay shrugged and headed to the front desk to give Janice, the receptionist, the files for billing. At twelve thirty, Mitch entered PVS with a tray holding six coffees. Kay sucked in her breath. No other woman could look as sexy in blue jeans and a tight black T-shirt. If Mitch was wearing cowboy boots, she'd melt into a puddle of lust at her feet. Too bad all she was going to get to do was look.

Kay swallowed and pushed out a few words. "I'm surprised to see you."

Mitch smiled sheepishly. "Callie told me to meet her at PVS and bring her a cappuccino."

"She promised us she'd bring lunch."

"That's what I'm here for."

"You're not a big cook then? No chef's apron hanging in your closet?"

"I barbecue, but I'm sure if it weren't for Callie, everything else I eat would come from cans and the freezer. Do you cook?"

Kay leaned on the counter. "Well, there's French toast and I can put together a decent salad, but that's pretty much where it stops." She amazed herself by having a weirdly casual conversation. Their last meeting was fraught with sexual energy and annoyance. She rubbed her palms on her jeans and plotted her escape.

An instant later, they saw Callie's SUV pull into the parking lot. Mitch set the coffees on the counter and jogged outside to help Callie.

"Lunchtime," Val said.

Kay jumped, surprised to discover Val behind her. Val snagged the tray of coffees off the counter and led Callie and Mitch to the lunchroom. Kay went to Lauren's office. "Callie's here with lunch." She grinned at Lauren's immediate blush triggered by the arrival of Callie, not the food. "Mitch is here too. Callie invited her for lunch."

Lauren grimaced. "When Callie cooks, Mitch appears."

"What is it between you two? Mitch is always nice to you, but your hackles go up every time she's near you."

"Long story."

Kay raised an eyebrow and waited for more detail.

"She's overprotective. Thought I wasn't good enough for Callie and tried to rescue her from me. She thought I was just messing around and would run off and break Callie's heart." She caressed her abdomen. "As you can see, I'm not going anywhere. But it still irks me, and I can't seem to let it go."

"Thanks for the warning. I'll keep that in mind." So, Mitch ran off the fun women? How boring was that? Kay followed Lauren to the lunchroom and slipped into a chair beside Mitch. It was a tricky gamble. The last time they'd seen each other it was beyond awkward and she'd scurried off to school before Mitch woke up. She squirmed in the unnerving warmth wafting off Mitch in waves, but it was preferable to sitting across from her and attempting not to make eye contact.

Some of the lunchtime conversation rehashed Lauren's accident, but mostly the others talked about Becky and Gwen and plans for the new baby. Mitch joined in, but Kay concentrated on her food. Kids and babies didn't interest her. She'd just finished her lunch when Janice stuck her head in the room with a question.

Kay jumped to her feet. "Lauren, stay and eat. I'll get this. Thanks for lunch, Callie."

"Just a second." Mitch got up and followed her out.

"I'm needed on the phone."

"Quick question. Sonny told me she can't make it on Thursday, so I was wondering if you'd have dinner with me?"

"What happened? Wait, never mind. Sure, okay, I have to get the phone." Kay hurried away surprised that she wasn't more disappointed. She wasn't a person who wasted time, so why was she still so intrigued by Mitch? She took a deep breath to steady her pulse and focused on the phone.

After helping the customer on the phone, Kay checked on her morning surgeries. She glanced up as Lauren hobbled into the treatment room and perched on a stool Val pulled over for her.

"Ian is here this afternoon, so I'm heading home with Callie," Lauren said as she fingered the orthopedic tools Val had cleaned and spread on paper towels to dry. "I'm glad you're here. PVS needed a surgeon."

"You did the small animal surgeries before your pregnancy," Val said.

"Not orthopedic surgery."

"Ready to go?" Callie entered the treatment room and slipped her arm around Lauren, as she bent and kissed her.

"Ready to go anywhere with you," Lauren said.

Val grinned. "Have a nice afternoon. Gwen and Becky are working on a project, so Becky won't be home for a couple of hours."

Lauren blushed and Callie winked as they left arm in arm.

Val glanced at Kay. "They're madly in love and I take credit for it. I pushed them together." She shrugged. "And Callie pushed Ronnie and me together. We're good matchmakers." Val tilted her head and focused on Kay.

Kay held up her hands and stepped back. "Don't even think about it. Not interested."

"Not at all?"

"Nope. You four do the nesting and the love thing. I'm happy as I am, and I've got plans that don't include someone else in my space." She backed away, turned, and ran to her office before Val could marry her off. There would be no nesting for her.

She dropped into a chair and groaned as she started to write out her notes. The rest of the veterinary world had moved to electronic records, but PVS was still stuck in the dark ages with handwritten ones. When it buzzed, she grabbed her phone to see if the cute woman from the coffee shop had texted her back. No such luck.

Instead, Sonny had emailed her to cancel on Thursday. She had some urgent work to do and couldn't make it to the conference after all. She'd taken a rain check on dinner. "Well, so much for that."

"So much for what?"

Kay looked up and discovered Mitch leaning against the doorjamb of her office. The casual way Mitch shifted to cross her ankles and arms was unbelievably sexy. She bet Mitch had no idea how enticing her muscular leanness was. "I just got Sonny's email canceling." She tried for a nonchalant shrug.

"Will I do? You never answered."

Kay smiled. "Will you do what? My laundry? Wash my car?"

Mitch straightened, looking only mildly exasperated. "Will you have dinner with me on Thursday night? I have the day off and can meet you in the city whenever and wherever you wish."

Kay laughed. "You'd drive all the way to Saskatoon for a meal?"

"I'd drive all the way for a cup of coffee with you."

Kay squinted at Mitch and found sincerity in her warm hazel eyes. "I'd like that." She didn't have the desire to decline and didn't want to, however much a waste of time it was. "I'll text you with a time and where to meet." It was clear after the club that they weren't on the same page, but she couldn't help it. Mitch was gorgeous and sexy, and she wanted to know her better, at least for a night or two. Dinner was a start.

CHAPTER SEVEN

M itch sat at her table and sipped her soda. She tried not to fiddle with the cutlery or straighten the collar of her shirt again. She glanced at her phone, but the time had moved only three minutes since she'd last checked. Kay wasn't late, but maybe she wouldn't show at all? Maybe she'd met someone at her conference and joined them for drinks? Kay had wanted to meet with Sonny, not her.

Mitch looked toward the restaurant entrance and smiled as Kay arrived. She was beautiful and had clearly dressed for the conference in a suit of cream-colored slacks and tailored jacket. Her blue shirt and matching shoes softened her outfit and gave it a feminine air.

Mitch stood as Kay approached the table. She wasn't chauvinistic or old-fashioned, but she liked courtly manners and fussing over a woman. "Hi, Kay. Good day at the conference?"

Kay sat. "Yes, interesting presentations."

"I slipped into your lecture. I didn't understand much but you sounded good."

Kay squinted at her. "How did you get in?"

Mitch grinned sheepishly. "My badge lets me go where I want."

"I'll bet it does. Well, I'm glad you enjoyed it and I hope I didn't sound nervous."

"Not at all."

"Good." Kay leaned toward her. "I was terrified. I teach the veterinary students, but I've never presented to other veterinarians."

"What's the difference?"

"I'm more knowledgeable than students and that gives me confidence, but with other veterinarians I can't predict their questions, and there's always the risk they'll stump me."

When the waitress appeared, Kay ordered sparkling water and Mitch another soda. "Do you like teaching the vet students?"

Kay sipped her drink and looked thoughtful. "I enjoy almost everything about lecturing."

"Almost everything?"

Kay shrugged. "People who talk through the lecture or sit in the front row and fiddle with their phones annoy me. Why come if you're not going to listen?"

"What do you do?"

"I punish them. Ask them tough questions." Kay opened her menu and tipped her head toward their waitress as she walked by. "That's her third trip past our table since I got here. I feel like a guilty child. We better have our entrees chosen by the time she returns, or she'll stand us in the corner."

Mitch chuckled as she opened the menu. A second after she and Kay had closed their menus, the waitress appeared, and they gave her their orders.

"Thanks for the invitation to dinner. I'm sorry it got so weird after the club," Kay said.

"A colossal misunderstanding."

"That all it was?"

"Yes. You were up for more than me." Mitch studied Kay. "If I hadn't taken you home, would you have hooked up with another woman?"

"Probably with half a dozen." Kay laughed. "Just kidding. It's okay if you're not interested in me. We can be friends."

Mitch reached to straighten her collar again, but let her hands drop. Kay was clear on what she wanted, so why was she still pushing? Was it just a feeling that Kay might change her mind? She'd met wounded people who pushed others away out of protection. "I am interested in you, but I want another date and to spend time with you. I want to know you better before anything more."

"We're not romantic kids." Kay thumbed the condensation on her glass.

"No, we're not kids and because we're not kids, we shouldn't leap into bed. I prefer to be more than sexually attracted to a woman. What if we're compatible in bed, but we fit nowhere else?"

"That would be enough for me."

Mitch sighed. She had a feeling that's where things stood. "Sex isn't enough for me. I want to be in a serious relationship and I'm not afraid to admit it."

Kay pointed at her. "Are you a nester like all your friends?"

"These days I am." Mitch scanned Kay's body and didn't hide her admiration. Changing the subject seemed like a good idea. "You're in good shape. What do you do for exercise now, besides kayaking?"

"I swim two or three times a week and I go to the gym."

"Sonny has a bad knee too and Ronnie introduced her to cycling. It forces her knee through repetitive circular motions but puts little weight or pressure on it. She says it's great exercise."

"What happened to Sonny?"

"Bad car accident when she was in Alberta. Some drunk crashed into her and smashed up her knee. It slows her down, but it doesn't stop her. Someday she'll need a new one."

Kay sipped her water. "I'll need a new knee someday too. I worry about the time away from my career, about the risks of surgery and contracting MRSA at the hospital. And there's the time spent in physiotherapy and waiting for the new knee to heal well enough so I can work. I've already kept my knee five years longer than the original surgeons told me I would."

Mitch nodded. "Not too many surgeons on crutches."

"Exactly. It's better to rest my knee whenever I can. Val's organized PVS so I can sit while I spay and neuter cats and small dogs. When she leaves for university full-time, I'll miss her."

"Lauren will miss her too. She relies on Val."

"As a technician and as her voice of reason, according to Val." Kay laced her fingers together and leaned forward. "Enough about the others. What's your life plan? Detective? Detachment commander?"

Mitch choked on her dinner and raised her hands in mock horror. "Not commander. Well, someday, but right now I like getting out of the office."

"Will you live in Thresherton forever?"

Mitch shrugged. "My friends are here. My mother and my sister are only in Regina, but we don't get along well."

"Why's that?"

"Take your pick. Cop thing, the lesbian thing. The last time I was home my mother told me to 'quit playing with girls and find a man.'"

Kay scowled. "Are you kidding? She thinks you'll marry a *man*?"

"She's hoping. Doesn't matter that I've never even *dated* a man, she still thinks she can bully me into marrying one."

"I'm sorry about that. It hurts when family doesn't understand us."

The sadness in Kay's eyes told her story. "What about your folks? Your brothers?"

"I don't visit Prince Edward Island often. I don't see eye to eye with my parents. They don't believe in me." Kay shrugged. "I do miss my brothers though."

"Don't believe in you? But you're a doctor. They must be proud."

"Maybe, but they don't say so. They sort of steered me toward the army. Thought it would be safe and give me direction. Nobody saw 9/11 or the war in Afghanistan coming. They feel guilty that I was injured, so now it's even weirder at home."

"Well, they should be proud. I'd be. You've accomplished a lot and you're not done." Mitch rested her knife and fork on the edge of her plate. "And after you're done here, you're headed to the US."

Kay nodded. "That's the plan. I love surgery, and when my residency is over, I'll move on. I like working at PVS and it'll do until something better comes along."

"So, PVS is just one step along the way." Was avoiding commitment Kay's approach to everything and everybody? Was each woman and each job just a transitory step? Mitch leaned back. She didn't want to be anyone's stepping-stone, but she liked Kay. Maybe friendship would be enough after all. She needed to steer them to more neutral conversation. "If you're up for it, I wouldn't mind a stroll along the river after dinner. Will your knee be okay?"

"Sure."

After paying for dinner, Mitch took Kay's hand and led her the block from the restaurant to the paved path beside the river. Soft streetlights illuminated their way. Mitch looked into the dark water of the South Saskatchewan River as it flowed through the middle of Saskatoon. Which brilliant person had the foresight to save the strip along the river as parkland?

She strolled with her hands in her pockets and Kay rested her hand in the crook of her arm. It felt natural. She shortened her stride to accommodate Kay and they walked in silence as the sun set.

Thirty minutes later, Kay slowed at a bench and they sat. "How do you feel, right now?"

Mitch tilted her head and regarded Kay. "I'm fine."

Kay grinned. "Fine? Freaked-out, insecure, needy, and emotional?"

Mitch grinned. "I'm content, peaceful, and happy. Better?"

"What if I kissed you?" Kay looked up at Mitch. "Would you jump away or throw yourself in the river?"

Mitch smiled and shook her head. "Not at all."

Kay leaned toward Mitch and she met her halfway. They shared a passionate kiss and slipped their arms around each other. When they separated, Mitch paused for a minute lost in her thoughts. She studied the river and reveled in the amazing kiss, and wished it came with more emotion than lust. Her pulse was thrumming in her ears and she wanted more, but Kay wasn't offering what she wanted.

"I used to think we'd met before, but now I'm sure we haven't because I'd remember kissing you." Kay looped her arm through Mitch's and rested her head against her shoulder. "This is nice."

"Yes." Mitch forced the one word past the lump in her throat. Clearly that kiss was enough for Kay. She liked Kay, liked her a lot, but maybe too much. On one hand she wanted to get to know her better, but even if Kay were willing to commit to a relationship, she was leaving. With difficulty, Mitch calmed her mind and tried to enjoy the peaceful interlude. It was a clear night, and she watched the reflection of the stars as they twinkled in the river. Hell, but she was tired of being alone.

CHAPTER EIGHT

While Gwen and Becky were staying with friends, Callie and Lauren hosted a dinner at Poplarcreek. Kay dug into the tasty home-cooked food and stole occasional glances at Mitch. Their dinner two nights ago, after the conference, was friendly and there'd been one amazing kiss, but she wasn't optimistic there would be more. She let the conversation flow around her while she imagined taking Mitch to bed. Fantasies were harmless.

After passing around plates of dessert, Callie leaned against Lauren and clasped her hand. "We have an announcement to make."

Kay stopped eating and put her fork down to focus on Callie.

Callie threw her arms wide. "We're getting married."

Val laughed. "About time, Callie. You knocked her up and now you have to marry her."

Callie grasped her crotch and wiped at her nose. "You know it, man." It was a sad macho imitation, and Callie's reward from Lauren was a gentle hug.

"Yikes, Callie. Please, never do that again," said Mitch.

"Why not, Mitchy?" Callie swept in and grabbed Mitch's face. She kissed her on each cheek and Mitch grinned.

Kay winked at Mitch and mouthed, "Mitchy?"

Mitch winced and shook her head.

"It amazes me how quickly Lauren became pregnant," Ronnie said. "Weren't you just talking about a baby at Christmas and about Lauren going first because she's older?"

Lauren kissed Callie's hand. "We got organized right away and Callie caught me with one try." She winked. "The first time out."

"*I am the woman.*" Callie strutted through the kitchen still doing a poor macho impression.

"Never do that again either," Mitch said.

"Congrats to both of you," Sonny said.

"Yes. It's great." Kay forced some excitement into her voice. She was happy for them, but why would anyone want to be married or tie themselves to one person forever?

"I'm crazy excited for you two. When?" Val bounced in her seat.

Lauren scanned the group. "We plan to marry in a month. We're hoping for early July. We'll have to work fast because I'm already four months and I want to have the wedding before I'm monstrously huge."

"It's a big job organizing a wedding," Val said. "I'll help, but I've never been married."

Lauren opened a notebook and Callie groaned.

Lauren searched Callie's face. "Should I put it away?"

Callie kissed Lauren's cheek and then patted her shoulder. "Go ahead."

"We started a list and we have jobs for everybody who can help. Ronnie, we want to marry in a church in Thresherton or outside at Poplarcreek. Can you find us a location and somebody to officiate?"

Ronnie nodded. "On it."

"Val, can you help us with the reception? Food and dishes?"

"Absolutely." Val snagged a piece of paper from Lauren's book and wrote, her pen flying across the page.

"Kay, you're a wiz with the computer and email. When we select a date, can you design an invitation and send it to everyone? We'll follow up with a paper invitation by mail."

Kay barely knew Callie and Lauren, but touched to be part of the big day, she smiled. "I'm happy to help."

Val looked up from her growing list. "Do you have a photographer?"

"Becky has already volunteered, and Gwen will help her," Callie said.

Mitch cleared her throat.

"We have a job for you, Mitch. Don't worry." Callie stepped behind Mitch and squeezed her shoulders. "Will you and Sonny organize a pre-wedding party, please? We don't have much time, so we'll have to fit the engagement party, stag and bridal shower into a single pre-wedding party. You can hold it near Thresherton or in Saskatoon. I'll leave that up to you."

"I'd love to help," Sonny said.

"Lauren, is your family coming from Ontario?" Ronnie asked.

"I'm sure my brother and sister-in-law will bring my mother. Callie's family is driving from British Columbia. Summer's a busy time of the year at Wilkins Berry Farm so we expect they'll only stay a few days."

Callie rubbed her hands together. "Now for the wedding party. My sister and Lauren's brother, and Sam and Becky." Callie clasped Lauren's hand. "And Mitch and Val, we'd love you two to stand up with us."

Val leaped from her chair, ran around the table, and flung her arms around Lauren's neck.

Lauren returned Val's hug. "You decide what to call yourselves. You can be best broads or maids of honor or one of each."

Callie hugged Val. "We gave Val the biggest job, so she's welcome to call on anyone for more help."

"My mom will help me," Val said. "She knows everybody in Thresherton. Should we book Thomas and Marcus to do the food?"

"Good idea." Callie nodded. "I'll work on the preparations too, but I should clean up the backyard and plant a few more flowers. I also intend to finally paint my poor neglected porch. We're having the reception at Poplarcreek."

"I'll help with the cleanup and painting," Ronnie said.

"Thanks, Ronnie. Oh, and I'm hunting for volunteers to go with me to the bridal show in Saskatoon next weekend."

"Me, pick me." Val hugged Callie.

"Anyone else should let me know if they want to come with us. Lauren hid under the bed when I invited her." She kissed Lauren on the top of the head. "I'm taking a bucket of cash and we'll buy whatever we need, including a dress."

"For you or Lauren?" Mitch snorted.

Lauren's head shot up, and she scowled at Mitch.

Kay blinked as Mitch focused on her plate. "You'd look awesome in a dress," Mitch said.

Lauren squinted and her eyes drilled into Mitch. Kay leaned back, afraid to come between them. Mitch was Callie's good friend and should be in the bridal party, but clearly that didn't mean Lauren would be the butt of any jokes. Kay glanced at Callie and caught her rolling her eyes at Lauren and Mitch.

"The dress is for me," Callie said. "It would be great if Mitch and Val spoke at the reception."

Mitch raised her head and smiled at Callie and Lauren. "Thank you. I'm not much of a public speaker, but I'll say a few words." She faced Lauren. "They will be kind and respectful words. I promise."

"Kay, want to come to the bridal show?" Callie asked.

"Hell, no! I mean, no thank you." She'd been about to suggest she'd prefer to date two smelly men simultaneously, but bit back the joke. Fortunately, the group laughed.

"It's just Val and me then."

The wedding announcement was a great deal of information to absorb. Everyone wrote lists, made plans, and quizzed Callie and Lauren on their preferences. Kay sat and watched the activity. She'd tackle Lauren for the emails of her friends and family later.

Mitch pulled Sonny aside and gestured for Kay to join them. "Can you please help us with the invitations to the party?" Mitch asked. "Based on the timeline, we're inviting people by email. We considered using Facebook, but email is easier. Anyway, the Rainbow Club rents their lounge for private functions. We'll start there. Lauren and Callie have a ton of friends who'll celebrate with them. I'll text Rachel. She'll help."

Sonny scratched the back of her neck. "What if I phone Rachel?"

"Sure, but why?" Mitch asked.

Sonny waggled her eyebrows and Kay grinned. She licked her lips in anticipation. At a wedding there would be a buffet of women all dressed up and looking pretty. Bring it on.

"Kay, are you there?"

She turned to focus on Mitch. "Did you say something?"

"I asked if you were staying at Poplarcreek all weekend and did you want to do something tomorrow?"

"With who?"

"Me." Mitch slapped herself in the forehead. "This used to be easier. I'm sure it did."

"Okay, but how about something as friends." Ten seconds ago, she was picturing the selection of women at the party, and now she was going out with Mitch. They weren't on the same page, but she was still drawn to her. There was something solid and safe about Mitch. "What did you have in mind?" The words escaped before she could stop them.

"I don't know yet."

"How about I pick something?" Kay groaned inwardly. Now planning tomorrow was her project. She'd have to think of something tame and neutral and friend-like. Food was safe. "Meet me at the diner at ten."

Mitch looked so pleased it made Kay smile, but she couldn't help but smack herself mentally. This was a bad idea.

That night Kay lay in bed, desperately searching for peace. She didn't recognize herself. Where did the single-minded professional go? Was it just wedding fever that had made her accept Mitch's invitation? Wasn't there some biological urge that made people want to pair up at a wedding? Well, she'd remain immune. She was happy for Lauren and Callie, but she wasn't a nester. She had big plans that didn't involve settling down, ever. Even if the woman was hot, and kind, and sexy, and a great kisser…

Chapter Nine

M itch was walking along the street and spotted Kay in the diner. She was third in line at the small counter and most of the twelve tables and booths were full of diners. The décor was an old, tired sixties theme with turquoise vinyl seating, but it was spotless and the food good.

Mitch considered not stopping but scolded herself for being chicken. On Sunday, she and Kay had enjoyed a pleasant meal together at the diner. Kay hadn't wanted to talk about the upcoming wedding and had expressed a disconcerting repugnance for marriage and nesting. Still, Kay's sense of fun, her beauty and intelligence, drew her in like a ship about to wreck on a rocky shore. Brunch had ended with a peck on the cheek and they'd gone their separate ways. It felt less like a date than a quick bite with a new friend, and maybe that's how it should stay. She accepted her fate and slipped into the diner to wait by the door.

"Thanks," Kay said as she paid her money and picked up her bags of food. "Hey, you."

Mitch buried thoughts of danger and warmed to the welcoming smile that made her glad she'd stopped. "Do you have time for lunch?"

"Sorry, I'm buying lunch for everyone and taking it back with me. We have a full afternoon and Lauren's still finishing morning appointments. She said she had to keep going or she'd never get caught up."

Mitch made herself smile to hide her disappointment. "That's too bad."

Kay nudged Mitch's shoulder with hers. "I had fun on the weekend, and I'd stop if I could, but we're buried in work today." She stepped toward the door. "I'm on call tonight and staying at Poplarcreek. That reminds me, I need to text Callie." She shrugged. "Maybe I'll see you there for dinner?"

Mitch brightened. "What time will you be there?"

"It'll depend on when we finish. A veterinarian's life is unpredictable. Ask Callie." Kay disappeared from the restaurant with a wave.

Mitch had arranged to visit a pig farm in the afternoon, so she plotted a route past Poplarcreek. Criminals stole from farms because farmers left their equipment outside in plain view while they drove into town or disappeared into their fields. This time, thieves had entered an unlocked barn at the pig farm and taken a generator. Unfortunately, the thieves had returned two weeks later for the replacement generator. Rural Saskatchewan used to be safer, but these days everyone needed to lock their barns and homes.

After lunch at the diner, Mitch purchased a coffee for herself and a cappuccino for Callie and drove to Poplarcreek. To her, cappuccinos were watered-down coffee, but Callie preferred the milky drink to regular coffee. Mitch seldom called ahead and just hoped she could find Callie, but it was risky because she could be anywhere on the farm or in the fields. She knocked on the door to Callie's house and pushed open the unlocked door. "Callie? You home?"

An instant later, Callie entered the kitchen wearing only a towel.

"Geez, Callie." Mitch turned her back. "What if I'd been the feed salesman?"

Callie laughed. "I'd have gotten a free bag of calf feed."

Mitch listened to Callie laugh as she climbed the stairs, presumably to get dressed. She had wrapped her long hair in a towel, and she had a second one around her body that stopped mid-thigh. Hell, but she was gorgeous. Mitch settled at the kitchen table with the two coffees and sipped hers.

Ten minutes later, Callie returned and picked up her coffee. "Thanks. Does yours need heating?"

Mitch looked up. Callie wore denim cutoffs, a T-shirt, and nothing on her feet. With her wet hair tied in a ponytail, she looked about twenty. "No, thanks."

Callie slid her cappuccino into the microwave. "I'm glad you dropped by for a visit." When the timer dinged, Callie removed her coffee and settled into a chair across from Mitch after plopping a baking tin between them. "What's up?"

Mitch sighed. The tin would contain cookies or something else delicious. Callie could quit at one cookie, but not her. Better to leave the tin closed. "Why're you using the downstairs shower?"

"We're having guests for the wedding, so I'm painting the upstairs bathroom, and don't change the subject, Suzanne."

"Please, don't call me that." She put a whine in her voice that always made Callie laugh.

Callie squeezed Mitch's hand. "Spill."

Mitch swirled the liquid in her cup. Callie was her best friend, and she could trust her with her thoughts. Her mind flashed back to Kay's opinions about love and marriage. Maybe Kay could go through life without it, but would she be happy? It had been many years since Callie was this happy. Mitch had stood at Liz's shoulder at their wedding and in a few weeks, she'd stand beside Callie. Some people must just be the type others wanted to marry. She'd never been asked or done any asking.

"Why didn't you and Lauren get married before she got pregnant?" Mitch asked.

"It's all legal stuff to do with my RCMP benefits and ownership of Poplarcreek." Callie sighed. "Lauren wanted us to do wills and a prenuptial agreement so nobody could say she married me for the farm. As if." Callie laughed. "Anyway, the lawyers took longer to get organized, and it took me no time to get Lauren pregnant, but when the paperwork was done, she suddenly wanted to get married before the baby came. She's blaming it on hormones."

"Good for Lauren for insisting on a prenup. It wouldn't have occurred to me, but she's right to do it."

"You think Lauren is *right* about something?" Callie comically gaped at her and grabbed her phone. "I have to call my mom and post on Facebook or maybe Twitter, if I had a Twitter account. I know, I'll text Val and get her to tell everyone at PVS."

"Stop it. Stop it, please."

Callie sat poised with her finger above her phone. "I will, if you get to the point. What did you really want to ask me?"

"What do you think of Kay?"

Callie nodded and leaned back with a smug expression. "Have you eaten?"

"Yes, a late lunch at the diner. I ran into Kay fetching lunch for the clinic and she said Lauren was still on morning appointments."

"They're swamped at work. I'm not sure how they managed before Kay joined them." Callie stood and stepped to her refrigerator. "I'm starved." She selected food from the refrigerator and set it on the counter. "Lauren says Kay's a great surgeon and a hoot to work with."

"A hoot?" Mitch laughed. "Lauren's word or her grand-mother's?"

"Ours."

Mitch cleared her throat. "Kay is funny, which is great, but she's only serious about her work."

"Very true, and in a different age she'd be some hippie in a beat-up van roaming the country."

"She was telling me about a friend who converted a van into a home and drives around the west doing locums for other vets."

Callie returned with her salad and a couple of hard-boiled eggs. "What a great idea. Kay could set up a surgery suit in an RV and drive from clinic to clinic doing complicated surgeries. Lauren says Kay's really good at bone stuff."

"Orthopedics?"

Callie pointed her fork at Mitch. "That's it. Quit stalling. Why're you really here? You didn't come all this way to bring me a coffee."

"I have to see a farmer about another stolen generator."

"Again? Why doesn't he lock it up?"

"He'll have to figure out something this time. His insurance company won't keep replacing them. And speaking of, your front door should be locked when you're alone."

"I suppose."

Mitch took a deep breath. "Should I invite Kay to dinner at Thomas and Marcus's restaurant?"

"Why not? She's smart, cute, and seems interested in you. After all, she took you home after the club for *French toast* over a week ago."

"It was delicious."

"Pardon?" Callie squeaked and dropped her fork.

"The French toast, the French toast. What did you think I meant?"

"Well, I assumed—"

"Since dating Marion, I'm more careful before getting involved. I want to get a real sense of a woman first. We fell into bed on the second date, and within a week, I was emptying half my dresser for her clothes."

"I know, sweetie. And it took you three years to get rid of her."

Mitch shook her head. "That last year when we went to the Rainbow Club, Marion spent all her time with her friends and left me standing around alone or fetching drinks. I was just useful to her."

"She was a leech and I'm glad you figured it out. I never liked her."

"You never told me."

Callie shrugged. "I was tempted, but in the beginning, she made you happy and I liked that."

"That's why I want to get to know Kay first, but she's made it very clear she's not into anything serious. She's even said we should be friends."

"That's too bad. I thought there was a connection between you two." Callie squeezed Mitch's forearm. "I get that she's attractive and smart, but watch you don't set yourself up for another disappointment."

"I sort of got a sense she might change her mind, but it's probably wishful thinking. It's just that she's amazing." Mitch glanced at her watch. "I'm late. Hell, I'd better get going."

"Please be careful. I don't want you to get hurt again, but I want to see you happy." They hugged their good-byes and Callie kissed Mitch on the cheek. Mitch climbed into her cruiser and drove toward the farm with the missing generator.

So, Callie and Lauren both liked Kay. Everyone liked funny Kay, but Mitch saw the toughness and the vulnerability. She'd cradled Kay in her arms while she slept. She'd felt warm and protective, and it was a feeling she liked. But Kay sounded increasingly like a bad idea.

❖

"Unbelievable." Mitchell drove toward Thresherton after a discouraging afternoon. The pig farm still didn't intend to lock up the next generator. They said it was too much hassle to have to lock and unlock the barn. She'd spent an hour taking pictures and looking at grainy video surveillance tapes. Later, she'd driven around to the four neighboring farms, but nobody had seen anything. What a waste of time.

Mitch glimpsed the clock on the dashboard. Almost dinnertime and she'd be passing back by Poplarcreek. Callie would have a wonderful meal on the table. Lauren was tired of her, but she had an open invitation from Callie and Kay might be there. She called in to work and told them she was taking a dinner break. She'd just seen Callie, but right now she could do with some company.

She pulled into Poplarcreek and smiled at the warm lights beckoning her from Callie's kitchen. She parked at the house and headed inside. "Knock, knock. Where is everyone?"

"Hey, you." Callie popped into the kitchen and fiddled with a pan on the stove before she gave Mitch a big hug and a kiss on each cheek.

"Something smells good."

"Omelet with mushrooms and cheese."

Mitch glanced toward the small pan on the stove. It wasn't a family meal. "You're happy. And why's your T-shirt inside out?"

"I was upstairs, Mitchy. Kay took more of the afternoon work, so Lauren could come home early."

"Lauren is upstairs, and Becky is? Wait. She's away for the night?"

Callie winked. "Becky is staying with Gwen at Val's. And Kay didn't ask to stay so she must be heading back to Saskatoon after work."

Kay had said she'd be at Poplarcreek, but clearly her plans had changed. "Right, I'm out of here."

Callie kissed Mitch on the cheek, handed her a tin of baking, and propelled her through the door. "Night, Mitchy."

Mitch climbed into her cruiser and set the tin on the seat beside her. No family meal for her tonight, but she wouldn't begrudge Callie her fun. She was in love and well-loved, and she was happy for her, if a little envious. She looked again at the warm lights coming from the house and sighed as she pulled away into the darkness.

Mitch straightened and pointed the cruiser toward PVS. Maybe she would follow Callie's example and settle down. If not with Kay, then with somebody else. For now, she needed to get rid of the baking tin full of calories. Maybe she could just catch Kay before she left. Some friendly company would be better than a future of meals for one.

CHAPTER TEN

K ay heard the doorbell and walked to the front door of PVS which she'd locked for the evening. She peered through the glass door. Outside, Mitch shuffled from foot to foot and occasionally glanced at her cruiser as if considering her escape.

She opened the door. "Hey, it's the cops. I want to report a stalker. This woman followed me to the diner on the weekend, ran into me at lunch at the diner today, and now she's shown up at work."

Mitch looked as if she was searching for an answer, but clearly none came to mind.

"You must admit all these meetings are getting a little stalky?" Kay laughed. "Stop looking so hunted and come in. I'm kidding." It was surprising that Mitch kept showing up. Hadn't she scared her off with all the innuendo and flirting? But maybe Mitch was coming over to her side. She grabbed Mitch's sleeve and with the barest of tugs pulled her inside. "What a surprise. I'm glad you're not another emergency. It's been a long day and Val wants to go home."

"I just came from Poplarcreek. Callie sent me away with a tin of baking. It's heavy and I'm afraid if I take it home, I'll eat it all."

Kay squinted at Mitch and shrugged. "I don't understand."

"It's Callie's baking." She said it as though the meaning was clear.

Val entered the waiting room. "Hey, Mitch. Thought you might be another emergency."

Kay pointed to the tin in Mitch's hand. "Mitch has baking from Poplarcreek."

"It's sort of an emergency. I need help to eat this."

Val laughed. "Callie's baking? Awesome. Follow me."

Kay locked the door behind Mitch and followed Mitch and Val to the lunchroom. "It's too late for coffee. Mitch, do you want water or a soda?"

Mitch slid a carton of milk from a bag and displayed it as if the carton were a bottle of fine wine. "It's a good year for milk."

"Perfect." Kay grabbed plates, forks, and glasses and they settled at the table.

Mitch lifted the lid off the tin with reverence. She tipped the lid open two inches, so the others couldn't see the contents. She peered inside and breathed deeply through her nose.

Val pointed at Mitch. "Quit teasing. You brought it to share."

"You'll spoil your dinner, Valerie."

"Not a chance. Gimme." Val lunged for the tin, but Mitch raised it above her head. Val crossed her arms over her chest and pouted.

Mitch and Val were behaving like toddlers. Kay had seen Val silly before, but she enjoyed this new side of Mitch.

"Corporal Mitchell. Before you are two women who haven't eaten since lunch." Kay made a show of looking at her watch. "Five hours ago. If you continue to torment us, we will retaliate."

Mitch locked eyes with Kay. "What're you gonna do, blondie?"

Kay smirked. "Want to test me? You're big, but if we team up, we could take you."

"Where're you going?" Mitch asked as Val darted from the room. "I'm kidding. Val, come back. I'll share."

"Now you've done it," Kay said.

"Should I go and get her?"

"I'll go in a minute if she doesn't come back."

Val returned with a little kitten held against her cheek. "Look who I've got? Mr. Paws is about six weeks old and so cuddly. Aren't you, Mr. Paws?"

Mitch's face softened. She set the tin on the table and held out her hands to accept the kitten. "Hi, sweetie. You're so tiny."

"Well done, Val," Kay said as she watched Mitch cuddle the kitten. "The cute kitten is a devious weapon."

Val grinned with her mouth already full of chocolate brownie. As she ate, Kay focused on Mitch's large hands as she cradled the kitten and caressed its head. Her mouth went dry, and she gulped her milk as she relived Mitch's hands caressing the bare skin of her back as they danced at the club. A tremor skittered up her spine as she imagined the power in Mitch's long, strong fingers.

"Hey, Mitch, do you mind if I take some brownies with me?" Val asked.

Mitch shook her head without taking her eyes off the kitten. It purred and rubbed its head against her chin. "Help yourself."

Val squeezed Kay's forearm. "Are we done? Or do you need help with the poodle again?"

"No, thanks. I've got it covered. Hey, did you get more ketamine? You told me to remind you." She astonished herself by remembering the ketamine when all she could think about was Mitch's caresses.

"I did, but we're tearing through it. I ordered two bottles this time." Val laughed. "Thanks, Mitch. See you tomorrow, Kay."

Kay glanced at Val but returned to focus on Mitch's hands. "Have a good night." She absently ate her brownie, no longer hungry for food. The sight of Mitch caressing the kitten rendered her speechless. She would purr too if Mitch caressed her and made those cooing noises. She yearned to say something flirty, but her brain couldn't find the words and their last conversation had been about friendship. When she finished her brownie, she reached for the kitten. "I can take him."

Mitch reluctantly relinquished the kitten, lifted her fork, and attacked her brownie. "Thanks for helping me with the brownies. I'm afraid to take the tin home. I could eat chocolate and Callie's baking all day long. Combine them and I'm helpless. Callie can eat it because she farms and works hard, but I'm five years older and my job's not as physical."

Kay nodded. "There's always baking at Poplarcreek, but you don't look as if you eat any."

"You don't either."

Kay cuddled the kitten and searched Mitch's face. "So, you dropped by to bring us baking? To leave the demon tin with us?"

Mitch laughed. "The lights were still on in the clinic." She forked brownie into her mouth.

Kay smirked at Mitch until she squirmed. Mitch could stick to her story of dropping by to share the brownies, but she could've taken the brownies to the police station if she'd just wanted to get rid of them.

Mitch studied the milk in her glass. "What's your plan tonight? Are you heading to the city?"

"I've more to do tonight and I want to check on my patients in the morning. I can't start my day until I've seen how they did through the night. It's a bit obsessive, I know."

"No, it's dedicated."

"Anyway, I have an open invitation to stay at Poplarcreek. We were so busy I forgot to text Callie that I wanted to stay tonight after all."

Mitch scratched the back of her neck. "Might be a problem. I dropped in at Poplarcreek, at dinnertime. Lauren was upstairs, and Callie was in the kitchen, barefoot, with her shirt on inside out, and her hair a mess. She was making dinner for two and Becky is staying with Val."

Kay grinned. "Once, in the middle of the night, I met Callie in her kitchen fetching a snack. Her expression was peaceful, a complete contrast to her crazy, messy, hair." She laughed. "So, I'm sure they've had sex before when I was there, but now you've made it feel weird."

"Sorry, I—"

Kay playfully punched Mitch in the shoulder. "Just kidding. Thanks for the warning. I'll leave them their private time. Well, apparently, I'm bunking here. Ian has a folding camp cot stashed somewhere."

"Stay at my house."

Kay blinked in surprise as she regarded Mitch. "Your house?"

"I'm on dinner break now and off at ten, but you can drive over anytime. The spare room is the room closest to the front door and the sheets are clean."

"That's an intriguing offer, for your spare room."

"It's just a place to stay. Just one friend helping another." Mitch continued to eat her brownie. "Or Val has a couch, and the motel on the highway isn't too bad. If you decide to stay at my house, you'll need to bring food. I've only got peanut butter and stale bread left."

"I'll put the kitten in his bed. Back in a second." Kay stood and headed to the cat room. She buried her nose in the kitten's soft warm fur and caught the subtle scent of Mitch's cologne. The familiar scent brought back a sense of longing. Should she stay with Mitch? "What do you think, Mr. Paws? She is sexy but we want different things. I can stay with a friend without it being an invitation for more. Right?" The kitten mewed. "Oh, what do you know, you're just a baby." Maybe staying with Mitch was a terrible idea, but a real bed would mean a better night's sleep.

Kay kissed the kitten and set him in his bed. She popped into the dog room and untangled a puppy from his IV line. She replaced his soiled newspapers and refilled his hot-water bottle. When the puppy snuggled against the bottle, she tucked a blanket over it and caressed its head. "Sleep now, little guy."

She dashed back to the lunchroom. "I accept. Thanks, Mitch. I appreciate it."

"Great." Mitch stood. "I should go. I'll be home at ten fifteen unless I get caught up at work." She pointed to a hand-drawn map and a house key on the table. "I have a spare key at the detachment, so lock the door behind you and help yourself to anything."

"To peanut butter and stale bread. Thanks." She smiled. "I always bring an overnight bag to Thresherton, so I'm set there, and I'll bring something to eat." Kay closed the tin and handed it to Mitch. "Thanks for these."

Mitch reached for the tin then pulled back. "No, thanks. Leave it here, please. Lauren will take it home when it's empty." They walked to the front door and Mitch looked at her for a few seconds before striding away.

Kay arrived at Mitch's house after work, dropped her bags in the spare room, and headed into the kitchen with her groceries. Val had given her the farm-fresh eggs and sworn Kingsway's eggs were the best on the planet. She rummaged in Mitch's cupboards and cracked two eggs into a frying pan, after dropping a slice of still-okay bread into the toaster. Mitch wasn't kidding about her empty refrigerator. After dinner, Kay washed her dishes and put them in the dish rack to dry.

She suppressed the urge to snoop in Mitch's bedroom and settled for exploring the rest of the small bungalow. The house consisted of three bedrooms and a kitchen and living room. One bedroom held an elliptical, a bench, and free weights. The hand weights were set at an impressive fifty pounds. The tidy living room held a worn couch centered in front of an enormous television.

She scanned the large prints of the prairies hanging on Mitch's living room walls. She'd covered another wall with a mixed collection of pictures of people in a variety of frames. Some were family pictures. She leaned closer to examine a photograph of a man, a woman, a boy, and two young girls. Mitch looked about six in the picture. The man, presumably her father, appeared to be Canadian Aboriginal.

The rest of the pictures were of friends and other RCMP officers. She was sure the room temperature had shot up five degrees as she paused in front of a large picture of Mitch. In her day-to-day police uniform, Mitch was hot, but in the red-serge jacket, she was edible.

Kay rubbed her left knee. She needed to jump into a hot shower and get to bed. Fifteen hours on her feet was enough for one day. An hour ago, she'd been ready to curl up and sleep on the floor of PVS. She'd struggled to keep her eyes open as she drove across town. Now she was in Mitch's house and wide-awake. A hot shower would help. She fished through her overnight bag for a minute, then dumped it on the bed. She groaned as she pictured her bodywash, shampoo, and conditioner sitting on the edge of her bathtub at home.

Kay stripped off her clothes and walked naked to the bathroom. Perhaps she should've grabbed a towel first, but she was alone. She plucked Mitch's bodywash off the edge of the tub, popped the top and breathed in the subtle scent of rosewood. The scent that had wafted off the kitten after Mitch cuddled it.

Little, except a lover's hands, felt as exquisite as hot water flowing over her tired muscles after a long day. She massaged her knee and groaned with relief. As the bathroom filled with steam and the smell of Mitch's products, she imagined Mitch's hands sliding over her in the shower. What if she were still here when Mitch arrived home? Kay laughed at herself. "For one, I'd be freezing cold because all the hot water would be gone."

Kay returned to her room and dressed for bed in shorts and a T-shirt. Mitch would be home soon. She considered waiting up but crawled into bed, exhausted. Several surgery articles on her tablet distracted her, and as she immersed herself in science, the world disappeared. When the crunch of gravel announced a vehicle, she clicked off the tablet and held her breath.

She registered a key in the lock and sock feet treading along the hall to the bathroom. She listened to the shower and quiet whistling. An instant later, she pictured Mitch naked and coming to her in bed. These foolish thoughts were guaranteed to ramp up her libido and steal more sleep. She'd been offered the spare room, not a place beside Mitch in her bed. They were friends and there was no point in thinking of anything more.

Quiet sounds in the kitchen brought her fully awake. She abandoned all hope of sleep and got up. She padded down the hall and skidded to a halt as Mitch cracked three eggs into a frying pan. She scanned Mitch's body, and covered her mouth to conceal her ragged breathing. She wore a tight black tank top and matching boxers. Kay melted into a puddle of lust. No way could she remain sane in the same room with her, especially if Mitch didn't want to have sex. She turned around and snuck back to her room. As she slid under the covers, she sighed with regret. If Mitch had caught her spying, anything could've happened.

"Kay, are you up?" Mitch called softly.

Kay froze. Mitch must have heard her in the hall. The choice was before her. Acknowledge Mitch or pretend to be asleep? Her libido was about to speak when her saner self clamped her hand over her mouth. The after-club visit to her apartment was a mess of misunderstandings. She wouldn't do that a second time. Next time she would make sure she and Mitch were on the same page and right now they weren't.

A few seconds later, Mitch tiptoed away. Kay listened to clinking dishes in the kitchen, followed by a door closing. Had it been the right decision? The pulsing between her legs told her the answer was no. As she listened to the house creak, she reconsidered her decision and screamed into the pillow she held over her face.

At five thirty, Kay's phone alarm buzzed, and she shot awake in her bed at Mitch's house. She'd showered before bed, so she dressed and left. After a quick visit to PVS she drove to Saskatoon to start her day of meetings and classes.

In the office Kay shared with three other residents, she collected her computer and notes for the meeting at ten. She yawned and rubbed her eyes. She'd not slept well. She'd tossed and turned while picturing Mitch naked in the shower and in her bed.

When Mitch had invited her to stay that night, life had become charged with possibility, but it had only amounted to one friend helping another. "Friends. We're just friends." Kay shook her head. Thanks to her attraction, Mitch was already more than a friend, but that's where it had to end. Mitch wanted what she couldn't give. Wouldn't give. As usual, her life was her career and she worked hard. A month ago, that had been enough, but was it today? Trying to figure out her connection to Mitch was like walking through thick mud. She was making progress, but it was a hard, painful slog.

CHAPTER ELEVEN

Four days later, Kay was back in Thresherton and had settled in for a day of surgeries. None were emergencies, which was good, and she made her way through them without incident. She'd been able to put some of her latest classroom learning into play, which was a bonus.

Two hours later, Kay rolled her shoulders and bent to massage her left knee. That was her last scheduled surgery for the day, and they were low on ketamine again. Was Val rationing it? She wouldn't have enough to sedate a large dog if one rolled in for an emergency.

Kay splayed her fingers over her stomach when it growled. She was starving and hoped Val would hurry back with lunch.

Val stuck her head into the treatment room and raised a white paper bag. "I'm back."

"Thanks. Be right there."

"I'll fetch Lauren," Val said as she darted from the room.

Kay used the bathroom and washed her face and hands. She loved the ritual of lunch at the diner or sitting in the lunchroom, chatting with the women she worked with. At the college, lunch was often a sandwich at her desk. Lunch with her PVS friends was a highlight of her week. She hadn't had such good friends since her classmates in vet school back in PEI.

Kay entered the lunchroom and sat on an empty chair in front of a Caesar salad with chicken. The diner prepared a tasty salad with fresh ingredients. In Saskatoon, she only managed two meals from a head of lettuce before the rest turned black and mushy. It was easier to stock her kitchen with cans and frozen dinners. Kay grinned. She and Mitch could compete to see who had the emptiest refrigerator.

Kay ate as she listened to Lauren and Val chat. They were good friends, as close as sisters.

Val nudged Kay. "Have you seen Mitch lately?"

"Not since the evening she dropped by." Kay focused on her plate and fiddled with her salad. "Is she dating anyone? She's never mentioned anyone."

"No, but women crowd around her at the club," Val said. "Mitch dates, but I've never seen her serious or with somebody her own age in years."

Lauren dropped her elbow to the table and rested her chin in her hand. "Mitch doesn't tease me as much anymore. The last few months she's even been opening doors for me."

Val patted Lauren's arm. "She opens doors for you because you're pregnant. She's a very thoughtful person."

"How are preparations coming for the baby? Is Little Corny's room ready?" Val asked.

Lauren grimaced. "Please, quit saying that or it'll stick to the child. Corny Cornish. Might as well enroll them in karate at birth."

Val pointed at Kay. "She started it."

"Guilty." Kay laughed. "So how is the baby's room coming?"

"Callie stripped off the old wallpaper, painted the walls, and sanded and refinished the floor. I offered to help, but she refused to let me. She said, 'You might be awesome with a scalpel and passable with a paring knife, but put anything else sharp or dangerous in your hands and there will be blood.' How nice is that to hear from your fiancée?"

Kay laughed. "Now I know why she does all the cooking."

Janice popped into the lunchroom. "Officer Mitchell's here and wants to talk to you, Val."

"Sure, send her back," Val said.

Kay finger-combed her hair to make it fuller. She cursed herself for not stopping to fix it after her last surgery, but it couldn't be helped now.

Lauren snorted as she watched, then looked down at her salad when Mitch came in.

"Hey, all."

Kay sat a little straighter and smiled. "Stalking me again?"

Mitch sat across from Kay. "You keep saying that, and I'll have to stay away. Anybody want an ice cream? I picked up a selection."

"Oh, goody, goody. Thanks, Mitch," Val said.

Mitch handed the bag to Val. "You're welcome."

"You've got, like, eight in here."

Mitch waved her hand, but never took her eyes off Kay. "Some for later or tomorrow."

Val selected a treat and passed the bag to Lauren. "I saw a couple of peanut butter chocolate ones."

"Thanks, Mitch." Lauren dug into the bag, tore the wrapper off, and took a bite. "So good."

"Kay?" Mitch pushed the bag toward her.

"Maybe later. I'm stuffed now, but you go ahead."

Mitch stood and put the bag in the freezer compartment of the lunchroom fridge. "Kay, do you have a minute to talk, outside?"

Kay nodded and followed Mitch to her cruiser. Mitch leaned against it and Kay did the same and waited as long as she could. "Thanks again for the place to stay the other day."

"Oh, you're welcome. The eggs were a treat. I'm afraid I've eaten them all."

"Good. I left them for you." Kay studied the people moving along the sidewalk and waited for Mitch's real reason to drop by. "Have we got somebody under surveillance?"

"Pardon?"

"We're just standing here, so I assumed we were watching somebody. That old lady with the two grocery bags looks suspicious. Should we question her?"

"That's the mayor, and she's very honest."

Kay leaned close and splayed her hand against Mitch's stomach. "Okay, how about those two kids?" she whispered "The ones with the bicycles. They have a shifty look about them."

Mitch seemed like she was going to say something.

Kay quickly stepped away. She rubbed her hands together to dispel the tingle created by the sudden tightening of Mitch's muscles beneath her palm.

Mitch gave a quick laugh. "I'll go question them. See you at the club this weekend?"

Kay shook her head. "Nah, I'm on call this weekend, but I'll be at Poplarcreek. No doubt you'll be there for dinner."

"I don't always go."

Kay snorted. "I hear Callie always makes extra for you."

"Probably. Anyway, see you later." Mitch got in her car and left.

Kay watched the cruiser pull out of the parking lot. What had Mitch wanted to talk about? Surely, she hadn't dragged her outside to talk about nothing. Was she supposed to do something? Mitch had clearly rebuffed her interest in anything physical. It was time to back away, no matter how intrigued she was by Mitch. Kay shrugged. She'd been sure Mitch was going to ask her out. Probably not a good idea, so why was she so disappointed?

She'd been plenty clear about her goals. Now was not the time to waver. She squared her shoulders and headed inside. What she didn't need was to be drawn from her path. She'd worked too hard. She was in her kayak paddling a peaceful river with treacherous waterfalls called Mitch. Now was the time to pull her boat and portage around the danger.

CHAPTER TWELVE

"Hey, Mitch, you have the day off, right? Are you busy? Because Kay needs rescuing." Callie said.

Mitch's hand squeezed her phone as if to crush it. "What happened? Is she all right? Where is she? Does she need an ambulance?"

"Whoa, she's okay. It's just that her car broke down. It's ancient, and belongs at the wrecker, not on the road." Callie chuckled. "But students can't be picky. Anyway, Kay called Lauren, but she's stuck at work. Lauren wanted me to go, but I'm waiting for the electrician and I have to be here when Becky gets home."

"I'll go."

Callie told her where Kay was broken down. "Thanks. Good luck."

Mitch tapped the details into her phone and listened to Callie laugh as she hung up. It was Friday, and Mitch was off duty until Monday morning.

She laid her hand on her stomach and her mind flashed back to meeting Kay at PVS three days ago. Kay had caressed her stomach and it had sent her pulse skyrocketing. When she'd undressed later, she'd expected to find singe marks the shape of Kay's fingers on her skin. It had been off the scale intense and made her want to be around Kay even if it was a bad idea. When she'd chickened out and decided not to ask her on a date the other day, she'd reminded herself that it really was a bad idea to get attached to someone who would be gone soon enough. When was the last time just thinking about a woman had sent her into such a deep tailspin?

She grabbed a pair of coveralls and her tool kit. She hopped in her pickup truck and drove to where Kay waited.

When Mitch arrived, Kay climbed from her car smiling. An instant later, the smile switched to a grimace. "Hi, Mitch."

"Callie called me." Was Kay disappointed she was the one to come out? It hurt to think so.

"Sorry to bug you, but my car needs a boost. Or maybe a big fire to put it out of its misery."

"Let's have a look." Mitch popped the hood and examined the old car. The right fender and right door were green, and the rest of the car was blue. It had parts not made for the make and model and a hose patched with duct tape. Kay shouldn't be driving it anywhere, let alone on the highway between Thresherton and Saskatoon. "Sorry, there's more wrong here than I can fix. You need parts."

"It figures. It was an old car when I bought it." Kay sighed. "I prefer biological systems because they can heal themselves."

Mitch arranged for a tow to the Thresherton Garage. The garage owner promised to examine the car at once and give Kay a call. "Sorry, I couldn't fix it," she said.

"Thanks for trying. Maybe I should've just told him to drop it at the wrecker's." Kay laughed.

"What'll you do now?"

"I'm headed to Poplarcreek for the evening. I'm on call tonight and I work tomorrow."

"I'll drop you at Poplarcreek."

"I don't need more help, and I've bugged you enough."

Mitch made an exaggerated show of scanning the road in both directions as if searching for another vehicle. "You got another ride coming?"

"Is there a bus?"

The fact that Kay would prefer to take a bus than get a ride from her made it clear where they stood. She wasn't sure what she'd done to make her step back, though. "You'll have a long wait. Next bus is Monday morning and it's headed into the city."

Kay winced. "Once again, I impress you with my organizational skills. Will you drive me to Poplarcreek, please?"

Mitch winked, trying to get her to relax. "If I deliver you to Callie, she'll invite me for dinner."

"Sneaky, but your keen investigative technique had no doubt deduced that I'm arriving in time for dinner. We're coconspirators."

Mitch laughed as she loaded Kay's overnight bag and computer in her truck. They climbed in and headed to Poplarcreek.

Mitch drove but kept stealing glances at Kay. She was beautiful in a tiny, feisty way. She bet Kay wouldn't appreciate being called feisty. Small women seldom did.

Mitch didn't mind helping with the car. She liked taking care of people, sometimes even if they didn't appreciate the help. The hair on the back of Mitch's neck rose, warning of danger. Kay was not another woman who needed rescuing. Right now, she was helping a new friend, nothing more, nothing to read into. *Yeah, right.*

Kay shifted in her seat and studied Mitch. "You're staring. What's up? Something on my face or are you mentally comparing me to a wanted poster?"

Mitch took a deep breath. "Will you have dinner with me this weekend, if you're not too busy?"

"That would be fun. We should ask Lauren and Callie to join us." Kay shook her head. "But I'm on call and that makes it risky. There's always a chance I might have to leave."

Mitch waited for a yes or no, but it wasn't coming. A dinner with Callie and Lauren along sounded nice and she owed them for so many meals, but it wasn't a dinner with friends she'd been after, though she should've been. She struggled for something pertinent to say but failed. "Kay's an interesting name. Easy to spell."

"Back to the personal questions?"

"Personal?"

Kay laughed. "Just kidding. My first name is Katherine. My parents call me Kathy, which I hate. In high school they called me Katie, and in the military, Kate. At vet school I reinvented myself and morphed into Kay. I'll have to stick with Kay because the only other names I can make from Katherine are Therine or The."

"I like Kay." Mitch took a deep breath. "You never answered. Would you have a drink or dinner with me this weekend?"

"It's nice of you to ask."

"Sorry, I forgot you quit drinking."

"It's okay. Like I said that night at the club, I'm not an alcoholic, but I was headed that way when I got back from Afghanistan."

"You had a rough time and were wounded. Anyone sensible would understand using alcohol as pain relief or an escape."

"Would they? Would you?"

Mitch nodded. "Sure. Why not? I indulge myself after a hard day at work."

Kay dropped her eyes to her lap and examined her nails. When she raised her head, she locked eyes with Mitch. "What about prescription painkillers?"

"If you need them, and likely you do." Warning bells began to ring quietly.

Kay continued to stare out the window as she began to speak. "The pain in my knee was excruciating after I got back from Afghanistan. I took a ton of painkillers, but when the pain settled down, I didn't stop. I faked the pain so my doctor would prescribe more. Eventually, I realized I was addicted and had to find help." She drew circles in the condensation on the window with her fingertip. "I quit drinking because my counselor suggested my body and mind might shift to using alcohol once I gave up pills. She warned me a new addiction could replace an old one."

Mitch's thoughts spun in circles. She'd seen drugs destroy people. She'd cared about people who had suffered from an addiction. She wouldn't risk getting into a relationship with an ex-addict. Didn't they always relapse? Didn't it always cause heartache?

"You're quiet. Did I shock you?"

Kay's laugh was half-hearted. Mitch glanced at her and caught the overpowering vulnerability in Kay's eyes. She needed to say something quickly, but it had to be the right comment.

"You're looking cartoonish. Your mouth is hanging open and I'm waiting for your eyes to pop out." Kay laughed weakly. "Are you really as shocked as all that? I took oxycodone for my destroyed knee and it's notoriously addictive. Don't tell anyone."

Mitch pulled off the road and studied Kay as her eyes flew from astonishment, to anger, to pain and hurt. She wished Kay had stopped at anger. It was hard to see the hurt in her eyes. "Thank you for telling me. It must have been a rough time and it's your story to tell." Vague platitudes weren't her style, but nothing else came to her as she processed Kay's history of addiction.

Mitch pulled her truck back onto the road. She tried several different topics of conversation in an attempt to lighten the moment, but Kay shook her head and wouldn't look at her. They rode in silence for the rest of the trip until she parked at Poplarcreek. Kay had her door open almost before the truck stopped.

"Whoa. Careful." Mitch placed a restraining hand on Kay's arm.

Kay studied Mitch expectantly and then she jumped from the truck with her shoulder bag and charged into the house.

Mitch groaned as she carried the rest of Kay's gear inside. She arrived in the kitchen just as Kay disappeared into Callie's office and closed the door. Mitch set her bags outside the office door. "I'll leave your stuff here." She waited for a reply that didn't come and then headed into the kitchen and dropped into a chair.

"How'd it go?" Callie asked as she worked away at the stove. "I asked Kay, but she flew past me."

"I couldn't fix it. It's at the garage for whatever they can do."

"So, she's annoyed? That why she ran past?"

"No, I—" Mitch glanced at the outside door as it opened. What could she say? She'd told Kay it was her story to tell. But keeping things from Callie felt weird. She hated secrets.

"I'm home!" Lauren kicked off her shoes, headed inside, and kissed Callie. "Mitchell, I see you're here too."

Mitch winced at the lack of welcome. Apparently, she wasn't wanted anywhere right now.

"Mitch helped Kay with her car and drove her here. I invited them both for dinner."

"Right, yes. Thanks, Mitch. How'd it go?" Lauren asked.

Mitch shrugged. "I had to have the garage tow it."

"Sit down, Mitch. You're staying for dinner," Callie said

"Yes, stay." Lauren smiled. "Thanks for trying. I'm sure if you couldn't get it going, I wouldn't have stood a chance. I'm just going to change." She headed upstairs.

It was a day for firsts. Lauren invited her to stay and complimented her. One day they'd be friends. One day.

"Can you tell Kay we're ready to eat? Lauren won't be long."

Mitch knocked on Callie's office door. "Kay?" She waited but Kay didn't answer. "Callie said dinner's ready in five minutes." She waited in silence for a minute and then headed back to the kitchen.

When Lauren returned, everyone sat for dinner. Most of the conversation pertained to the wedding. Mitch had hoped Kay would take the chair beside her or across from her, but Kay was quiet, and had positioned herself with Gwen and Becky between them. The girls seemed to live at one another's houses.

Just as Callie passed out plates of dessert, Kay snatched her ringing phone off the table. "Sorry, it's the garage." She stepped away from the table and returned a minute later. "My car will be ready by noon tomorrow, but I have to be at PVS by eight."

"My mom's picking up Becky and me tomorrow and you can have a ride, but she won't be here until nine," Gwen said.

"Thanks, but that'll make me late."

Mitch shrugged. "I don't work until Sunday night. I'll sleep here and run you into Thresherton in the morning." She looked at Callie, who nodded.

Kay didn't answer as her eyes shifted from Callie to Lauren and back. "Thanks, I appreciate it."

After dinner, Gwen and Becky ran upstairs to play. Kay and Lauren disappeared into the living room to discuss an article they were coauthoring. Mitch stayed with Callie to help clean up the kitchen.

Callie nudged Mitch with her elbow. "You were quiet tonight. Good conversation on the way here?"

"Interesting."

"So, have you decided whether to ask her out?" Callie asked.

"I tried to invite her to dinner, but we got sidetracked and she didn't accept."

"So, try again."

Mitch set down the dish she'd been absently drying to consider Callie's words. "I have to think about it." A drug addiction, even in the past, was a red flag.

"Okay. Now, that dish is dry enough. If you're done rubbing the pattern off, I have another ten for you to dry."

Mitch smiled and picked up a second plate. She dried the dishes, but her mind lingered on Kay and on the decision that waved back and forth in front of her. Was it a bad idea to ask her out? Kay was only interested in fun, leaving in less than a year, and she'd been an addict. Why was she still so determined to try to strike something up between them? Why was friendship such a hard line to keep from crossing? Was she giving off mixed signals by not sticking to the friendship angle?

Mitch put a plate in the cupboard and fetched another one to dry. There'd been a millisecond when she'd thought Kay wanted to accept her offer. She shook her head. She was just fooling herself. And besides, Kay hadn't spoken two words to her since they'd arrived at Poplarcreek.

Callie brought Mitch bedding for the couch. She would've offered her a bedroom, but the spare rooms were in a messy state because she was rearranging furniture and redecorating to get ready for the wedding and the baby.

By the time Mitch had settled on the couch for the night, she had no answers. Her only accomplishment was a headache and she longed to sleep. She switched her mind to dismantling her bike piece by piece which worked better than counting sheep.

Chapter Thirteen

Kay lay in bed and counted the tiles in the ceiling of Callie's office. She'd used exhaustion as the excuse to get out of working on the article with Lauren. It was only half-true. She couldn't concentrate on Lauren's words because she was straining to hear the conversation in the kitchen as Callie and Mitch did the dishes. How much had Mitch told Callie? She couldn't make out the words, but the deep tenor of Mitch's voice had reverberated through her.

For a second, she'd been drawn to her in the truck, but thankfully, she'd tamped down her attraction. Mitch was shocked and repulsed. She didn't blame her.

Kay reached for her tablet on the table beside her and winced as she moved her knee. Too much standing at work these days. She should've grabbed her ice pack from Callie's freezer, but Mitch had still been in the kitchen and she wanted to avoid her. She rubbed her knee. The ice would've helped with the swelling and she wouldn't be lying awake in pain.

She started reading an article. She was at the last paragraph but remembered nothing. Netflix and mindless sitcoms were what she needed tonight. Something light and distracting, but there was no such relief available.

Kay woke and stretched as she glanced at her phone. Two a.m. At least she'd slept for three hours. She flexed her knee experimentally and found it still sore and hot with inflammation. She should've iced it before bed, but she'd do it now. She turned on a lamp and dug through her bag for the retractable walking stick she sometimes used as a cane. Cane in hand, she quietly exited the office and headed to the kitchen to fetch her ice pack.

The moonlight bathed the room in a warm glow, and she stopped at the kitchen window to admire the full moon.

"Who's there?"

She jumped and dropped her cane. It had rubber padding and made little noise when it hit the floor. As she lost her balance, Mitch put an arm out to steady her. She fell against her and clutched her muscular bicep. "You startled me. I didn't hear you."

"Sorry, sock feet. Are you steady?"

Kay gripped the counter on either side of her as she balanced and looked up at Mitch and compared her to the pictures at her house. The years had added lines around Mitch's eyes. Lines that deepened when she smiled. If anything, she was even more handsome than she'd been when she was younger. And as the moonlight illuminated Mitch's face, she registered her wariness.

"Your cane fell."

Kay looked around and discovered her cane wedged in the gap between the counter and the refrigerator.

"Can I grab it for you?"

"I can get it myself."

"I'm sure you can, but may I get it for you?"

Kay focused on a spot above Mitch's shoulder. "Yes, please." She was unsteady without the cane and not just because she was standing and trying not to put weigh on her knee. Mitch's proximity made her uneasy, and the warmth that she emitted made her skin tingle. She'd almost forgot that Mitch's body radiated heat like a furnace.

Mitch retrieved the cane, brushed the dust off, and handed it to Kay. She accepted it and leaned heavily on it. Her physical balance restored, she took several deep calming breaths and pushed out a few mundane words to fill the silence. "Trouble sleeping?"

"No, bathroom."

Kay needed to know. "How freaked-out are you about my confession tonight? I'm no longer addicted."

"I'm glad and I think you're very brave."

"You're not disgusted?"

"Not at all." Mitch shook her head sadly and lifted her hand as if to touch Kay's hair and Kay swayed toward her. It would be so easy to fall into those welcoming arms and lay her head against Mitch's shoulder. She leaned away at the same time Mitch stepped back. Weren't they a pair of indecisive fools?

"Well, good night." Kay winced as she turned to open Callie's freezer.

"You're hurting. Your knee's still bad then?"

Kay pushed aside frozen meat, ice cream, and other items searching for her ice pack. "Not all the time. Only when I overdo it. Can you hit the light, please? I'm trying to find my ice pack."

"Is that it in the door slot?"

"Well done." Kay set the ice pack on the counter. "Sometimes it aches so much it's impossible to sleep." She hadn't been sleeping for more personal reasons, but Mitch didn't need to know all her secrets. Kay fiddled with her ice pack. "I don't take any pain medication. Not even over-the-counter products. I have other ways to deal with the pain. Sometimes just moving around helps." She shrugged. "It's no big deal. I always fall asleep when I'm more tired than sore."

Kay kept talking to keep Mitch there because she was reluctant to break their connection. She turned to face the window. "I walked by and was drawn to the window. You can appreciate a full moon in the country. In the city, we have too much light pollution and you never notice the sky."

Mitch stepped behind Kay and peered over her shoulder. They weren't touching, but they were close enough she warmed in the heat pulsing off Mitch's body. Being this close to her in the truck had been like standing in the way of a moving car. This time, in the moonlight, as the compassion radiated off Mitch, she felt like a hundred-car train was barreling toward her.

She shivered at the intensity of the sexual energy flowing between them. Was Mitch aware of it? Did she feel the same?

"You're cold. I'll fetch your shawl," Mitch said.

"No, I'm okay." Kay turned, but Mitch had vanished. A minute later, Mitch returned with Kay's shawl and spread it over her shoulders.

"Thanks. How did you find it in the dark? I forgot where I left it."

"I pay attention."

Kay chuckled. "Am I under surveillance, Corporal?"

"Not for any official reason."

Kay turned and looked up at Mitch. "Well, you need to sleep, and I'd better go back to bed. Long day tomorrow." Her mouth and her head said the words, but her body ignored her and refused to move.

"Can I help?"

"How do you mean?"

"Can I help with your knee? I've noticed you rubbing it. Does massage help?"

"Yes," Kay whispered. An instant later, she trembled as she envisioned Mitch's strong hands easing the pain in her knee and the rest of her body. She longed for her touch.

"Yes, it helps, or yes, I may help, or yes, please, massage it?" Mitch stole closer and matched her tone to Kay's.

Kay looked up at Mitch. "Yes, to all."

Mitch raised her hands to the level of Kay's waist. "May I pick you up?"

"Yes." Mitch took her cane and leaned it against the counter and gripped her around the waist, lifted her, and placed her on the end of Callie's kitchen table. Kay's breath hitched in excitement and she subtly took deep calming breaths.

Mitch scanned the kitchen and snagged a bottle of hand lotion sitting by the sink. She held it where Kay could read the bottle's label. She nodded and Mitch pulled a chair close and dropped in front of her. Mitch folded the edge of Kay's long T-shirt to mid-thigh. Kay struggled to keep from moaning at the sensual glide of the fabric against her skin as Mitch uncovered her. Mitch squirted lotion on her palms and rubbed her palms briskly together to warm the lotion. Frowning in concentration, Mitch glanced at her for confirmation.

"Please," she whispered.

Mitch coated Kay's knee and calf in lotion in a gentle soothing motion. "Tell me what to do."

Kay hunted for words, but still found none. Mitch sat below her, and the moonlight flowed in, glinting off Mitch's tousled brown hair.

Kay tried again to speak, but her mouth was dry. Her words emerged in a croak. "Massage it and be...firm." She almost said hard, but that was too intense. The word made her long to slip off the table and straddle Mitch's lap.

Mitch glanced up as she massaged her leg. "Tell me if I'm hurting you."

"It hurts now, but I'll tell you when to stop." Her knee was a mess of scars, but it was a fact of life, and although Mitch had hesitated for a second, it didn't stop her from touching Kay's knee. At least that was one thing Mitch wasn't repulsed by.

Mitch massaged her calf and knee and partway up her thigh. Kay sucked in a breath when Mitch's hands climbed higher on her thigh.

Mitch lowered her hands. "Sorry, I got carried away."

Mitch's hands sliding along her body had unnerved her, and her flesh begged for more contact. Did Mitch know? How did she feel? "Amazing. Thanks. You have strong hands, but gentle."

Kay traced her lips with the tip of her tongue. She was living a favorite fantasy of moonlight and a hot butch at her feet. Mitch's hands were on her and now she hungered for those hands everywhere. Her control slipped as she caressed Mitch's bent head and sifted thick hair between her fingers. Mitch looked up, and she cupped her face with her hands and tugged. She spread her thighs in invitation when Mitch rose.

Mitch didn't move in. She placed her hands on the table on either side of Kay and leaned toward her for a kiss. Kay moaned, amazed a woman with such a hard body possessed such soft lips. She deepened the kiss, linked her arms around Mitch's neck, and pulled. Mitch's arms trembled as she kissed her eyelids and the sides of her mouth working her way back to Mitch's lips.

Mitch stepped back, her chest heaving. "If I put my arms around you, I'll need to take you to bed. I could ignite I want you so much."

"Come here then," Kay said. Mitch settled between Kay's legs and enveloped her in strong arms. Mitch met her lips with hard kisses. Kay linked her fingers behind Mitch's neck and curled her legs around her waist.

Mitch slid her hands under Kay's backside. "Can I take you to bed?"

Kay's last ounce of control fled. "You better." The room had filled with a sexual hunger and the energy they created shot between them. Kay craved this. Smart or not, she'd packed her brain away. Libido and lust were in charge.

With little effort, Mitch scooped Kay into her arms and carried her to the bed in Callie's office. This time, Mitch set her on the bed with great care and stared down at her. "What should I know?"

"Know?"

"So as not to hurt you or annoy you again." Mitch grinned.

"Put no weight on my left leg and knee. My knee is a mess of arthritis. Don't put your weight on me. Oh, and expect me to be on top, a lot." She scowled at Mitch. "And I'm serious about this one. Never put your handcuffs on me. It will never be sexy."

"I'll be careful." Mitch shifted to Kay's right side and slipped in beside her. "I wish I was wearing a strap right now."

"We'll get to that, eventually." She bent and captured Mitch's mouth. She kissed Mitch's face, neck, and throat while Mitch's hands roamed her body. When Mitch rubbed her nipples, she straightened to give her more access as she clasped the bottom of her T-shirt preparing to remove it. If this was the only time they'd have sex, she damn well planned on it being memorable.

CHAPTER FOURTEEN

A second later, somebody knocked on the door. "Kay, are you there? We have an emergency at the clinic," Lauren said. "The answering service called me because you didn't answer your phone."

"Sorry, I didn't hear it."

Mitch grabbed the phone off the bedside table and passed it to Kay.

Kay peered at her phone. "They called while I was in the kitchen. I'm sorry."

"Can I come in or will we keep shouting through the door?"

Mitch stood, unlatched the door, and strode past Lauren without a word or a glance.

Kay sat on the bed, uncomfortable and embarrassed about Mitch being in her room. She lifted her chin. She and Mitch were single, consenting adults. It wasn't Lauren's business what they did, but it was her house.

Lauren entered, her eyebrows raised. "The answering service says it's a dog hit by a car."

Mitch returned, handed Kay her cane and departed without speaking again. She didn't make eye contact with Lauren and Lauren didn't acknowledge Mitch's presence.

Kay winced at the frigid air between Lauren and Mitch. If they were dogs, they'd circle each other with their hackles up and teeth bared. She hobbled to the desk and grabbed some clothes. "I'd better hurry."

"Do you need help?"

"Would you call for help if it were you?" Kay spoke with a bite in her words and immediately felt remorseful for snapping at Lauren for being kind. "Sorry about that. I can do it." She refused to have people speculate on whether she could do her job. How humiliating that Lauren thought she needed help.

"I've asked for help when I need it. A patient's suffering is more important than anybody's ego. I'd assess the patient and if it can't wait, I'd call Val to help me. We've done surgery in the middle of the night, but if you go that route call her cell phone."

Kay scanned Lauren's face, shocked that she'd read her so well. "What about Gwen?"

"Depends on the day. On the weekends Gwen watches and helps. On weeknights, she used to sleep on the folding cot Ian stores at the clinic. These days, Val slips out and leaves Gwen because Ronnie's usually there."

"Thanks for the suggestion. And you're right, if I need help, I'll call."

"Okay, good luck." Lauren left.

Kay dressed as fast as possible and grabbed her bag. She limped outside and searched the parking lot for ten seconds until she remembered her car was in the shop.

Mitch gestured to the open passenger door of her truck. "I'll give you a ride."

"I'll borrow Lauren's truck." Kay groaned inwardly at her ridiculous suggestion. She couldn't bother Lauren now, and why ask to borrow her truck when Mitch was ready? "Seems I need rescuing again."

They drove to Thresherton in silence. Kay stole glances at Mitch, but her eyes were on the road. Did Mitch regret what had almost happened? Kay only regretted being interrupted. She could still feel Mitch's fingers on her nipples. She sighed. Being interrupted at all hours of the day or night was an occupational hazard for a veterinarian. But damn, she'd been so close to getting what she wanted. Getting who she wanted, but was it what Mitch wanted? Had she maneuvered her into bed? As much as she longed for Mitch, she wanted it to be right for her too, with no regrets. Mitch may be a tough cop, but no doubt she could be hurt too, and Kay wanted no part of that.

When they arrived at PVS, Kay dashed in the side door and keyed off the alarm. She didn't take the time to notice if Mitch followed or drove off. Her hands shook as she buttoned her white lab coat. She'd done plenty of surgeries but hadn't had sole responsibility for an animal. At the veterinary college, others did the triage and emergency care work.

She dug through the drug cabinet to organize her premed drugs. If she needed to sedate the dog for X-rays or surgery, she wanted to be ready. Still only half a bottle of ketamine? Val was slipping as school took up more of her time. Clearly, she'd forgotten to order the ketamine. She'd order it herself in the morning. It wasn't a drug to be short on.

When the clinic's front doorbell rang, she took several deep breaths and marched to the front door of the clinic.

Kay unlocked the door to a woman and a man. "My name is Dr. Gallant. Please, bring your pet and follow me." The two people led their dog to an exam room. Kay studied the dog as it walked. It was favoring its right hind leg.

"Let's put your pup up on the exam table."

"We're Ellen and Robby Watson. Our dog is Gus. Robby was checking on a cow due to calve. Gus always goes with him to the barn, but instead he ran barking into the road and a car hit him. They just drove away after hitting him. The bastards."

Kay nodded and slipped the earpieces of her stethoscope in and examined the animal. He was moaning in pain, but his eyes were bright and his heart and lungs strong. She felt along all his limbs and only elicited a whimper when she palpated his right hip. He lifted his head and licked her chin as if asking for her to be gentle. "Good boy, Gus. You're not bad at all." She looked at the Watsons. "I think it was a glancing blow. It might just be a big bruise, but I'd like to keep him here today and X-ray him when my staff gets in. Would that be okay?"

"Thank you, Doctor."

"I'm going to find the fucking asshole who hit him. They could have killed him." Robby looked at his dog while he cursed loudly.

Mitch rushed in and Kay jumped in surprise.

Mitch shrugged. "You didn't lock the door. Is everything all right?"

Ellen pointed at Mitch. "You're RCMP, aren't you?"

"I'm Corporal Mitchell."

"We saw somebody run our dog down, on purpose."

"Where was your dog?"

"He and Robby were going to the barn and then Gus saw a car parked on the road and ran toward it, barking. They just started their car, plowed into Gus, and drove off. They deserve to go to jail."

"I'm sorry about Gus. I'm in the detachment office Monday morning. Please come in and give me the details."

"We have a dairy farm, but we'll be there after morning milking." Ellen clasped Robby's hand and dragged him from the clinic. "Come on, Robby."

After Ellen and Robby left, Kay led Gus to the treatment room and settled him in a kennel. She collapsed into a chair and rubbed her knee while Mitch looked into the kennel. "Poor Gus. Do you really think somebody hit him on purpose?" Kay asked.

"No. It was dark out and Gus ran into the road. Still, I want to find them and give them a chance to apologize for hitting Gus and leaving. And I'm curious about why they were parked in front of the house. We've had a rash of thefts at farms."

Kay laughed. "People stealing cows?"

"Sometimes, but lately it's been farm machinery, tools, generators. Farmers tend to leave barns and sometimes houses unlocked."

"Well, Gus looks comfortable. Would you like a cup of tea, Mitch?"

"Please."

"Lock the front door and meet me in the lunchroom."

Kay unearthed the herbal tea from the top cupboard and made them each a cup. She preferred strong coffee but sucked at making it. Moldy leaves would be tastier than herbal tea, but they ought to have something warm and comforting.

Mitch entered the room and collapsed into a chair. "Door's locked."

"Thanks for your help tonight and your offer of a ride in the morning." Kay glanced at the wall clock. "But it's almost six, so I'll just stay here. Minnie will be in at seven." She studied Mitch as they sat in silence and sipped their tea.

With exaggerated care, Mitch set her cup on the table and regarded Kay. "What happened in Callie's office wasn't my style."

Kay almost spilled her tea at the abrupt topic change. "You don't like girls anymore?" The intensity in Mitch's expression made her nervous, and she resorted to a lame joke as cover.

"I like women and I want to get to know you better first. I've said that before, but I meant it then and do now." One side of Mitch's mouth quirked up, and she focused on Kay. "You're very beautiful, and tonight, I lost my head. Touching you and…well, I want to try this again. Kay Gallant, will you have dinner with me sometime?"

"Are you asking me on a date?"

Mitch grinned. "Yes. Why are you so against having something real?"

Kay shrugged. "It just seems like something I could never have. I've been good on my own."

"What if you didn't have to be?"

Kay sighed. Mitch knew all her secrets and she wasn't running away. That was good news, but now a date was back on the table. She grinned. There had almost been sex on the table, but a date? Were they back in high school? She wanted Mitch. This dating plan was trying her patience, but how could she say no? Did she want to? Should she? All this thinking in circles was making her seasick. She let her instincts speak for her. "Thanks, I'd like that." She waited for a pang of anxiety about their conflicting goals, but it never came. *Interesting.*

CHAPTER FIFTEEN

On Monday morning, Mitch met with the Watsons at the RCMP detachment office. "How's Gus?"

Ellen smiled. "Dr. Gallant says he has a big bruise. Nothing broken, but we still have to keep him quiet."

"That's great news. Did you figure out who hit him?"

Ellen did most of the talking and presented Mitch with a surveillance tape. After the dramatic increase in equipment thefts, many local farmers installed surveillance cameras at the entrance to their farms. The tape showed what the Watsons described. Mitch saw a dark road, and the lights of a car roar past their laneway. The picture was too blurry to read the license plate or determine the make or model of the car.

"I'll keep your information on file, but there's too little detail for me to identify the car or driver."

Ellen waved a piece of paper under Mitch's nose. "I've got more. Somebody left this letter yesterday. He reached through his car window to sneak it into our mailbox but dropped it. He parked, walked back, picked it up, and put it in. We have him on video." They watched the second video. In the daylight, Mitch saw a tall, thin young man at the mailbox, but she still couldn't make out the license plate. But then, she didn't need to. She knew where to find that particular car.

Mitch examined the letter and Ellen's video. The letter was a heartfelt apology for hitting their dog. The author wrote: *I was sitting at the side of the road texting. I drove off without checking first. Sorry about Gus. I never meant to hurt him. I hope this helps with the vet bill and that he's better soon.* In the envelope, they left one hundred and twenty dollars in cash. So clearly not somebody searching for things to steal.

After the Watsons left, Mitch signed out of the detachment office, drove to Kingsway Farm, and knocked on the front door. Kingsway was a thousand acres of wheat fields with a large farmhouse, machine sheds, and other outbuildings. It also had a large vegetable garden, a small flock of chickens, and sold free-range eggs.

"Hello, Mitch. How are you?"

"Fine, thank you, Mrs. King. Is Maggie at home?"

"She's in the shop."

Mrs. King didn't question why the police were visiting her granddaughter. It never occurred to her because Mitch often visited Maggie. "Thank you, Mrs. King." She strode to the workshop and found Maggie working on a motorcycle. "Hey, kid."

"Hey." Maggie avoided eye contact. Maggie remained on her knees by her motorcycle, but her hands stilled, and she gripped her tools so tightly her fingers went white.

"I have cold drinks for you girls," Mrs. King called from the backstairs of her house.

Mitch jogged over to the house. "Thank you, Mrs. King." She returned and handed a soda to Maggie. She popped the tab on hers and took a long drink of the cold liquid. "Come on, Maggie. Let's talk." She kept her tone soft and coaxing.

Maggie led the way to a small, crowded office on the side of the shop where they sat on a sagging couch. Maggie was eighteen and done with school. Her friends had moved away to attend university or were in relationships with local guys. Too thin for her height of six feet, Maggie was all angles and sharp features with a compelling androgynous appearance. Her blue eyes were striking, and her shoulder-length dark brown hair meant that if she'd wanted to, she could've modeled men's or women's clothing.

Mitch stretched her legs out. "What happened Friday night?"

Maggie's shoulders slumped. "It was an accident. I was chilling in my car at the side of the road, smoking and listening to music. I couldn't sleep, so I just got away for a while. And then Gus was barking, and I saw him running toward me. I panicked and drove away. I never meant to hurt Gus. Will he be all right?"

"Kay says it's a big bruise and he's sore, but no broken bones." Mitch had hoped to be wrong. She'd recognized the profile in the video of a tall, thin youth, with the bulge of small breasts under the hoodie.

Maggie slumped with her head hanging between her knees and cried. After a minute, she sniffled and wiped her eyes on a dirty rag she pulled from her pocket. "I didn't mean to hurt him. I love animals."

Mitch empathized. She'd seen the worst that adults did to each other, but seeing the innocents of the world hurt, like animals and children, really bugged her. "Who was with you?" She didn't buy the story of smoking and listening to music or the one in the letter about texting. Maggie had abundant space at home. Mrs. King didn't allow her to smoke in the house, but she had an office and her shop in the barn. She didn't have to park on the road. She envied her the space. When Mitch was young, she couldn't breathe without her family knowing.

Maggie lifted her head and swiped at her eyes. "I was with Naomi."

"Naomi?" Mitch knew most of the young people in town and all the gay ones. They gravitated to her for advice or protection, and for a compassionate ear. Given the right circumstances and the right person, people talked about what bothered them. And talking helped.

"Naomi's the assistant manager at the grocery store in Karlberg."

Mitch groaned. Naomi Marken was thirty, with two kids and an enormous husband. "You didn't stop that night because you couldn't let the Watsons see Naomi?"

Maggie's eyes clouded with guilt, and she hung her head. "Yes. I'm sorry about Gus."

Mitch rested her hand on Maggie's shoulder. "Gus will be all right. Kay knows her stuff."

"Kay?"

"Dr. Gallant. The new surgeon at PVS."

"She's hot. Is she on our team?"

Mitch bristled at the questions and scowled at Maggie.

"Sorry, Mitch. No disrespect."

"Yes, I agree, and yes, she is, are my answers. Now, I'm closing this topic." Mitch waited for Maggie to nod and continued. "So, about Naomi. How serious and how long?"

"Four months and we're in love."

Naomi might be a lesbian or bisexual and longing for more or different attention than she received from her husband. Mitch wanted to shake Maggie and implore her to run far and run fast from Naomi. But that approach never worked. These affairs ended in their own time. Maggie was in love, but someday Naomi would choose her husband and crush Maggie's heart, hopefully before the enormous Mr. Marken crushed Maggie's body. "I see why you didn't stop. The letter and the cash were thoughtful, but you ought to speak with the Watsons. A good neighbor wouldn't hit a dog and drive off."

"I had to leave because Naomi was with me." Maggie groaned. "And Ellen will kill me."

"Undoubtedly, but you need to ask how to make up for hitting Gus."

Maggie frowned, unconvinced. "Do I have to? I mean, I wrote the letter."

"How guilty do you feel?"

"Bad." Maggie hung her head again. "You know I'd never hurt an animal."

Mitch leaned toward Maggie. "The guilt will eat at you. Confessing will help."

Maggie pointed at her. "Cliché."

"Sometimes sayings become clichés because they're true. Do you need a bodyguard?" Mitch did a comical shudder. "I'll go with you and protect you from Ellen Watson."

"No, thanks, I'll tell my gran first, then go." Maggie raised her head in defiance. "I'm not telling them about Naomi."

"That's fine. That's between the two of you." Mitch rose. "Good luck. See you later." She walked away a few steps before turning back. "Drop by if you want to talk. I'll tell you about the older woman I dated at your age." Mitch winked and departed. Maggie needed to get out of that situation, but she was an adult and entitled to her own horrible dating mistakes.

Mitch climbed into her cruiser. What about her horrible dating mistakes? Were she and Kay any better suited than Maggie and Naomi? Kay just wanted sex, but that wasn't Mitch's style. But then Kay had agreed to a date, reluctantly. Mitch understood. It was easier to convince yourself you didn't want love than to risk the hurt of losing love. Why was she thinking about love? Love was a rare commodity, especially in her life.

Mitch phoned Kay. "Do you have time for a quick chat or lunch?"

"Swamped today. You just caught me between surgeries and Val's waiting."

"What if I bring you lunch?"

"Thanks. Any kind of sandwich except egg. See you about one?"

"One, it is." Mitch stared at the silent phone. Kay had gotten to the point and already hung up.

Mitch pulled out and headed back to town. At lunch time she pulled into PVS and called the clinic.

"Prairie Veterinary Services, Val speaking."

"Hi, Val, it's Mitch."

"Why're you sitting in the parking lot?"

"I'm meeting Kay. Can you please tell her I'll wait in the cruiser for her?"

"You're kidding? Come inside."

"Please, Val."

"Okay, woman of mystery. I'll pass your message along. She's just in the bathroom fixing her hair." Val chuckled. "Probably fixing it for you."

Five minutes later, Kay opened the front passenger door of the cruiser and slid inside. She looked around. "Am I supposed to be in here?" She laughed. "I hope nobody thinks I'm being arrested. That would shoot around town in ten seconds, and I'd never live it down."

"BLT." Mitch handed her the sandwich. "And if you're in the front, everyone will know you're a guest."

"In the back would be another story." She glanced over her shoulder. "I promised myself I'd never ride in the back of a cop car again. I'm starved. Okay if I don't wait for you?"

"Go ahead."

Kay unwrapped the sandwich and bit in. "Awesome, thanks. Long time since dinner last night. Any chance you can run me over to the garage, please? My car is ready."

"Sure." Mitch pulled out. "I found the person who hit Gus."

"You slap the cuffs on them?"

"She said it was an accident and I believe her. Maggie King is just an eighteen-year-old kid and wouldn't hurt an animal. I've known her for years and she can be trusted."

"You care about her?" Kay continued to eat like she hadn't had food in the last two years.

"I do. Maggie lives with her grandmother and looks after the farm. She's a responsible kid, but Kingsway is a lot of work. Maggie's grandmother raised her since she was a baby. Her aunt was awesome, but Angie moved to Edmonton a bunch of years ago. I've been looking out for Maggie since." Mitch shrugged. "She got into some trouble in high school. Underage drinking and skipping class. Also, she's a lesbian and her ex-girlfriend outed her. She struggled through a couple of rough years."

"You like helping."

"I do. I'm not a social worker, just a friend to talk to, but it helps. I unofficially mentor local LGBT youth. I check up on them and make sure they do their schoolwork. I could've used an older friend at their age."

"I'm impressed."

"I try."

"Good for you for caring." Kay cleared her throat. "So, you don't want me to tell the Watsons?"

"Maggie will tell them herself."

"I'd be afraid of Ellen. I'd want you for backup."

Mitch laughed. "I offered her protection, but she wanted to do it on her own. Anyway, I just wanted you to know that I took care of it, but I hope you'll let Maggie tell Ellen."

"I will. No problem."

"Thanks." Mitch pulled in and parked beside the garage. "You sure it's ready? Need me to wait?"

"It's ready. I checked." Kay collected her bag. "Thanks for lunch." Kay leaped from the cruiser as if it were on fire.

"Kay, wait."

Kay scooted in and perched on the edge of the seat.

Mitch searched her eyes. "You agreed to have dinner with me in the city. How about Wednesday? You still okay with that?"

Kay shrugged and looked everywhere but at Mitch. "Yes, Wednesday night is good."

"You seem uneasy. Is there something I'm missing? Something I can do?"

Kay playfully punched her in the arm. "Let's just relax and have fun. Make it low stress."

Mitch grinned. "I can do that."

Kay studied Mitch for a beat. "Pick me up at home? I'll be home by four." Kay slipped from the cruiser.

"Perfect. See you." Mitch watched Kay walk to the garage office. She would wait until Kay collected her car, in case there were complications. Kay looked professional and sexy in her white lab coat and scrubs. A strong, competent surgeon, and one who was leaving. Callie had asked her to be careful and not to let herself get hurt. Developing an attachment to Kay Gallant might not be wise, but she couldn't help herself.

Kay exited the repair shop and waved at Mitch as she walked to her car. Mitch pulled out of the parking lot and headed toward the detachment office. Wise or not, she had a date on Wednesday. Mitch groaned. She was like an out-of-control downhill skier who was picking up speed for a record finish or a spectacular crash. She was in so much trouble.

Chapter Sixteen

At four on Wednesday, Mitch knocked on Kay's door.

Kay opened the door. "Hello, you, come in."

"It's too early for dinner. Do you want to do something first or are you hungry? I made reservations for seven, but I can easily move them on a Wednesday."

"I had a late lunch. I could wait."

"What would you like to do? A walk along the river would be nice unless you have another idea."

"Well, I bought a new mattress and I've been trying to figure out how to get it home."

"And I have a truck." Mitch smiled. "Let's go." Here was a chance to help Kay again. She silenced the warning bells with ease.

Kay scanned her from head to toe, and Mitch felt the heat from Kay's brilliant blue eyes warm her in places that had no business heating up.

"But you're in your nice clothes."

Mitch slipped off her jacket. "I'll leave this here. I've got clean coveralls in the truck."

"Thanks," Kay said and hung up the jacket.

They headed to the bed store, picked up Kay's mattress, and brought it back to her apartment. With some grunting and bickering, they maneuvered it into Kay's bedroom and installed it.

"Thanks for your help," Kay said and dropped onto her back on her new mattress. "Want to help me break it in?"

Mitch laughed and started to haul the old mattress out of the bedroom. "Help me with this."

"Yes, Corporal. No slacking off for me."

They got the old mattress into Mitch's truck and tied it down. Mitch gave the mattress a punch. "When did you buy this?"

"A friend gave it to me." Kay squeezed Mitch's forearm. "How about I make dinner?"

"I invited you out."

Kay pointed to the old mattress. "Now I owe you. I have all the fixings for French toast."

Mitch accepted the invitation. She'd prefer to eat out, but Kay wanted to treat her, and no doubt couldn't afford the huge steak Mitch lusted after.

Later, Mitch refused another slice of French toast and pushed her plate away. "Delicious, but I have to stop." She stretched. "All that sugar is making me sleepy."

Kay winked. "The offer's still open to help me break in my new mattress."

"You flirt a lot. Are you ever serious about anything but being a surgeon?" It wasn't that she didn't appreciate the flirting, but with Kay, it felt like deflection more than anything genuine.

"Rarely, but I'll behave if you want to be serious." Kay rolled her eyes and sat primly with her hands in her lap. "What do you want to talk about, Officer Serious?"

Mitch smiled. "How did you like being in the army?"

"Too structured for me and no way was I going to kill anybody, ever."

"But you joined the army. Didn't you expect to?"

"Women aren't front line, and I told you my parents pushed me to join." Kay groaned. "They thought it would give me purpose and discipline, because as you know, I didn't have any."

"And did it?"

"Yes, some, but not for being a soldier. What about you? Did you join the RCMP because you wanted to shoot people?" Kay rested her chin in her palm.

"No, of course not, and thankfully, I've never had to."

"Same as me then, sort of. So why the RCMP?"

"I lived in Regina near the training depot. As a kid, I'd climb up to the roof and watch the recruits training outside. I wanted to be one. Wanted to be part of that gang of good guys." Mitch laughed. "We'd see them when they went out on the weekends. They seemed to be having fun and there was a sense of camaraderie. I wanted that too."

"To be part of the RCMP family?"

Mitch blinked at Kay's insight. "Yes, part of a family. Part of something bigger. Did you ever want to be?"

Kay tipped her head from side to side. "I have my brothers and their families. That's enough." Kay rose and carried the dishes to the sink. She turned and leaned against the sink and studied Mitch. "Some days, at PVS, with Lauren and Val and everyone, I am part of something bigger. We do good work. Not saving the planet work, but people are happy with the care we provide."

Mitch nodded. It was on the tip of her tongue to suggest PVS could be like a second family to Kay, but that would have been pushing. "I get that. I wanted to help people and that meant catching the criminals who harmed them."

"You wanted to protect people from all the bad guys."

"Initially, but later it was more than that." Mitch sighed. "It became more about drugs. I'd seen what drugs did to kids. I wanted to stop that. I'd spent a bunch of frustrating years on the job in Surrey, British Columbia, where the dregs of society harmed good people and got away with it. But the dregs often were or had been drug-addicted kids stealing or selling themselves to buy drugs."

Kay slipped back into her chair and listened intently.

Mitch shook her head. "Kids were dying of drug overdoses or I arrested them for possession. It wasn't right. We needed to catch the people selling the drugs, but they were too well hidden. There were bigger reasons for the kids to be on the street, but I tried to do my part. It was frustrating and I was burning out fast, so when the RCMP gave me the option of moving back to Saskatchewan, to tiny Thresherton, I took it."

"So, no drug problems in Thresherton then?" Kay laughed. "No Saskatchewan drug cartels?"

Mitch pointed at Kay. "Don't laugh. You'd be surprised at what I've seen. The days when rural kids were protected from the drugs and dealers of the city is long gone. They're nearly as prevalent here as they are in the city, believe it or not." She pulled up a picture on her phone and handed it to Kay. "That's my brother with my parents, my sister, and me. Johnie died of an overdose at fifteen. I was only thirteen, but I understood what happened."

Kay gasped. "I'm so sorry. That must have been so hard to lose a brother. I'd be crushed if I lost one of mine."

Mitch traced the outline of Johnie's face and cleared her throat to push down the feelings that after a dismal day at work could still overwhelm her. "His death devastated me and I pretty much hid in my room for three months. He was my best friend and my pal. He didn't push me away like an older brother might. We hung out and got into all kinds of trouble together."

"You still miss him?"

"I do, but not with the sharp pain of all those years ago. It's more of a dull ache. I wonder what kind of man he would've grown up to be, without drugs in his life. What he'd have done for a living. We both wanted to get motorcycles and fix them up. And sometimes I like to imagine he would've been a great dad."

Kay squeezed Mitch's hand. "How about your parents?"

"Johnie's death tore them apart. My dad wouldn't talk to us or to my mom. He just sat on the couch like a lump of clay. Not sure if my mom wanted to talk, she mostly screamed at him. She blamed my dad for bringing us to Regina to live. She said we'd have been safer in the small town in Alberta that we'd been living in before."

"Was it true?"

"Maybe a little, but drugs are everywhere from the smallest village to the largest city. But in Regina, my brother joined a gang. That ruined him."

Kay shook her head. "I bet he had a lot of potential."

Mitch straightened up. "All kids have potential. The potential to work, raise families, and be happy."

"You're right. I was thinking like my parents for a second. They didn't think I had *any* potential. I wasn't serious enough for them. Too into music and drawing and to quote my mother 'silly clothes.'"

"You were artistic?"

Kay laughed. "Artistic or flaky? I'll admit to artistic leanings, but no talent and no motivation to get any better. I tried a bit of everything, even writing, but lost interest. I still have my sewing machine, but I rarely use it."

"You made your own clothes?"

"I specialized in flowing hippie clothes that wouldn't have been out of place in the seventies."

Mitch looked around the apartment decorated in garage sale finds with lots of colors. It did look like a hippie palace. A beaded hanging door wouldn't have been out of place. "You sure do like color."

Kay nodded. "I do, and it helps disguise my crappy furniture. One day I'll have new stuff, but I'm happy with what I have for now."

"How did you end up in medicine, in vet school?"

"What little girl doesn't love puppies and kittens? I'd wanted to be a vet since I was a kid, but by high school nobody thought I was smart enough, including me. While I was recovering after Afghanistan, I walked dogs at the SPCA to strengthen my leg. I loved it there. Animals are way better than people. There's no judgment from dogs. If you're nice to them, they're nice back. They don't care if you're a chain-smoking skinny girl with straggly pink hair and the shakes. They just want their belly rubbed."

"You're really good with animals."

"At the SPCA we took in stray animals that were injured. One dog was hit by a car. She got an infection and needed a lot of nursing. I practically moved in to look after her and slept over some nights. I used to mash canned dog food with warm water and feed her with a syringe."

"Did she get better?"

"Yes, and we found her a nice home with a family."

"Why didn't you keep her?"

Kay paused and focused on the wall for a beat. "I don't know. Isn't that strange? My mother said she looked scruffy."

"So, your mom—"

Kay shook her head. "No, they wouldn't have stopped me. I'd almost died in a war. My parents would have given me anything. My mom fussed so much it drove me crazy some days. No, it was my decision. I didn't think I could look after her properly. I couldn't look after myself."

The profound sadness in Kay's eyes startled Mitch. Not even when she was talking about Afghanistan had Kay been as sad. She wasn't about regrets, but giving up on the chance to have a pet she loved was one. "What was her name?"

"She never told me." Kay laughed. "I didn't give her one. Too much of a commitment when I wasn't going to keep her, and I didn't want her to be confused when she found a forever home."

Mitch squeezed Kay's hand.

"Coffee, I think." Kay brushed at her eyes and leapt to her feet. "I make crap coffee, so my brother shipped me a Keurig machine. You have your choice of flavors."

So much about Kay's approach to life made sense to her now. Kay's nomadic life was all about moving from job to job and keeping people and love at a distance. But the most telling thing was that Kay could form strong attachments but didn't trust that she could make them last. She was scared and that was something Mitch could understand. She still struggled to get it right, but she didn't stop trying. Maybe Kay was willing to try again? If not with her, then with someone. She longed for Kay to be happy and be loved.

CHAPTER SEVENTEEN

One week before the wedding, Mitch and Sonny stood beside each other in the lounge at the Rainbow Club. Given the timeline, tonight was the only pre-wedding party Callie and Lauren had been able to make time for.

Kay squeezed between Mitch and Sonny and linked her arms through theirs. "Amazing job, you two." She wriggled with joy when Mitch and Sonny each kissed her on the cheek. Sandwiched in bed between these two gorgeous butches was fantasy material as she pictured them both entering her at the same time. She squeezed her thighs together, uncomfortable with the sudden arousal and then imagined one pair of talented lips at work between her legs and another pair of soft lips attending to her nipples. She took a deep breath and forced herself to concentrate. Fantasies were harmless, even though the ones she had about Mitch had shifted from totally erotic to something deeper. Now she imagined falling asleep in her arms after the mind-blowing sex, which was a totally new element but definitely reflected the time they were spending together in real life. Some days she just looked forward to hanging out and chatting. She couldn't have been more surprised if she'd won the lottery without buying a ticket.

"You organized a wonderful party with such a mix of people," Kay said.

"Thanks," Sonny and Mitch replied in unison.

Kay scanned the lounge. Gay and straight friends from Saskatoon and Thresherton crowded the room, as did members of the brides' families.

Mitch and Sonny had arranged for Thomas and Marcus to prepare trays of finger food. Mitch had planned to serve chips and popcorn, but Kay convinced them to go fancier. The bar sold the drinks, and the club handled the tasteful decorations. Guests had covered a table with presents. For a party that they'd pulled together quickly, she was impressed at how personal and intimate it felt.

"Hey, Rachel's here. Excuse me." Sonny darted across the room to Rachel.

Kay looked up at Mitch. "Great party."

"It's better now that you're here."

Mitch looked into her eyes and Kay smiled back. "I like being here with you."

"I asked the club to play more slow songs tonight. I hope you're ready for more dancing."

Kay popped up on her tiptoes and kissed Mitch on the cheek. All the fantasy material she required was right here.

"I'll take that as a yes," Mitch said.

Two hours later, Kay swayed on the dance floor with her cheek pressed against Mitch's shoulder. Mitch had removed her jacket and relaxed. The speeches were done, people were thanked, and the presents were opened. She and Mitch danced with Callie and Lauren, but they promised the rest of the night to each other. Kay shifted her head under Mitch's chin and brushed aside the edge of Mitch's crisp white shirt to kiss her collarbone. Mitch tightened her arms around her.

Kay squeezed Mitch's forearm. "It's midnight and I have to work tomorrow."

"You need your sleep."

"Not necessarily." Kay waggled her eyebrows. "But I need to get to bed soon."

Kay drew Mitch into a dark corner and kissed her until she had to stop for air. An intense throbbing between Kay's legs insisted she entice Mitch to come home with her. Forget chatting. Tonight, she would take Mitch to bed. Without regret, she'd declined offers from several others for company after the party. She trembled when she pictured Mitch's hands on her. She opened her mouth just as Mitch spoke.

"Let's end the night here." Mitch gestured between them. "There's something important growing between us."

Kay smoothed the collar of Mitch's shirt. She looked sexy in her dark suit. Kay had blown her budget and purchased a black strapless dress that stopped four inches below her knees, so she looked sexy and it hid her scars. They looked good together in their dress clothes, but how much better would they be without clothes? She wouldn't know because she was being sent home alone again.

Kay forced herself to smile, and for only a second did she regret declining the offer of the dentist still smiling at her. She'd have Mitch or nobody. Kay struggled to inject perkiness into her voice. "Okay, Mitchy. The party's over for us for tonight."

Mitch cleared her throat and directed a mock glare at Kay. "Only Callie calls me Mitchy, please. If you use it others will."

Kay laughed. "I promise." She was about to make another joke, but Mitch's expression grew serious again. Too serious for a party.

"I sense something real between us," Mitch said. "You're so elegant tonight and your shoulders are begging me to kiss them. My head will explode after I admit this, but what we're building is important and I don't want us to rush." Mitch dipped her head and gently kissed her.

"Good friends, remember?" Kay pushed against Mitch and slid from her arms. Her stomach flipped not from excitement but from fear. Mitch had looked at her with longing and even lust before, but not with an intensity so strong she felt Mitch could see inside her. "Night, Mitch."

"Wait, Kay. May I take you to the wedding next weekend? You're welcome to my spare room for the whole weekend."

Kay moved in and leaned against Mitch, pressing her forehead to her strong shoulder. She drank in the scent of her, the heat of her, and the strength of her until she found the power to speak. She looked up into Mitch's hazel eyes, so intense they were dark green.

"I'd—" She swallowed and tried again. "I'd like that." And she would. Nothing would make her happier than spending the wedding with Mitch.

"You look a little shocked."

"I was trying to remember the last wedding I went to. I usually find a reason not to. It was my brother's, just before I left for Afghanistan."

"We'll have some fun and keep it light."

"Thanks. I asked to have next weekend off from the WCVM. And Ian and Fiona have insisted on covering PVS, so I have nothing but time to party." She gave a weak smile and tamped down the fear. It was ridiculous to be afraid.

Mitch smiled "Thanks. I'll walk you out."

Kay smiled back at Mitch's broad happy smile. This was a woman who wanted her company, not just her body. Kay shook her head. "No, thanks. I can find my car. You stay, you're a hostess."

"But it's dark out."

"I see Ian and his wife leaving. I'll tag along with them." She kissed Mitch on the cheek.

"Are you okay? Are we?"

She smoothed the lapels of Mitch's shirt. "We're very okay. See you, maybe next week at PVS? I work on Tuesday."

"Count on it."

She kissed Mitch, stepped back, and walked to the coat check.

Kay rested her forehead against the steering wheel at a stop light. Her body thrummed with excitement or fear or maybe some intoxicating combination of both. A car honking woke her from her reverie, and she drove through the green light and headed home.

Kay frowned at Janice. The chronic ketamine shortage was getting ridiculous.

"Look who I found wandering around?" Val said as she entered the treatment room with Mitch in tow.

"I probably shouldn't be back here, but—Kay? What's wrong?" Mitch asked.

Kay kissed Mitch on the cheek. "Nothing, just frustrated." She gestured to Janice who was leaning against the counter. "Janice says our order didn't arrive. Val, I can't sedate with a hammer or magic, I need ketamine."

"But—but, I ordered it," Val said. "Are you sure?" she said to Janice.

"Yes, of course, and don't keep asking me. I'm reception, not in charge of your stupid drugs."

Mitch cleared her throat. "Ketamine's not stupid. It's dangerous and not a drug to lose track of."

Val nodded. "That's why we have it locked up."

"I do a lot of surgery, but still—" Kay said.

"You two figure it out. Not my problem." Janice pushed past Val and detoured around Mitch on her way out of the treatment room.

"It will be everyone's problem if we've lost it," Val muttered.

"Agreed, and Ian and Fiona would be in big trouble," Mitch said. "Not to mention the kids who get their hands on it. At a low dose they hallucinate and get dizzy. A higher dose can paralyze and kill. It's serious stuff."

"We use it for the temporary paralysis, so we can intubate." Kay patted Mitch's arm. "We get it. Don't worry, Corporal. Nobody's headed into a K-hole with our ketamine. We just need to get more organized."

"But I am organized," Val said in a small voice.

"I know you are. It's probably my fault." Kay laughed. "I'd lose my head if it wasn't attached." She squeezed Mitch's arm. "I'm buying lunch for everyone. You coming, Val?"

Val shook her head and looked miserably at her feet.

"Come on, I didn't mean that our ketamine muddle is your fault. I lose stuff all the time at home. If I just forget about it. It always shows up."

Val shrugged. "I brought some yogurt. I'll stay here." She trudged out of the treatment room after Janice.

"I hurt her feelings," Kay said. "I never meant to do that. She's the best vet tech ever and my friend."

"You didn't offend her, but she's as serious about her work as you are. She'll want to solve this."

"We both do. I've noticed that we've been low for a while. We'll figure it out. I'll bring her something back from lunch and talk to her again this afternoon."

"Good plan. We need to talk about Callie's wedding. It's only four days away, and my speech is as boring as dirt. I need help. Meet me at the diner?"

"There's nowhere else." Kay laughed. Nowhere that could serve them so quickly that they could linger over their meal and still get back to work in time. She kissed Mitch on the cheek again and almost did more. When Mitch left in her cruiser, she changed and followed in her car. She could walk to the diner, but that would take twenty minutes out of the sixty she had and every minute she wanted to spend with Mitch.

Mitch had asked Kay to go with her to the wedding, making her happier than she thought possible. Being pleased about being part of a couple for the day puzzled her, but it was only one day. "Where did that thought come from?" Correction, not a couple. Just a couple of friends, but not so long ago her plan was to get Mitch into bed. Now she wanted to spend time with her, just talking. What was happening to her?

CHAPTER EIGHTEEN

Friday evening, Kay pulled up to Mitch's house and parked. It was late, but Mitch's truck wasn't in the driveway. Maybe she'd been called in late to work. Kay tried the front door and found it unlocked. "Not very secure, Officer Mitchell." She headed inside and put her bags on the bed in the spare room and looked around. Mitch had painted it a soft shade of green, and the new light summer comforter matched.

Kay tentatively examined the basket of items on the desk. She read the card: *To make your stay more comfortable. Help yourself to anything that makes you happy.* "Anything, Officer Mitchell?" She lifted items from the basket. There were bath products, the ones she liked. Mitchell had done some investigating. It was even her brand of toothpaste.

Mitch had gotten more inventive with some snacks. Kay unwrapped the small box of chocolates and moaned as the first one melted in her mouth. Quality chocolates were an extravagance she rarely allowed herself. She lifted the bar of soap to her nose and breathed in the subtle citrus scent. The bath bombs she'd save for another day, but she desperately wanted a shower.

Taped to the edge of the card was a house key. She almost didn't want to touch it. She shook her head. It had no special meaning. Just a friend giving her a key to the house so she could come and go. She laughed at the motorcycle key fob and slipped it into her pocket.

Kay grabbed her small bag of groceries and carried it to the kitchen. She'd come prepared this time. She opened the refrigerator and gasped at the piles of fresh food. The two dozen Kingsway eggs and the huge bottle of maple syrup made her laugh. She put her stuff away, closed the door, and then discovered a note taped to the front.

Hi, Kay. I wish I was there to meet you, but it's go time. We're all at Poplarcreek setting up for tomorrow. Val rented all the equipment, but she needs an army to set it up and we've all been conscripted. Relax and help yourself. See you later, M.

Kay smiled. Her shower could wait. She glanced at her watch. If they were all still working at almost eight at night, surely, they could use her help. She shot Mitch a quick text. Kay placed an order for the four pizzas Mitch asked for and changed into old jeans and a T-shirt. Later, she arrived at Poplarcreek and paused on the laneway. The sun was starting to set and it was dark enough to see all the romantic white lights strung around the yard. From the house to the barn and hanging from the edges of a large canopy set up over an army of chairs, it looked like a fairy tale garden.

Kay jumped at the knock on her window. She wound the window down. "Hey, Ronnie. How are you?"

"Tired and hungry. Mitch said you were bringing pizza. Please tell me you have pizza."

Kay pointed to the boxes. "One has pineapple as instructed."

"You're a goddess." Ronnie opened the door. "Need some help?"

Kay laughed. Ronnie's hands were on the boxes that she was already holding close to her nose. "Thanks."

Ronnie jogged away with the pizza and headed for a table that looked set up for a buffet. People appeared from everywhere and descended on the pizza like ravenous vultures. She joined them and set down the case of cold beer she'd picked up.

Callie approached her and spoke around a mouth full of pizza. "Thanks so much. I usually do a better job of feeding people, but I got wrapped up on sorting out the table decorations and forgot to put anything on."

How could table decorations make Callie forget food? But she looked serious and stressed, so Kay kept her jokes to herself. Some women took marriage and weddings seriously. "I'm happy to help."

"Thanks, Kay," Lauren called over a plate heaped in pizza.

Kay waved back. Callie moved off and Mitch joined Kay.

"You should get some before it's all gone." Mitch took her hand and led her toward the food. "Stand down, you wolves, and let Kay in."

Kay snorted as a hole was made for her in the crowd. She took two slices on a plate and joined Mitch who was seated at the table. Mitch popped the top off a beer and downed half in one pull. "Oh my God, that's so good. Thanks." Mitch kissed her cheek. Kay smiled at Mitch and stuck her tongue out at Callie who was making teasing gestures at her.

"Where's Val and her clipboard?" Sonny asked.

Ronnie stood. "I'll get her. She wanted to count dishes or something." She jogged toward the house and returned a few minutes later with Val in tow.

"Hi, Kay, thanks for dinner." Val filled a plate and sat beside Ronnie.

"How's it going?" Kay asked Mitch.

"We're getting there. We need to finish setting up for the reception. We have to organize the tables still." She draped her arm around Kay's shoulders and pointed to the canopy. "You see they get married in the church, then come back here for pictures and snacks and stuff, and then we rearrange the chairs and tables around a central dance floor for the dinner."

"What can I do?"

"Pray for good weather. We've got more canopies, but they won't protect from a serious rainstorm. They're mostly for protection against the sun. But I suggest after pizza, you check in with Val. She's handing out assignments."

Several hours later, Kay stumbled into Mitch's house and collapsed on a chair in the kitchen. "How did you do that all day? Captain Connor was *relentless*."

Mitch laughed. "Val certainly had us hopping. She's very organized."

"She'll probably have a string of vet clinics in fifteen years, and we'll all be working for her. Thanks for the basket of treats, by the way."

"I just want you to feel at home." Mitch stretched. "I'm beat and we have to be back by eight."

Kay waved. "You take the first shower. I'm going to check emails and then I'm crashing."

"Thanks." She stood and hesitated. "Kay?"

She smiled up at Mitch.

"I'm really happy you're here." She gave Kay's shoulder a brief squeeze and left.

"Me too," Kay whispered. She dragged herself to the spare room, booted up her computer and answered the three emails that couldn't wait. She waited five minutes after the shower stopped and then grabbed the new bar of soap from Mitch and headed to the shower. As tired as she was, she couldn't help but think of how nice it would be to curl up against Mitch's hard body, even just to sleep. She shook it off and crawled into her own bed, alone.

She and Mitch were on the road by seven thirty the next day clutching giant travel mugs of coffee. They met Callie, Becky, and Gwen emerging from the barn when they arrived. All three were in coveralls and dirty rubber boots.

"You look very beautiful on your wedding day," Mitch called.

Callie did a little bow. "Ha, ha. Only haute couture for me. Morning, Kay."

Kay waved. She dropped her arm and moved half behind Mitch when Val spotted them. "Here comes Colonel Connor. We're in for it."

"She got a promotion?" Mitch whispered out of the side of her mouth.

"The scarier she gets the higher her rank goes." Kay smiled. "Morning, Val."

"There's a lot to do still. Mitch, find Ronnie. The chairs are set up wrong. Kay, follow me." Val turned and marched toward the house.

"Good luck." Mitch laughed and jogged away toward Ronnie who was moving the chairs and tables what appeared to be six inches to the left.

"Coward," she called after Mitch.

"We're in the house, Kay."

Val's voice cracked like a whip and Kay shot to attention, almost saluting. Val sounded just like her sergeant when she'd been in the military. She hurried over to the house and joined them inside. She looked around. "Where's Lauren?"

"She's with her family and we won't see her until the church." Val turned and focused on Kay.

Kay took a step back. Colonel Connor was fierce.

"Here's the thing. You're the only one not in the wedding party. I mean, Ronnie's just an usher, but we need her at the church early to seat people. After lunch, we'll head out to get cleaned up and changed. Can you stay here a while longer and finish up?"

"I need to go back to Mitch's and change."

Val waved her hand impatiently. "Yes, yes, give yourself time for that. You can leave when the babysitters show up. Callie hired three kids from the high school to keep an eye on the children who arrive with the guests for the reception. Their job is to keep an eye on everything here until we get back. They still haven't caught whoever's been stealing from the farms. And Callie and Lauren aren't taking any chances today."

"Okay, as long as I know what to do."

"I'll have a list for you. Now let's force Callie to decide on the centerpieces before she loses her mind."

Much later, after a quick lunch outside, Mitch said, "It's time for me to go get ready and head to the church. I've got Becky, Gwen, and Ronnie coming to my house to get ready as well. I guess Val's house is full of Lauren's family and they're changing there. Will you be all right?"

Kay nodded. "General Connor is busting my ass, but she gave me permission to leave in time to dress. I don't know how long it takes her, but I'll need an hour."

"Another promotion?" Mitch laughed. "See you at the church." Mitch kissed her cheek and joined Becky at her truck. They hopped in and left followed by Ronnie and Gwen in Ronnie's car.

Kay caressed her cheek where Mitch had kissed her and then with a huge sigh, returned to Val and her clipboard.

Later, Kay followed Mitch's advice and took the Thresherton taxi from Mitch's house to the church. She rubbed her palms together. Her hands tingled with nerves. She was meeting Mitch at a church and if she'd had to drive herself, she might not have made it.

Kay was one of the last ones to arrive. She slipped into the church, shocked at how full it was. She'd never have been able to come up with so many friends and family. Thank goodness she'd never need to.

"This way, Kay."

She leaned on Ronnie's arm, glad of the support for her weak knees as she was led to a row six from the front and to a seat beside Gwen. Her pulse was through the roof. It wasn't like it was her wedding, but it was terrifying, nonetheless.

She greeted Gwen and was introduced to Val's parents. She also nodded to the few clients sitting close.

Ronnie walked to the front and spoke with Mitch and tipped her head toward Kay. Mitch smiled at her and Kay's fear evaporated. She smiled back with a warmth that came up from her toes. Mitch was handsome in a full charcoal gray suit with a tie and sky blue cummerbund that matched the bridesmaid's dresses. Everything was elegant and beautiful. Callie and Lauren had gone for the classical wedding or as much as Kay could tell. She had no experience.

Mitch was standing on one side with Becky. Kay smiled. Becky looked like a mini version of Mitch in her gray suit and stood proudly beside her. Across from them, Lauren shifted from foot to foot and occasionally spoke with a man beside her who could have been her twin. Lauren was in slacks and a sort of softer, maternity version of a suit. Feminine but not girlie, and it suited her.

Kay rose with the music and watched Val walk down the aisle and stand beside Lauren's brother, then Callie's sister came in and stood with Mitch and Becky. Callie followed. She was dressed in heels and a simple long white dress, with a bateau neckline and one delicate sky blue bow at each shoulder. She looked very Audrey Hepburn and classy with her hair piled high.

Callie joined Lauren with a smile that lit up the room and linked her arm through Lauren's as they turned to face the minister.

Everyone could see how much in love they were. What would it be like to have that and how hard was it to hold on to?

A spattering of sniffles filled the church as Lauren and Callie said the vows that they had clearly written from the heart. Kay dabbed at her eyes and looked at her tissue in astonishment. Where was her protection against sentiment and the worship of relationships that encumbered so many adults and held them back? How many people could have accomplished so many important things if they had been allowed to focus on their careers? In her book, behind every successful person was space and room to breathe. And yet, the beauty in front of her was undeniable.

Breathing became a little more difficult when they all rose as the brides passed by. Mitch led Callie's sister out on her arm and took a second to smile at Kay. She returned the smile with warmth and flashed to a fantasy of walking down the aisle on Mitch's arm. She scolded herself and pushed the unwelcome thought away. She was never getting married and never settling down as long as there were different places to work and new places to see.

Kay followed the family outside and milled around while everyone chatted and watched pictures being taken in front of the church.

She shook her head. Lauren was married. She'd moved from a busy, fast-paced job in Toronto to tiny Thresherton, settled, married, and would now never leave. How could she be so certain that it was the right decision? What if she failed, or worse, missed an exciting job opportunity because she was tied to Callie and her farm? Kay tilted her head to study the brides from a different angle. They were so much in love. If Lauren was tied to Callie, it was because she'd tied the knot herself.

"Hello. You look very lovely."

Kay smiled up at Mitch. "And you look very dashing. You and Becky."

"Ah, yes. One of Callie's aunts tried to coax Becky into a dress, but when she saw me in my suit, she would wear nothing else. Callie left it entirely up to Becky to choose. The only stipulation was she had to dress up and she had to match."

Kay laughed. "There was a lot of matching."

"I'm so happy you're here. I have to travel back to the farm with the bridal party. Will I see you later?"

Kay frowned. "Of course. Did you think I was going to run off?"

"Maybe. Not really, but I didn't want to assume. Yikes. Val's waving at me. Time to go. Here are my truck keys." Mitch expertly wove through the crowd in time to join the bridal party in the cars decorated for the occasion. The wedding was old-school but suited Callie and Lauren.

"Want to come with us, Kay?" Gwen asked.

She looked around. There must have been a hundred cars and pickup trucks in the parking lot and up and down the roads and side streets. "I'm supposed to bring Mitch's truck back to the farm."

"I know where it is. Follow me." Gwen strode off and called over her shoulder. "Ronnie, I'm going with Kay."

Kay hurried after Gwen, a mini Colonel Connor. She'd have to tell Mitch later. Gwen filled Kay in on the schedule of events to come as they drove over, ticking them off on her fingers. At the farm, there were drinks, plates of hors d'oeuvres, and chatting. When the pictures were done everyone gathered for the buffet dinner. The dinner was based on a country barbecue theme, with lots of meat, fresh vegetables, and salads. The guests had been arranged so that Kay and Mitch could sit together.

Mitch made a respectful speech that wasn't close to boring. It was sweet and showed her love for Callie, her best friend. Val took a funnier route and added a few hilarious stories about how Lauren and Callie met over a calving in the freezing months of winter. "I have a pretty good idea," Val said, "that Callie married Lauren to have her own personal veterinarian on staff at Poplarcreek." When the laughing and clapping subsided. Val said, "Ladies and gentlemen, I give you Dr. and Mrs. Cornish."

Kay joined in the second round of applause and laughed with the rest when Callie stood and pulled Lauren into her arms for a deep kiss. After the traditional cake cutting, everyone sat again for coffee and dessert.

"I have to remember not to stuff myself," Mitch said. "There's dancing later."

Kay danced once with Lauren and once with Ronnie, but the rest of the night she reserved for Mitch, when Mitch could break away from the obligatory dances. She didn't mind as she got to watch Mitch move. She was so much better than she gave herself credit for. She was strong, confident, and a born leader. She'd even waltzed with Callie's mother.

It was a wonderful night, but when the first wave of tired adults and the children left the party, Kay settled in Mitch's arms and stayed there. She let the sentiment of the day settle over her and welcomed it. She opened every pore to the sensation and let her fears and insecurities be buried beneath the surreal feeling of peace and belonging enveloping her. Today was a special day and Mitch was an exceptional woman. And one day, she would make the woman she married very happy.

CHAPTER NINETEEN

Kay lounged against Mitch's shoulder as Mitch drove them home. "I'm so glad the weather cooperated for the wedding. Amazing day, wasn't it?" Kay said.

"Perfect. And thanks for your help with my speech. I'm surprised you didn't tell me to add some jokes."

"You could've, it was your speech, but serious was the way to go."

"You're right. Lauren wouldn't have liked jokes, but Val got away with it. Everyone laughed at her speech."

"She was hilarious, but she wasn't so funny leading up to the wedding. She was so stressed out." Kay yawned. "It's been a busy month and I loved seeing Callie and Lauren's wedding, but I'm glad it's over."

"I apologize for the mountain of work we dumped on you. Thanks for all your help."

"All of you left to change and left me at Poplarcreek. I almost didn't make it to the church before the brides." Kay laughed. "I wanted to run away when Val handed me the clipboard with the lists. In the military, I planned meals, cooked meals, and served meals to hundreds of soldiers. It was decent training for a wedding, but the army didn't prepare me for the level of fussiness and detail Val expected."

Mitch smirked. They'd been following Val's orders and directions for a month. Mitch glanced at Kay. "Are you tired?"

"Exhausted." Kay grimaced. "Val's a tough commander." She rubbed her left knee. "I can't wait to soak in the tub."

"Sore, eh?"

"Very. I wish I'd brought my cane with me, but it wouldn't fit in my silly little bag."

"I'll carry you inside." She smiled at Kay who was already half asleep.

Kay drew her dress up to mid-thigh and massaged her knee. "That feels good."

Mitch glanced down as Kay moaned. She'd felt the many raised ridges of scaring when she'd massaged Kay's knee at Poplarcreek. In the diffuse light in the cab of the truck, her knee appeared as if it had been through a meat grinder.

When they arrived at her house, Mitch parked and jogged to the passenger door of her truck. Kay eased into a standing position beside the vehicle. Mitch's pulse pounded in her ears as she picked her up. She carried Kay, cradled in her arms, into the house, but Kay spoiled the sexy moment by giggling as she delivered her to the spare room. "What's so funny?"

Kay grinned. "Sorry, I'm exhausted, and my mind is spinning. Who carried who through the door of the bed and breakfast Callie and Lauren rented?"

"I'm not sure." Mitch scratched her chin as she playfully considered. "I'm sure they might carry each other, for short distances. But Lauren is too pregnant to carry Callie, and Callie wouldn't risk dropping Lauren or hurting the baby." Mitch grinned at Kay. "I wish we'd put money on it, but I bet they entered hand in hand."

"Probably." Kay stretched. "Okay if I have a bath? I'm dying for a soak in hot water."

"Go on in. I'll fetch our stuff from my truck and take care of my chores."

"Join me? After your shower? For a chat? There's so much I want to tell you."

Kay's tone was strangely serious, yet soft at the same time. Mitch glanced one more time at her before dragging herself from the room. Kay's classy dress fell to mid-calf, but with a long slit up the right side, allowing Mitch glimpses of a strong, elegant leg, and she loved the color of the dress.

Mitch let the dogs into the backyard still not sure how it happened that Max, Dover, and Barney were staying with her. The three dogs got along if Max, the most exuberant of the three, didn't push the old men to play. She fed them on her patio and watched Barney and Dover amble through the backyard for another twenty minutes. Even on three legs, Max circled her backyard twice at top speed.

After depositing the dogs in their various beds in her living room, she headed to her bedroom. She yawned as she stripped off her clothes and hung up her suit.

Mitch headed to the bathroom in boxers and a tank top. The bathroom door was ajar and the room empty. The door to Kay's bedroom stood open. They'd been flirting all day and every time she glanced Kay's way Kay was studying her with an enigmatic grin on her face.

Mitch peeked into the room and sucked in her breath. Kay lay on her stomach with the sheets only pulled as far as her waist, displaying a generous expanse of muscled, naked shoulder and back. Her mouth went dry, and her hands itched to explore Kay's soft bare skin. She stepped back, needing a cold shower.

Mitch returned ten minutes later, showered, and wrapped in her robe. Kay hadn't budged. She flicked off the light, slid Kay's door closed, and stumbled to her bedroom. She yawned and rubbed her face. There would be other opportunities to talk, and judging by her lack of clothes, Kay had sex in mind. She was hard to resist, but Mitch backed away. They'd agreed on friends and she'd kept the wedding low pressure. And that's where it needed to stay.

Mitch woke when the sun peeked through a gap in the curtains and caught her in the eyes. She scowled at the clock. Six thirty. She stretched and yawned, pleased at the short but satisfying night's sleep. She'd expected to be restless and conscious of Kay in the spare room, but it never happened. Tension had filled the air while she showered before bed. Her bathroom had smelled of the soap and shampoo Kay used. A mixture of scents she'd delighted in while they danced, and which had infused her dreams.

"What the hell?" Kay shouted.

Mitch leaped from bed and raced to her room. She skidded in and her heart stuttered at the sight. Kay, with messy hair and her face full of sleep, was sitting up in bed. She was naked, with the sheets pooled at her waist. Mitch spun around until her back faced Kay. "Are you—are you—all right?"

"You can turn around."

Mitch turned slowly.

Kay sat frowning in confusion with the sheets carelessly raised to cover her breasts. "When did you get a dog?" Dover was resting his head on her bed, tail wagging and looking at her with adoration.

An instant later, the other dogs shoved their way into the bedroom. Kay laughed as Max leaped onto her bed. "Hello, Max. I know you." She petted Max and looked at Mitch. "Max is Callie's dog, so I assume you're babysitting for the wedding. Who're these two?"

Mitch introduced Dover and Barney as Ronnie's dogs and gave a little background on each.

"Good for Ronnie and Val. Anybody who'd rescue an old yellow lab from abuse is a hero in my books," Kay said.

"I shut your door last night, but clearly not tight enough because Dover found you. He's good at pushing doors open."

"But how did you end up with them?"

Mitch shrugged. "The dogs needed a place to go where they wouldn't be underfoot because Lauren's family is staying at Val's house. Anyway, Val said, 'You can billet the dogs or billet people.' It was no contest."

"I'll bet." Kay laughed.

"We picked them up on our way home to change for the ceremony, but they were outside when you got here, so you wouldn't have seen them." She scratched the back of her neck. "Sorry they bothered you. I'll let them outside. Hey, boys, come with me." She left the room and Max bolted after her. The two labs plodded after him.

Mitch stayed with the dogs in the backyard for fifteen minutes before heading inside. The sexual tension between her and Kay was creating a cloud it was hard to see through, but they needed to find a way. Kay had wanted to talk the night before but had gone to sleep instead. What was she thinking? The mixture of excitement and trepidation tied her stomach in knots.

She rolled her shoulders and headed inside, ready for anything, but Kay wasn't around. Mitch leaned against the counter and yawned while she prepared three bowls of dog food. The dogs pressed against her legs as they waited. A second later, they scurried away.

"Hey there, boys."

Mitch turned at the happy voice and studied Kay as she petted the three dogs and scratched behind their ears. Kay wore a short T-shirt and shorts, and her wet hair curled around her face. She was gorgeous and Mitch scanned her body until Kay caught her.

Kay winked. "Morning again."

Mitch refocused on her task. Ogling Kay wasn't conducive to a serious conversation about friendship. "I'll feed the boys and then feed us. I switched on the coffee. Help yourself when it's ready." Balancing three bowls of dog food on her arm, she almost ran outside with the dogs following.

She set down the bowls, took several deep breaths of cool morning air, and returned to the kitchen. She washed her hands and plopped into a chair across from Kay. She poured herself a coffee. "Sorry, again, about Dover. He's a sociable guy. I'm glad he didn't scare you. Val screamed the first time she woke to hot doggy breath in her face."

Kay tilted her head and scrutinized Mitch. "I hoped you might join me last night. It was a little anticlimactic to have a dog wake me."

Mitch froze with the cup halfway to her lips. She placed it on the table and stared into the cup for a few seconds before squinting at Kay. "I peeked in after my shower, but you were out cold."

"Fair enough. Exhaustion trumped—well, anything. I was too tired to get pajamas on. Val busted my ass yesterday. I saluted her twice without thinking."

Mitch laughed with Kay.

"I love it here," Kay said. "I never wake up laughing in Saskatoon. Life at the college is always about the next surgery, next article to read, or next lesson to teach. I always thought that was what I wanted."

Mitch set her coffee mug carefully on the table, afraid she might spill it. "What do you want now?" She spoke quietly to coax more conversation from Kay. Her radar was on high alert for something important. Maybe she hadn't imagined the connection building between them.

"I want...I mean I think I want to..." Kay hung her head.

Mitch waited, almost afraid to breathe.

"Mitch, I'm not very good at this, and in fact I suck, but you know how I've been kind of constantly after you for sex?"

Mitch nodded.

"What if we did it your way? Kept it just at friends and played twenty questions until we were, I don't know, sure, or more sure, of each other?" Kay shook her head. "I'm screwing this up." She started to rise.

Mitch grabbed her hand, turned it, and kissed Kay's palm. "I understand you."

"You do?" Kay asked.

There was wonder and a vulnerability in Kay's eyes that must have always been there if only she'd looked hard enough. "I do. We're going to spend some more time together. No pressure, just getting to know each other like friends do."

"We are friends."

Kay's face was pale, and her lips trembled. Was it fear? It was intense emotion and perhaps she needed a break. "We're expected at Poplarcreek at eleven for brunch, but it's only seven now." Mitch circled the edge of her cup with a finger. "I have the ingredients for French toast."

Kay guffawed then studied Mitch. "You're serious? No kidding? Okay, I'll make your breakfast."

Kay looked almost relieved to jump up and tackle a task she was comfortable with. Mitch sat back and diverted their conversation to the simpler topics in life such as musical preferences and movies.

She teased Kay for her love for anything Disney but agreed with her that movies about war were for other people.

After breakfast, they retired to the couch with coffee. As they chatted, Kay's eyelids drooped and popped open again several times. "Why don't you stretch out," Mitch said. She shifted and Kay lay across her lap.

"Thanks, this is comfortable," Kay mumbled as she drifted off.

Watching Kay made her drowsy. She yawned and set her phone alarm for ten in case she fell asleep. She brushed a blond curl off Kay's forehead and enjoyed the most perfect morning ever. How would it be to wake every day to Kay's smiling blue eyes? Maybe she could have what she wanted but only if someday Kay wanted the same thing. But Kay was still leaving. She banished the thought. She didn't have to deal with that right now. Today, it was just her and Kay, quiet and together.

When the alarm blared, Kay sat up and stretched. "I fell asleep on you again." She yawned. "Do we have to go?"

Mitch's shoulders slumped. "We're expected and it would be rude not to go."

"Okay, I'm moving." Kay scooted off Mitch's lap to sit beside her.

"What're you doing today? After brunch?"

Kay frowned and started to stand. "I thought I was spending the day with you, but that's okay if you have other plans. I shouldn't have assumed—"

"Whoa, Kay." Mitch grasped Kay's arm and gently pulled her to the couch. "Please, stay with me today, but I have to warn you, we'll have company."

"Pardon?"

"I offered to take Becky. She's coming with me after brunch, and I'll drop her at Val's in the evening."

"Oh." Kay smiled, but the smile didn't travel to her eyes. "Why doesn't she stay with Gwen?"

Mitch scratched the back of her neck. "I have her too. These days it's impossible to have one without the other. They're inseparable. So, will you spend the day with me?" Mitch scratched the back of her neck. "Before you answer, I should warn you we're going to a football game."

"*Football?*"

"The Saskatchewan Roughriders are playing the Montreal Allouettes in Regina. This game's a good choice because there'll be no rivalry. Although the rivalry and competition are the best part."

Kay shook her head. "I don't understand."

"Sonny's team is Edmonton, Ronnie supports Winnipeg, and I'm a Riders fan." Mitch winked at Kay expecting her to comprehend her clear explanation.

"Okay." Kay stretched the word to three syllables. "I don't get it."

"Well, since none of us supports Montreal we all root for the Saskatchewan. Brilliant, eh? Rachel's working this afternoon, but Sonny's coming, too. Ronnie can't come to this one, so I offered to buy her ticket for you and take Gwen, but I don't know if you like football."

"What makes you think I don't like football?"

Mitch smiled. "You mean you like football? That's awesome."

"Well, I don't, but why would you assume I wouldn't?" Kay punched her in the shoulder. "My family stuck to hockey."

Mitch almost danced with glee. "You like hockey?"

"Heck no."

"So, no to football and hockey." Mitch squeezed the bridge of her nose. "If you tell me you're a figure skating fan, I'll have to ask you to leave my house."

"I like ice dancing with all the pretty, pretty costumes."

Mitch squinted at her. "I'm not sure you can be my friend anymore. That's a deal breaker."

Kay collapsed onto the couch laughing. "You're so easy. I don't watch sports, but I'd love to go to a football game with you and Sonny and the girls. I'll even wear blue and gold, or pink and red, or whatever the colors are."

"Green and white," Mitch muttered through clenched teeth. "I have a spare jersey for you, but we should go soon. Val expects us at Poplarcreek in forty minutes. A few others are coming to the game with us. Some of the kids I mentor." Mitch winked and disappeared into her bedroom.

"What have I gotten myself into?" Kay called.

"You'll see," Mitch called back. She grinned as she dressed. Kay would know soon enough what she'd signed up for. Besides, if she wanted Kay to be a part of her life then Kay had better see what it was all about. And she wanted Kay to meet the kids she worked with, and for them to meet her. She laughed aloud as she dressed. When was the last time she'd been so happy?

Chapter Twenty

H ave fun, everyone." Val nudged Kay. "I hope you like football."

Kay shrugged. "I'm not sure, but I'm willing to try." And she would, if it meant spending the day with Mitch and she was curious to meet the kids that Mitch mentored. What was Mitch like with them? Was she a big sister, an aunt, or a drill sergeant?

It was a pleasant brunch and nice to see Lauren and Callie smiling with happiness. At one thirty, the football crew excused themselves from the party. Poor Ronnie watched them go with a wistful expression, no doubt conscripted by Val to help at Poplarcreek all day.

Mitch and Sonny each owned two-door pickup trucks, so Mitch borrowed Callie's SUV for the day because it had room for eight adults. When they arrived in Thresherton, Kay spied a group of three scruffy-looking youths loitering by the Thresherton Diner. They wore the clothes of typical teenagers. One was in a miniskirt, but she couldn't determine the sex of the others. One wore baggy jeans and the other a baseball cap on backward. To her astonishment, Mitch slowed in front of the group and the three piled into the SUV.

"Hey, Sonny, hey, Mitch." Backward Baseball Cap ruffled Becky's hair. "Hey, Anderson. Who's your girlfriend?" Becky swiveled and punched the youth in the arm while Gwen blushed.

"Whoa, no violence. You three, no picking on Becky," Mitch said.

"I won't." Miniskirt leaned around the seat and kissed Becky on the cheek. Becky blushed, not as red as Gwen, but she still blushed.

Mitch locked eyes with the teens in the rearview mirror. "Meet Dr. Kay Gallant. She's a veterinarian at PVS and she's with me."

"Kay, meet Jules, Jacks, and Bobby." Kay shook hands. Jules was in the miniskirt and Bobby in the baggy pants. Jacks, the cockiest of the group, wore her ballcap backward.

"Nice to meet you, Kay. No disrespect," Bobby mock-whispered, "but you are beautiful."

"Thanks, I think."

Jacks slung an arm around Jules who settled in against her.

Kay spoke little on the drive, enjoying the banter between Mitch and the youths. Gwen and Becky participated and sometimes Sonny spoke, but the three teenagers and Mitch carried the conversation. The teens alternated between quizzing Mitch and telling jokes.

The huge crowd at the Regina stadium with its cacophony of raised voices startled Kay. Since returning from Afghanistan, she'd loathed loud noises. Although she'd worked primarily at the base, she'd lain in bed at night listening to shelling and gunfire. In high school, she'd loved loud concerts, but today, the loud noise made her pulse race uncomfortably. She was safe and had nothing to fear from the crowd, but she stuck close to Mitch as they entered. When they located their seats, Kay sat beside Mitch, but moved over to allow Jacks to sit there and visit with Mitch. The other teens and Sonny sat behind them.

"So, you're a veterinarian?"

Kay swiveled to face Bobby. The flirty teenager had disappeared, and she was looking into intelligent blue eyes. Spikey, rough-cut, blond hair didn't hide the pretty face. The girl's features were delicate with a small nose and a wide smile. Her baggy clothes disguised her figure, which was probably the goal. Grunge clothes would discourage the boys, and besides, Bobby should dress how she was most comfortable.

"You must've spent years in school to be a veterinarian. Did you go to grad school? Mitch said you're at the WCVM."

"I am a veterinarian, but I'm not only doing graduate work. I'm doing a residency in small animal surgery. It has a research component."

"Cool."

"What're you interested in studying?"

"Not sure." She shrugged. "I like math and computers. I'm thinking of something in the IT field. Maybe design user-friendly software. I also enjoy games."

"You play computer games?"

"I *design* games. I've sold two already and I'm working on a third. I also have ideas for cool apps. My parents don't care what I do as long as I'm in at night and stay out of trouble." She shook her head. "They think I can't get into trouble on a computer."

"Your parents don't understand computers then?"

"They know how to use them. They both work at the Thresherton Hospital. Mom's a nurse and Dad's an X-ray technician. They use computers, but don't get how designing games translates into a living. Mitch is helping me educate them." Bobby smiled at Mitch.

Kay watched Mitch gesture as she argued with Sonny and Jacks about a call in the game. Kay swiveled to focus on Bobby again. "How do you know Mitch?"

She tilted her head and scrutinized Kay. "Mitch didn't tell you?"

"Tell me what?"

"The three of us are drug addicts, in recovery. Mitch helped us get off drugs. First by arresting us, and then by dragging us to addiction counseling."

Kay leaned away to stare at the youth and glanced at the other two teenagers. Why hadn't Mitch told her?

"Ah, she didn't tell you." Bobby tugged the hood of her sweatshirt over her face and hunched. She acted as if she longed to be smaller or disappear altogether.

Kay wanted to kick herself. Bobby was a nice kid, and it wasn't fair to put her own crap onto someone trying to get control of their life. It was time for damage control. "Mitch didn't tell me, but I'm okay with that."

Bobby pushed the hood off her face and contemplated Kay.

"Mitch considers such information your personal business, and if you wanted me to know you'd tell me. She respects you and wouldn't break your trust. She can keep a secret. Betrayal isn't in her nature." Kay patted her shoulder. "If she didn't trust you, Gwen and Becky wouldn't be here. You realize that, right?"

Bobby nodded. "She's crazy about Becky. Becky's mom is her best friend."

"Yes, Callie and Mitch are great friends." It was time for a topic change away from Mitch. "How's school going?" She groaned inwardly as she parroted her parents. Why did every multigenerational conversation degenerate into a discussion about school?

"We don't go to high school in town. The three of us, and two more, are homeschooled together. Our parents and Mitch teach us. And she arranges for others in the community to teach different subjects. Sonny helped us with a biology course. I know numbers and code, but plants and animals confuse me. Sonny dragged my ass through that course. She took me with her one day to autopsy a pig." She shuddered. "It was gross, but it helped. I understood the anatomy better when I saw it in 3-D."

They chatted for a while longer and then Bobby moved back to her seat. Kay enjoyed the football game, but it was more entertaining to watch Mitch, who slung her arm over Bobby's shoulders as they talked. Mitch was a kind and generous person and a good friend to teenagers and stranded veterinarians. Mitch had basically rescued her twice. Kay fidgeted in her seat, anxious for the chance to sit close to Mitch again.

When Jacks shifted to sit with her, she bumped into Kay's left knee and Kay gasped in pain.

"Sorry about that. Mitch told us to watch your knee. Did it hurt?"

"I'm okay."

She studied Kay's knee as if attempting to see something through her jeans. "How'd you break it?"

"I was with the Canadian military in Afghanistan. A bomb exploded under our vehicle, and my knee was mangled." Kay scanned the players on the field. She paid little attention to the game. Had it really been eight years ago? Some nights, alone in her dark bedroom with her flashbacks, it felt like eight seconds.

"Bet it hurt."

What should she share with these kids? She wasn't special and she was an ex-drug addict too. Kay did a mental head slap. Was that why Mitch had invited her? Did she bring her to inspire the teens? She was no role model. She'd only gotten off drugs when it was that or jail. But then…maybe it was time to stop barricading herself away from other people.

"It hurt like a bitch for several years. When I came home, they filled me full of drugs and I became addicted to them. When they cut me off those, I stole drugs from others until the RCMP arrested me." Strangely, it was a little easier to talk about this time.

"You took drugs?"

Kay wanted to laugh at the astonishment in Jacks's eyes, but she needed to be serious and careful. "I did for a few years, but not anymore."

Jacks sat back and stared. "But you're a *doctor*."

"I wasn't then, but everyone has the potential to abuse drugs, no matter what their profession is. Doctors included, and don't forget we have easy access and can be more tempted."

"What made you stop?"

"The judge gave me the choice of jail or rehab. I could've taken it up again, but I found something I liked better. What about you?"

Jacks shrugged. "I like motorcycles. Mitch is helping me fix mine up. That's our deal."

"That's an important skill. Fixing things."

"Wow, is it okay if I tell Jules and Bobby about you?"

"Yes, but stop there, okay? It's sort of private and I don't want all of Thresherton to know. I'm still a little embarrassed." That was the understatement, and it would be humiliating if the town found out.

Later, the teens went off for snacks and Kay snagged a spot beside Mitch.

"Are you enjoying the game?" Mitch asked.

"I don't understand the rules, but I'm really spending more time talking to Jacks, Jules, and Bobby."

"I'm glad. I wanted them to meet you."

"So I could tell them about my drug addiction?" She made sure there wasn't any judgment in her tone, but she couldn't help but wonder if the invitation had been about something other than them simply spending time together.

"No, of course not. Just because you're you and kind of cool."

Kay shrugged. "Well, I told them. I don't like to talk about it, but if in some small way it could help, I wanted to."

"You're very generous."

Kay shook her head. "Not me, not usually. I asked them not to tell anyone else."

"Then they won't. They have kind of a pact to keep what they tell each other private. It's a recovery thing."

Kay held on to her spot beside Mitch and accepted a hotdog from Jules with thanks. She sat a little straighter and let Mitch talk her through the rules of the game. It was exciting and she did a little dance with Gwen when the Riders scored a touchdown.

Kay leaned into Mitch and sighed when Mitch put an arm around her. She'd never intended on immersing herself in the lives and loves of the people she'd come to know in Thresherton. She had a plan. But as she relaxed against Mitch and laughed with the others, she wouldn't deny it felt awfully nice being part of something instead of apart from it.

Chapter Twenty-one

The Wednesday after the wedding, Kay pulled out of PVS and drove to the highway. She yawned and sipped the coffee she'd taken from the clinic before leaving. In an hour and a bit, she'd be home in bed. She could've stayed at Poplarcreek, but there was no reason to stay tonight. And she'd promised herself a day working in the college library. She had been neglecting her research, preferring to work at PVS. If she didn't catch up, she'd never finish her residency.

She saluted a motorcycle as it passed her doing at least ninety miles per hour. They were lucky. She kept her car to fifty, sixty if she was in a hurry, afraid if she pushed it her wreck of a car would start dropping parts along the highway. She laughed. A street sweeper should follow her home.

Kay gasped and slammed on the brakes as the motorcycle flew off the road and catapulted the rider into the wheat field. Only a black rubber skid mark on the asphalt remained in view.

Kay parked on the shoulder, put her hazard lights on and got out. The motorcycle was half-buried in the mud of the ditch. She looked up and down the highway for other drivers but saw nobody. "Shit, shit, shit." This time of day she was more likely to see Santa Claus than another car.

She slid down into the ditch and crossed into the wheat field. It was thankfully warm and sunny today, after two days of rain. The farmers had been happy to have the rain to feed the crops, but it made the field muddy.

Kay stopped. "Hello? Are you there?" Only the sound of insects and the distant hum of farm machinery broke the silence. "I can't see you. Can you tell me where you are?" She waited for a beat and then walked toward a flat patch in the wheat field.

She kneeled beside the slender person. They were breathing, but too still. "Hello?" They didn't answer, but she rejoiced at finding a strong pulse and no obvious bleeding. She pulled out her phone, said a quick prayer for a cell signal, and dialed 911. She told them she was on the highway, headed west toward Saskatoon, and gave a description of her car, but that was the best she could do. Wheat fields stretched in every direction with no landmarks in sight.

She gently touched the person's arm. "Hi there, my name is Kay. I've called for an ambulance. Please stay still. It's the best thing to do because you might have hurt your spine." She spoke a few more times, just in case they could hear her, but they didn't answer. When she heard the ambulance, she stood up and waved her arms over her head.

She got out of the way of the paramedics. A minute later, an RCMP cruiser skidded to a stop. Mitch jumped out and jogged toward them.

"Kay, are you hurt?" Mitch asked.

"No." Kay pointed to the person on the ground. "They crashed their motorcycle."

Mitch nodded and bent to speak with the paramedics.

Kay walked back through the field and made a couple of unsuccessful attempts to climb out of the muddy ditch.

"Need some help?" Mitch asked.

"Yes, please." Another person might have just grabbed her. Mitch asked first, then cupped her elbow and helped her out of the ditch. "Rescued again. Thanks."

"Can you wait for a minute and tell me what happened?"

"Sure." Kay perched on the bumper of her car. A few minutes later, Mitch and the paramedics struggled up the ditch with the stretcher, loaded it into the ambulance, and the paramedics drove off, back toward Thresherton.

Kay waited for Mitch, but she didn't move, just stared into the distance after the departing ambulance. She approached her. "Mitch? I didn't see much. Just the—Are you okay?" Mitch's expression was stricken, and her eyes filled with anguish. "You look like you need a hug."

Mitch launched herself into Kay's arms. The hug was so tight it stole Kay's breath, but she hung on.

After a minute, Mitch stepped back and swiped at her eyes. "Sorry about that. So unprofessional, but that was Jacks."

"Jacks? From the football game?"

Mitch nodded. "She's in bad shape. I need to call her parents. Can you wait a few more minutes?"

"Absolutely." Kay returned to her car, thinking of Jacks's cocky grin and intelligent eyes. Eventually, Mitch walked over, and Kay gave an outline of what she'd seen. "Can I do anything?"

"You look like you're headed home," Mitch said.

"I can come back." Her readiness to stay astonished her, but only for a second. Mitch was her friend, and if she needed her, she'd stay. And although Jacks wasn't related to Mitch, she cared about her. "What if I go to your house and wait for you? You'll want to be with Jacks."

"Will you be there tonight?"

"Yes, whatever you need."

Mitch wavered. "I have to go, but…"

"Yes?"

"Thanks. I'd like to come home to you."

Mitch jumped in her cruiser, turned around, and charged off in the direction of Thresherton. A fresh spray-painted mark at the side of the road, just above the motorcycle, marked its location. She hadn't seen Mitch do it, but how else would anyone find it in an endless sea of wheat fields?

Kay got in her car, carefully turned around, and headed back to town. "I'd like to come home to you." What a loaded phrase, full of meaning that could be misinterpreted. She parked at Mitch's house and went in. She put her bags in the spare room and dropped on the edge of the bed. She should work, but no way could she concentrate. She grabbed a soda and sat on the couch and tried to watch television. She sent Mitch a couple of texts offering to come to the hospital. Mitch answered the second one and said she was headed home soon.

She organized some food for making sandwiches and waited for Mitch. An hour later, she gave up and made herself a sandwich, but only managed two bites. She waited another hour for Mitch before crawling into bed. She refused to pester her with more texts. Mitch was probably staying longer at the hospital and that was fine. She'd be at her house when or if Mitch needed her. She'd planned on a day in the college library tomorrow, so no one would miss her if she stayed in Thresherton.

Much later, she heard Mitch come home and then the shower run for a few minutes. She got out of bed and padded down the hall. Mitch wasn't in the kitchen. She knocked on her bedroom door. "Mitch, are you okay?"

"Come in."

Kay pushed the door open and slipped in. Mitch was slumped on the edge of the bed in shorts and a T-shirt. She sat beside her. "How's Jacks?"

Mitch shook her head.

Kay gasped. "Oh no, she's not—"

"No, no. She'll be fine. She has a concussion and a broken leg. They'll keep her in the hospital for a while." March dropped her face into her hands. "She could've died."

Kay wrapped her arms around her, and Mitch shifted until she was half-lying across Kay's lap. She held her, and then propelled Mitch into bed. "Would you like me to stay with you?"

"Not for—"

"Of course not. Just for company." Kay slid in and gathered Mitch in her arms. Mitch told her more of the details of Jacks's injuries. She caressed her hair and subtly rocked her until Mitch fell asleep. She'd seen vulnerability in Mitch and even a little hurt, but the devastating pain of Jacks almost dying stripped away the last barrier of reserve between them. She curled around Mitch, prepared to hold her as long as she was needed.

The next morning, the unmistakable muffled crashing of weights woke Kay, and she was a little bummed not to have Mitch in bed beside her, still curled into her. She found Mitch in her home gym, nodding to the music in her headphones. She tapped her on the shoulder. "Want coffee?" she mouthed.

Mitch set her weights down and pulled off the headphones. "I'll make it."

Kay was going to make a joke about how Mitch wouldn't let her make coffee after the first batch had been thick enough to patch car tires, but now wasn't the time. She sat at the kitchen table and waited. Mitch gave her a coffee and they sat across from each other sipping. "How's Jacks?" Mitch would've checked as soon as she'd gotten up.

"The tough little shit is wide awake this morning. Only her leg is broken, but I might break the other one."

"What? Why?"

"She was high. Got a hold of some ketamine and thought if she drove super-fast her bike would start flying. Fuck, I hate drugs. She bought it at a party a couple of weeks ago from some woman. It was dark and the woman had a ballcap pulled down low, so she can't identify her." Mitch slammed her fist into the palm of her hand. "When I catch her, that supplier…" She shook her head. "Did you and Val sort out your ketamine mystery? Did you find it?"

Kay bit back a sharp retort to the thinly veiled accusation. Mitch was upset and needed her compassion. "Val's got that covered. We're not your source."

"Good."

Kay swallowed. Mitch's expression was ferocious. She'd prefer to face down a rabid rottweiler than Mitch in the mood that went with that face. "Anything I can do?" she asked weakly.

Mitch scratched the back of her neck and looked away. "Thanks for staying last night even though I was a big baby."

"Jacks is your friend. It's okay to be upset." She playfully slapped Mitch's forearm. "Quit being a tough little shit and give yourself a break, will you?"

Mitch smiled. "What're your plans today?"

"Can I stay and work here? I'm back at PVS tomorrow. Or I could go to Poplarcreek."

"Please stay. I have to get to work, but after dinner I'm going to the hospital to see Jacks."

"I'll come with you, if I'm welcome." She'd only met the teens once and didn't want to presume.

Mitch squeezed her hand. "Always."

Kay worked on her computer at Mitch's and went to the hospital with her in the late afternoon. Bobby and Jules were there too. It was uncomfortable at first, full of awkward conversation as they stood around Jacks's bed, but Kay kept making jokes and eventually everyone relaxed.

"Thanks, Kay, for, you know, finding me," Jacks said.

"Glad I was there."

"And, Mitch?" Jacks said tentatively.

Mitch looked at Jacks, her expression tender and fierce at the same time, and maybe a little disappointed. "Yes, Jacks?"

"I'm sorry about the special K. I was doing so well and then I…shit." She turned her head into the pillow.

Mitch's expression softened and she gently squeezed Jacks's shoulder until she turned and looked up at her. "You *were* doing amazing, and you *will* do it again. Today you start over, okay?"

Jacks nodded and coughed to cover a sniffle, but Kay wasn't fooled. This was the protective instinct that Lauren had talked about. Mitch protected the ones she cared about. Looked after them when they needed help. And Mitch had looked after her too.

Kay stayed with Mitch for the rest of the week. She went back to the college for one day but returned to Mitch in the evening. She didn't attempt to cook, but got some nice takeout, and Callie and Ronnie dropped off a couple of meals. It was peaceful hanging out with Mitch in the evenings. Kay didn't flirt with Mitch, and they slipped comfortably into a solid friendship. She was conflicted about that development but went with it.

❖

On Monday, Kay closed her computer when the front door opened. She got up to greet Mitch with a friendly hug, although she was always struck by how sexy she looked in uniform. "Hello. Dinner's in the oven." She laughed. "That sounded domestic. Next I'll be asking how your day was."

"Crappy. We can't figure out where the ketamine came from that Jacks got. I can't stand that she relapsed. She's been doing so well." Mitch dropped onto the couch. "I arrested her for possession ten months ago. Gave her the choice of jail or rehab." She shook her head. "I thought it would work. It worked for you."

Kay nodded. "Probably saved me, but it was humiliating. Dad wouldn't look me in the eye for two months. Only my mom visited me in rehab, and she always looked like she'd been crying."

"That sounds rough, but I wish somebody had stopped my brother, even if it was humiliating. God, I hate drugs."

Kay rubbed her hand up and down Mitch's arm. "What can I do?"

Mitch's stomach growled. "Apparently, I'm hungry."

"I can take care of that." She gently tugged Mitch to her feet and led her to the kitchen table. Mitch slipped off her utility belt and set it on the chair beside her. Kay placed a plate heaped with food and a glass of milk in front of her. "Callie's cooking again. Smells good."

"Thanks." Mitch began to mechanically eat. A little while later, she pushed her plate away. "Did anyone tell you about my good friend Liz Anderson?"

Kay set down her fork. "Only that she was Callie's first wife and that she died."

"She pulled some creep over for speeding. He shot her and ran away. They found a bunch of drugs and cash in his car. He shot her because she'd have found them. Freaking lowlife drug dealer. Freaking lowlife murderer."

Kay leaned back as the anger and pain wafted off Mitch. She stared at the metal fork Mitch slowly bent between her fingers.

Mitch straightened the fork but didn't resume eating. "Sorry about that."

Kay patted her hand. "It's okay. You were close."

"She was the big sister I never had."

"But isn't your sister older?"

Mitch shrugged. "Liz, Callie, and Becky, and now Lauren and the baby, are the family I chose. My sister and mother are the family I'm stuck with."

"Is that why you're a nester? Looking for a permanent relationship and close family? Because you didn't have it growing up?"

"I never thought of it that way. Probably why I want to stay in Thresherton, because we moved so much when I was a kid. I felt like I never had a home. Here I have roots and people."

The light and fun drained out of Mitch's eyes as she slipped into a sad place, so Kay searched for a lighter topic. "What're you doing this evening?"

"It's warm. I was going to take my bike out and blow the cobwebs from my brain."

"Can I come with you or do you want to go on your own?"

Mitch smiled for the first time in two days and Kay wanted to do a little jig.

"Please, come with me."

After dinner was tidied away, Kay changed into jeans and headed outside. She paused and held her stomach against the fluttering. Surely, she couldn't be hungry again? She splayed her hands over her stomach. The fluttering wasn't hunger. It was the excitement and anticipation of being wrapped around Mitch on a motorcycle.

She accepted the helmet and strapped it on, then climbed on behind Mitch and wrapped her arms around her. The bike roared beneath them and Mitch set off slowly, getting a sense of the machine with a rider on it. Kay hadn't ridden a lot, but enough to know how to move with the bike, and soon they were roaring down the backroads. Mitch slowed at one point and nodded toward a herd of deer that watched them go by, and eventually they pulled off into a clearing at the side of the road.

Kay climbed down and stretched. "That was fun. I haven't been on a bike in years." She looked around. "Why're we stopping here?"

"To watch the sunset."

Mitch kicked out the bike stand and removed her helmet as she climbed off. Kay took a deep breath. Why was each thing Mitch did just a little bit sexier than the last? She tipped her head toward the cars parked at the opposite end of the clearing. "That what they're doing?"

"Sort of." Mitch walked to the edge of the clearing and sat.

Kay moved in beside her. They were on the edge of river valley. "This is amazing. I thought Saskatchewan was totally flat." She set her helmet on the grass beside her.

"Val told me the glaciers carved out the valley. She says it's the best place to see the sunset and that in high school this place was called the Hang." Mitch scratched the back of her neck. "It's kind of a make out spot, but please don't read into that."

Kay sighed. She'd been about to say something flirty, but they were there to watch the sunset and because Mitch needed a break. "It's spectacular." She pulled her coat tighter around herself. She'd forgotten how breezy it got on a bike.

"Cold?"

"A little. Should've put a sweatshirt on under my jacket."

Mitch raised her arm in invitation. Kay shifted and snuggled in against her. The heat poured off Mitch in waves, better than a furnace. Mitch rested her arm around her, and Kay pulled it tighter. She searched for a topic of conversation and then gave up. Mitch appeared to be content to just sit quietly and she would too.

After a few minutes, Mitch spoke. "I come here to relax," she said in a dreamy voice. "I come after a hard day when I've seen stuff that no one should have to. This sight reminds me that there is still beauty in the world, you just have to look for it." Mitch looked down at her.

Kay smiled. "I get that. Thanks for bringing me."

Mitch squeezed Kay closer and looked out over the river valley as the sun set in the west. She raised her face and the orange glow caught the handsome plains of her face. Kay itched to caress her cheek but held back. Now wasn't the time. Mitch had brought her to her special spot. It couldn't have been a more intimate moment if they were in bed together. Mitch didn't hold back. She was an open book if Kay chose to read. How did she manage to do that? It was a skill Kay didn't have, but in that instant she wanted to learn.

Chapter Twenty-two

M itch parked her cruiser and took several large gulps of her coffee. She and Kay had gotten back late from the motorcycle ride the night before and then had sat up talking. She'd had a few too many beers and then Kay had tucked her into bed. There'd been a gentle hug and soft kisses followed by the thankful oblivion of sleep.

She shook her head and then grabbed it as it felt like it might explode. It was bright and sunny, and today of all days she would appreciate an overcast sky. At eighteen, she'd be falling-down drunk, crawl into bed at three a.m. and be up and wide-awake for work by eight a.m. These days she had some wrinkles and a few gray hairs, a stark reminder that she wasn't a kid anymore and needed her sleep.

Mitch took a deep breath, exited her cruiser, and approached RCMP constable Joanne Scott. "Hey, Jo. Who was here first?"

Jo pointed to a tall thin male RCMP officer interviewing two people farther along the road. "Phil got here twenty minutes ago."

Mitch counted three other police cruisers with lights flashing. She'd responded to the call, but as the fourth officer to arrive, she had no role, she was simply curious about what was going on. She walked up and stood where Phil could see her.

When Phil had a chance, he spoke to her. "Hey, Mitch. Two folks in a car swerved to miss a kid on a bike. Unfortunately, they still hit him and they crashed their car. It's a mess. All three have gone to the hospital. The kid's dog was hit running beside the bicycle. The poor animal's not dead but I wish I had the guts to shoot it and save it this misery."

Mitch straightened and scanned the area. Paramedics had taken care of the people and now an animal needed help. "The dog's alive? Where is it?"

Phil pointed toward the side of the road. "Will you take care of it?"

Mitch jogged away.

"Thanks, Mitchell," he called after her.

Mitch skidded down into the ditch. She saw a dalmatian lying on its side panting. It had blood on its face, and it whimpered in pain. The animal watched her with wide eyes as she crept closer. "Hey, puppy." Her stomach roiled at the dog's pain.

Mitch reached for it, intending to pet his head where she saw no blood. "Whoa." She fell back on her butt as the dog snapped at her with sharp white teeth that had appeared from behind curled and bleeding lips. The dog would've bitten her if he'd not been in too much pain to move. He whined in agony and didn't understand why it hurt. Her words were gentle as she reached again, but he lunged for her hand.

Mitch fetched a thick blanket from the trunk of her cruiser and outlined her plan to Jo. "I'll catch him, and you drive us to Kay, I mean to PVS." Kay was working at PVS today and that meant the dog would have the best surgeon in the province.

Jo threw her hands up. "I don't know if you're brave or crazy, but I'll help."

Mitch tossed the blanket over the dog's head to prevent him from seeing her. "Don't bite me, please, big guy." She grabbed his head while she slipped an arm under his body and lifted him. The poor animal snapped at her, then struggled, and howled in pain. She carried him to the cruiser parked closest to the ditch and slid into the back seat with the dog in her lap. Jo drove her with lights and sirens to PVS.

When they pulled into the parking lot at PVS, Jo jumped out and met Minnie at the door of the clinic. Mitch watched them talk, then Minnie darted away. Val and Kay appeared with a rolling stretcher.

Mitch looked at Kay's startled face. "This dog's been hit by a car. He tried to bite me and will now if I let him go."

"Can you slide out and still hang on to him?"

Mitch nodded and slid across the seat. The dog whimpered and growled as she moved. "Can you drug him or something? I don't want him to bite you."

"I want to examine him first." Kay grasped Mitch's arm and helped her from the car. Mitch lowered the dog to the stretcher and hung on to him.

Val appeared with a leather muzzle and Kay reached for it. They paused for a second, each clinging to one end of the muzzle. Kay tugged on the muzzle. "I'd prefer he bites me."

Val let go and at Kay's nod slowly pulled the blanket back. Mitch registered the dog's sharp white teeth as Kay slipped the muzzle on its snout. She held the dog while Kay and Val wheeled him into the treatment room. When she stepped back, Val took her place.

Minnie motioned Mitch to follow her back to the waiting room. "It's okay. Dr. Gallant's awesome. She'll look after him. What happened and what's his name?"

"He's not my dog and I don't know his name. He was hit running beside a boy on a bike. The child's in the hospital." Mitch described the accident to Minnie. "I'll be responsible for him, for now." She signed the papers at PVS, left a deposit, and went home to shower and change. Blood, urine, and feces covered the front of her uniform, and had soaked into her bra and underwear. The poor dog couldn't help it. He was in rough shape, but taking him to Kay was the right move. Mitch couldn't help but think of the way Kay had been there for her, too, as she'd worried over Jacks and allowed guilt to eat at her. She felt like she'd failed in her duty as a mentor, but having Kay around had eased the pain and helped her move forward without a ton of self-recrimination. Mitch had always been a rescuer, but these days, it looked like Kay was right there beside her.

Kay was examining the X-rays when Minnie joined her and Val.

"How is he?" Minnie asked.

"We have him on IV fluids and pain medication. The impact fractured his pelvis." Kay pointed to X-ray. "Transverse fracture of the ilium and ischium. The good news is the only damage appears to be to his pelvis. But we still need to watch for internal bleeding."

Val petted the dalmatian. "He's not trying to bite anymore. What's his name? I've been calling him Puppy."

Minnie shrugged. "Mitch told me the dog was running beside a bicycle when a car slammed into him and a child. She didn't know the boy's name or the dog's name."

Kay looked from Val to Minnie. "So, we don't have an owner?"

Minnie raised her hands. "Don't worry. Mitch gave us five hundred dollars before she left. I promised her it would be enough for emergency care and to stabilize him until she located the owner."

Kay looked off into space and smiled. Mitch cared about a dog she didn't know or own and that intrigued and impressed her. But it probably shouldn't. Mitch cared about the struggling LGBT kids, and people who were stranded, and everyone else she came across. Rescuing a poor dog was standard operating procedure for Officer Mitchell, but still it was extraordinarily generous.

Val had to leave at lunch to take Gwen to the dentist and just afterward, Kay met with Mr. Vanderdeen, the owner of the dog. He said Officer Mitchell told him where Cody was. Kay told him Cody had a fractured pelvis and offered to repair him for two thousand dollars. His eyes flew open wide as he registered the cost.

"After Cody's surgery there will be months of aftercare, especially for the first four weeks. He'll require extra help for four to six months, until he recovers."

He ran his hand over his face. "How is he now?"

"He's stable and we have him on medication for the pain. There's no evidence of serious internal damage, but we need to operate tomorrow. If we wait much longer, his tissues will tighten up, and it'll be harder for me to manipulate the bones."

"We could probably find the money, but our son's going to need a lot of care while he recovers. He has a broken leg, a broken arm, and a concussion." He shook his head. "I'll talk to my wife and come back after lunch."

Kay nodded. He had a lot to deal with at home and it was a lot of time to commit to his dog, but she prepared for the surgery anyway. She would save Cody with or without his consent. And somehow, she'd find the money to pay PVS back. She couldn't rescue every animal, but she was going to try. Kay snatched her phone off the counter and called the veterinary college. She arranged to stay in Thresherton another day so she could take Cody to surgery.

Minnie interrupted Kay's preparations. "I have Mitch on the phone. She's at the diner picking up lunch. She offered to bring us something. I have my lunch already, but she insisted on bringing me a piece of pie." Minnie blushed at the admission.

Kay scrutinized Minnie. Wasn't Minnie straight? She lived alone on a small hobby farm and never mentioned a partner, but she'd have told them if she was a lesbian, wouldn't she? "Thanks, Minnie." Kay considered declining. Mitch had done so much for her she was starting to feel like a leech, but hell, she had no lunch with her, and she was hungry. She'd only had coffee for breakfast, and she wouldn't have time to get to the diner. "Please, tell her I'd love a grilled cheese on brown and a house salad."

Kay turned her attention to her other patients and then headed to her office. She'd barely sat down to write her medical records when she heard the bell of the clinic door and Minnie greeting Mitch.

Kay popped out of her office as Mitch arrived at the counter. "Hello."

"Hi." Mitch held up a white paper bag. "They wrapped it in foil for you, but it'll be cold soon."

Kay followed Mitch to the lunchroom. Kay selected a variety of sodas from the refrigerator and placed them on the table and she slipped into a chair and shot Mitch another grateful look. "Thanks."

"Yes, thanks, Mitch." Minnie picked up her pie and disappeared.

Kay tore the foil off her sandwich, took a large bite, and a second larger bite. She shrugged at Mitch who grinned while she devoured the food. Mitch hadn't taken one bite of her sandwich. "I skipped breakfast. Lunch is perfect."

Mitch unwrapped her sandwich. They ate sandwiches and salads in companionable silence. Afterward, Mitch passed her a bag containing four large cookies, and she selected a peanut butter with chocolate chunks.

When Kay finished her cookie, she leaned back in her chair and rested her hands on her full stomach. "Thanks. That was good. I'm stuffed."

"Me too and you're welcome. How's Cody doing?"

That Mitch had learned Cody's name, didn't surprise Kay. "He's stable and in no pain, but the impact fractured his pelvis. When I told Mr. Vanderdeen, it would cost at least two thousand dollars for Cody's emergency care and surgery, I thought he might faint. It doesn't look good for poor Cody."

Mitch glowered at her and she leaned back, but Mitch was angry at the situation, not her.

"Life's not fair. Cody deserves to live," Mitch said.

Kay covered Mitch's hand with hers. "I agree, but the surgery's expensive and Cody needs six months of home care. Mr. Vanderdeen told me his son will need around the clock help at home, and healthcare won't pay for everything. He said his wife might have to give up her job to stay home." Kay shook her head. "Cody is too much for the family to cope with right now. Their son comes first."

"What if I keep him?"

"Cody?"

Mitch nodded. "I rescued him from the ditch and brought him this far. Cody deserves a chance."

"I'll speak with Mr. Vanderdeen. He'll have to agree if he's not prepared to take care of Cody. I'll try to get half the money from them, at least. And I'll talk to Ian and ask how much I can trim off the bill if I don't charge for my time."

"You don't have to do that. I'll pay what I have to."

"But I want to help Cody and you. It's very generous of you to take on his care. It could be six months before he's up and around fully."

"I can look after him, if you show me how."

"I'll help you all I can. Thanks, Mitch."

"Why're you thanking me?"

Kay swirled a finger in the condensation her can of soda had left on the table. "Because I was afraid I'd have to adopt him and I'm not sure I have room in my life."

"And you're moving."

Kay nodded, although in truth she hadn't given her plans of moving much thought lately.

"Well, I'm happy to keep him. And I believe in you."

"Thanks. I know I can fix him."

They both stood at the same time. Kay looked into Mitch's warm and welcoming eyes and moved in for a hug. They remained holding each other for a few beats, until Kay pulled away. "Cody's surgery is tomorrow morning and I'll call you as soon as we're done."

"Will I see you tonight?"

"You're going to have to let me pay for the bed and breakfast. I don't want to be one of those friends that comes for a day and never leaves." Kay forced a smile and wished she could pull back her words. Something in Mitch's wistful expression told her that was exactly what Mitch wanted. Kay took a step back. "I'd better get back to work."

"I don't need any money, but we need milk, eggs, and bread, if you have time to shop. See you." Mitch gave a little wave and left.

Kay watched the police car drive away. She'd warned Mitch that taking care of Cody would cost two thousand dollars and be six months of work. Mitch had accepted responsibility for Cody's costs as if it were no trouble. Assuming responsibility for Cody's home care was generous. And that was just like Mitch.

Kay turned and headed for the treatment room to check on the ketamine supply. Val was awesome, but she'd kill somebody if there wasn't enough for Cody's surgery tomorrow. Fortunately, there was enough, but she still couldn't help but feel there should be more.

That afternoon, Mr. Vanderdeen gave a thousand dollars for the surgery and signed Cody over to Mitch. Over dinner at Mitch's house that night, they discussed the issues surrounding care and Mitch made a list of things she'd need. The domesticity of what they were sharing was getting dangerously close to normal, and Kay went to bed unsettled.

The next morning, Val assisted Kay with the surgery. Kay straightened the pelvis and screwed metal bone plates across the fractures.

After the surgery, Kay phoned Mitch. "Cody's doing well and can go home on Saturday. Val or I will make regular house calls to save you bringing him to the clinic. He needs his sutures out in two weeks. In four weeks, he has to come back to PVS for another set of X-rays to assess the healing."

"I'm glad he's okay. Thanks for everything."

"Sorry, it's still a big bill."

"No problem. You did your best."

"Mitch, can I stay again tonight? Tomorrow's a work on the computer day and I'd like to check on Cody in the morning." She really needed access to the library at the college, but she hated leaving Cody and Mitch. She told herself it was so she could keep an eye on both of them and make sure they were okay, but deep down, she knew it was something else. "Mitch? Are you still there?"

"I'm here. Sorry, I have to go. There's an emergency. I can't wait to see you and you're welcome to stay as often as you want."

Mitch hung up and Kay stared at the receiver. Cody was a lucky boy and had just found an exceptional new home with Mitch. And who wouldn't want to live there?

Kay headed back to the treatment room to check on Cody. "Hi, Cody, you have a new mom. Mitch rescued you and you're going to be just fine." She adjusted his IV and gave his ears a scratch. A woman who rescued and adopted a wounded dog was a woman Kay respected and a woman she could love. Why was she even thinking of love? Where had that come from? Mitch impressed the hell out of her, but love would never happen. Love suited nesters like Callie and Lauren. Love was not for her.

CHAPTER TWENTY-THREE

Kay had to get back to the college for a day, so she left the rest of Cody's post-op care in Minnie's and Val's capable hands. She texted Mitch to let her know the plan and then she focused on the surgeries the college had booked for her. When she got home after ten hours at the college, she had the urge to phone Mitch. She was slowly losing the will to live alone. Instead of seeing it as having peace and space, all she had was pressing silence. What could she do? Tell Mitch that she wasn't ready for a relationship or a commitment of any kind, but she wanted the companionship they were building? Even the thought was terrifying, and for a second, she wanted to run. Instead, she wrote down her plans the way she used to when she'd begun this journey. *Finish school. Apply for jobs in the US. Move. Learn. Be independent.*

The list looked strangely bleak, and she put it in a drawer.

On Friday night, after she left the college, she packed a bag and headed for Thresherton. Minnie told her Cody walked outside to pee and that they'd had no problem getting him to eat. His nose was grazed, but healing quickly, and it didn't slow him down.

She pulled into PVS at six p.m. and parked beside Val's car. She unlocked the back door and called out immediately so as not to scare Val. "Hi, Val, it's Kay."

Gwen bounced out of the treatment room. "Hi, Kay, Mom and I are examining the puppy."

Kay laughed. "When did we get a puppy?"

"It's Cody."

Kay followed Gwen into the treatment room. Val was on her knees leaning into Cody's kennel. She had a stethoscope on so Kay waited, not wanting to interrupt.

When Val backed out, she looked up. "He's doing well. His heart rate is normal, and his lungs are clear. There's no fever and Minnie said Cody's eating like he's never been fed before."

"You were at school today, but you wanted to check on him?"

Val blushed. "You did too."

"Cody, you have a fan club." She petted his head. "You're a good boy, Cody." She smiled when he licked her hand.

Val stood and brushed down her lab coat. "He's not fully grown. Did you see the size of his feet?"

Kay laughed. "I know, right? Mitchell adopted a pony, not a puppy. Cody's big for a dalmatian. Oh well, I hope she's up for it."

Val pointed at her. "Hey, you're not working tomorrow. I could've discharged him."

Kay shrugged. "I took this Saturday from Lauren and she was grateful for the break."

"What's your plan now?"

"Not Poplarcreek."

"Do you have another option?" Val waggled her eyebrows.

Kay shook her head. "Didn't text her either." There was no reason not to stay with Mitch, but after holding her when Jacks crashed, a different energy had developed between them. It was nothing she could put her finger on, but it made her nervous. She needed her head examined. She didn't want to be alone and had rushed back to Thresherton, but now she was afraid to text Mitch. This kind of muddle and confusion was what happened when you let yourself connect too closely with people and forgot your career goals. She needed some space. "I don't think I'll stay with Mitch tonight."

Val looked at her with a question on her lips, but instead gave her a quick hug. "Then come home with us. All I can offer you is the couch for a bed, but Ronnie's cooking a fabulous dinner."

"And I made a chocolate layer cake," Gwen said.

Kay smiled at Gwen. "Then how can I refuse? I would love some cake."

She had a wonderful evening chatting with Val's happy family. She filled up on Ronnie's good cooking and had two helpings of Gwen's cake. She'd never been drawn to kids, but had discovered she loved the stories about the adventures and misadventures of Gwen and Becky.

After everyone headed for bed, Kay had a quick shower, pulled on pajamas, and returned to the living room.

"I hope you'll be comfortable," Val said.

"I'm sure I will. Thanks again for a great evening and the bed."

"Everything okay with you and Mitch? I mean, you're always welcome here, I just thought..." Val shrugged.

Kay motioned for Val to sit. "She's pretty great, it's just that I'm spending too much time away from school. It's a lot of work to keep up and move ahead. Well, you know that."

"I'm not in vet school yet. Introductory biology is great, but the biochemistry and physics courses I'm taking are a bit of hell. I thought I'd have the upper hand with all my experience, but not today."

"It will help in vet school, but vet school will still be a ton of work. I don't think I read a book for pleasure in the four years I was in college and I worked two jobs every summer."

"Mitch won't get in the way of your career. She respects you too much." Val patted Kay's knee. "I can see it in her face. She's impressed by you."

"Thanks for saying that, but I already feel like I'm letting her get in the way. If I lose focus, I'll lose Cornell and Davis."

"Is that all that's worth keeping? Nothing else you don't want to lose?"

"Maybe, I don't know. I'm confused. I used to know what I wanted, or I think I still do." She wanted to scream in frustration. She needed some space from Mitch if she was ever going to get on track again.

"'Night, Kay." Val smiled knowingly and left.

Kay crawled into the bed Val made up on the couch. Did she know what she wanted? Absolutely. She had her goals. But picturing Mitch's warm hazel eyes kept her awake until the vision lost the war with Val's cozy house and she closed her eyes.

Kay woke refreshed. Fortunately, she'd slept well because this Saturday at PVS was going to be busy.

At closing time on Saturday, Mitch appeared at the clinic in faded jeans with a torn knee and a hoodie with frayed cuffs. She tugged at her hoodie and smiled wryly. "These are my old clothes and seemed right for this job."

Kay dropped her head. She'd been staring. She liked casual scruffy Mitch as much as dressed up or uniformed Mitch. She probably liked Mitch dressed in anything, or undressed. "Sure, of course. Would you like some help to get Cody settled at home?"

"Thanks. I thought Val was going to help because you weren't working this Saturday."

"Change of plans and Val's gone home for the day. Will I do?"

"Yes, I didn't—please, help me."

Kay laughed. "It's okay. I get it. Now, let's settle your bill. They left it all ready for me so there's only a slight chance I'll muck it up."

Mitch swept Kay into a tight hug and kissed her on the top of the head. "I'm very happy to see you."

Kay looked up. Her mouth had suddenly gone dry and all she could do was nod stupidly.

The next kiss was on the lips and Kay struggled to keep professional as she gently pulled away, her fingers touching her lips. "Your bill's this way." She led the way on shaky legs and ducked behind the cash register, needing a little space between her and Mitch.

Mitch paid her bill and brought Cody's new pet carrier to the treatment room. Kay and Mitch loaded him in the carrier. Mitch carried him outside, and tied the carrier into the bed of her truck.

Kay closed and locked the clinic and followed Mitch home. Panic welled up in her on the drive. She was going to be in Mitch's house again and that was dangerous territory.

"Before we take Cody inside, can you please show me how you've organized his space?" Kay asked.

"Absolutely."

Kay followed Mitch inside. She suggested a few changes, but Mitch had common sense and had followed her directions. She'd emptied a spare room for Cody and purchased everything Kay advised her to.

"Cody has to live in his kennel for four weeks," Kay said. "You can take him outside, but only on a short leash and you must carry him up and down the stairs."

"Yes, ma'am." Mitch saluted.

"Stop that." Kay playfully slapped her forearm

They carried Cody in and slipped him into the kennel.

"It looks tight in there," Mitch said.

"A little, but we don't want him to move while he heals. You can tell a person to stay in bed, but a dog has to be forced to remain still. Later, we'll move him to a bigger kennel. Because it's tight, I left the cone off, but let me know if you catch him licking his sutures. He has to leave them alone to heal."

"Will do." When Cody had settled, they left him sleeping and Mitch closed the door to his room. "Are you hungry? Callie knew I'd be busy with Cody, so she brought me two homemade meat pies. One chicken and one beef."

Kay tapped her lower lip and pretended to consider the offer. "The last time I ate a slice of Callie's meat pie, I had to have a nap to digest."

"Stay, unless you have plans in the city. My spare room is still available."

"Are you telling me you have nowhere to be?"

"My plan this weekend is to care for Cody." Mitch scuffed the floor with the toe of her shoe. "But maybe you have a date."

"Nope, not me." Kay was stung by the remark and the idea that Mitch might think she was interested in somebody else. Could the exciting energy between them be her imagination? Then again, even if Mitch felt it too, Kay had made her plans clear and there was no reason for Mitch to think they'd changed. They needed to lighten the mood, so she playfully punched Mitch in the shoulder. "Now lead me to the food. I haven't eaten for at least four hours. And later I want to watch the silliest movie you own."

Mitch pulled her into a quick hug, kissed her on the top of the head, and headed into the kitchen. "It's a deal."

Kay stood swaying at the front door. The tight hugs and the kiss had almost undone her. What had happened to her goal of sex and fun and then moving on to a new job? How did being held in Mitch's arms against a soft, faded hoodie have her reeling emotionally?

She squared her shoulders and followed Mitch to the kitchen. They cut slices of pie, warmed them in the microwave, and moved into the living room. She settled on the couch and ate. "The pie is awesome. Thanks for dinner and the offer of a bed for the night. I'm like a vagabond sofa-surfing through the county."

"You're welcome here anytime. I like having you."

"Why?"

"I refuse to answer that." Mitch grinned and pointed at her with a fork. "You've got some jokes all lined up."

Kay lowered her plate and regarded Mitch. "Right now, I'm serious. Why do you want me here? I was once a drug addict and I've heard you rant about drugs and addicts." Never in her life had she felt the need to open the doors to her past, but in this instant, she wanted Mitch to know everything.

Mitch set her dinner on the table. "You were addicted to prescription painkillers. You were a veteran with an injury. It made sense."

"But it was more than that. I stole prescription drugs from my parents and their friends, and I bought a variety of drugs from dealers as I fell deeper into addiction."

Mitch was silent for a moment as she looked thoughtfully at her drink. "Why all the other drugs?"

"Pain in my knee was my excuse, but it was more hopelessness and a wish to disappear. I blocked my memories with drugs. When I was on drugs, my mind blanked, and I never flashed back to the war. I was reckless and didn't care, so eventually the RCMP in Charlottetown arrested me." Kay shook her head. "I never want to be in trouble with the cops again. That was enough humiliation to last a lifetime."

"You never told me about the other drugs. It's a lot to think about." Mitch sat with her arms loose and her head hanging.

What did Mitch think of her? Was she disgusted? Had it been a mistake telling her everything? Mitch already knew too much. Kay wanted to run from her shame. She jumped to her feet, spun, and lunged for the door. She cried out in pain as her knee collapsed and the floor rushed up to meet her. She expected to crack her head or snap her wrist when she broke her fall. It never happened. A strong arm encircled her waist, and she was lifted, but when she tried to take the weight on her left leg she crumbled. Another strong arm slid behind her knees and Kay was weightless. Mitch sank into the couch with Kay cradled in her arms. Mitch had moved lightning fast to catch her.

"Let me go, please. I can go."

"You don't have to leave."

Kay hid her face in her hands. "You must think I'm a disgusting waste of time. I do."

"Not at all. You were a kid and that was years ago. You just caught me off guard with the new information and—and I was picturing how much you must have been hurting to go looking for random drugs. Today, you're smart, talented, and caring, and I know you will never go back there." She rested her head against Kay's. "Yes, I'm aware that relapse can never be discounted. I'm not naive. I just believe in you."

Kay struggled for a second and Mitch loosened her grip. Mitch wouldn't hold her against her will. Kay sighed deeply and her eyes burned as she struggled to contain her tears. Mitch wasn't horrified but was brave enough to trust a recovered addict not to relapse.

Kay swiveled in Mitch's lap and put her feet on the floor. After trying twice to stand, she collapsed defeated into Mitch's lap again. She lowered her head into her hands. She wanted to escape with her shame and her hurt, but her destroyed knee had trapped her. She could hold out against the pain, but Mitch's kindness and understanding had undone her. She could take no more. While she wept, Mitch held her and dropped sweet kisses along her nape. Mitch's kindness and gentleness almost broke Kay's heart.

Kay buried her face against Mitch's neck, but she didn't cry long. She was done feeling sorry for herself. When she sat back, she caressed Mitch's wet cheeks in astonishment. "You were crying too?"

Mitch shrugged.

"I'm okay, honey." She fidgeted, not sure why Mitch remained quiet. "So, you don't loathe me for having been a drug addict? You're not disgusted?"

Mitch shook her head and her eyes widened in surprise. "Never. Addiction is an illness, not compromised morals. You medicated your pain and went to a dark place, like a lot of returning veterans do. And you're clean now."

Kay winced at the faith she had in her. Mitch's expression was filled with compassion for Kay at twenty-three years old with one good knee, no purpose, and no future. "Thanks, Corporal." She leaned in and kissed Mitch on the lips. The kiss wasn't a prelude to sex but a kiss of caring and connection.

Mitch held her for a few more minutes until her emotions settled. Holding Mitch was all she'd needed.

"Did you just hurt yourself?" Mitch asked.

"Yup." Kay grimaced and surprised herself by not being afraid to admit it. "My knee doesn't rotate well because the joint is no longer designed for spinning, lunging, or running. My leg is strong enough, but my damaged knee couldn't handle the sudden motion. Nothing broken, but my knee is painful." She rubbed her left knee and grimaced in agony.

"What do you want to do now? May I help? I have ice. I massaged your knee once, and it helped. We could try that again."

Kay gasped as heat surged through her body as she remembered where the last massage had almost led. She couldn't help herself and didn't want to. She licked her lips and nodded. "I could use some help. And a massage would be nice, thanks."

Mitch carried her to the spare bedroom. She stood on one leg and Mitch balanced her with hands on her shoulders. She held

Mitch's eyes as she unbuttoned her pants, slid the zipper down, and slipped her jeans off her hips. She perched on the bed and arranged her T-shirt to cover her lap as Mitch slid her jeans the rest of the way off.

"I have a bottle of lotion in my bag," Kay said.

Mitch darted from the room and returned with Kay's bag. She fished out the lotion and handed it to her. "What you did last time felt awesome."

After the massage and at Kay's request, Mitch stretched out beside her and they curled together and chatted more.

Kay yawned. "I warned you what a piece of meat pie would do to me." She yawned more deeply.

"Sleep then."

Kays sighed as her eyes closed. "Please stay here with me?"

"Of course," Mitch whispered.

She drifted off, thinking how nice it was to be taken care of this way.

❖

No, no. I'm too hot. It hurts. It hurts. Stop. Stop. Make it stop. She tried to crawl but couldn't escape the pain. She was going to be sick. Strong arms picked her up and ran from the cave with her cradled against a solid chest.

Kay's eyes flew open, and her heart pounded from the nightmare. Her mind flashed to the cave with the dirty carpet hanging over the entrance. She remembered little detail of that time except the vivid sense of too much heat and a burning thirst. The end, though…this was the first time the dream had been different. The first time she'd been saved.

When Kay's head cleared, she discovered she was lying in Mitch's arms.

"You had your nightmare from Afghanistan," Mitch said.

"Back with a vengeance." Kay winced. "At least I didn't punch you."

Mitch grinned. "I ducked this time."

"Good work." Kay smiled and burrowed in against Mitch's chest. "We'll get up in an hour and check on Cody."

"I'll set an alarm."

Kay sighed. Her flashback had been mild, and her dream had ended with Mitch chasing the bad guys away and carrying her to safety. In Mitch's arms, she was safe. She relaxed fully and allowed herself to be comforted. She was accustomed to looking after herself, but with Mitch she wasn't giving up control or risking her pride. She was just, for that instant, borrowing Mitch's strength. Surely, that was harmless enough.

CHAPTER TWENTY-FOUR

"Hello, everyone." Mitch squeezed Kay's shoulder and flopped into a chair beside her. Kay, Lauren, and Val had driven to the Thresherton Diner for lunch and Kay texted Mitch an invitation to join them. She'd been glad to get the invite and didn't deny that it felt an awful lot like one a girlfriend might extend.

"Hi," Lauren said.

"Hey, you." Val leaned to give Mitch a one-armed hug. "How's Cody?"

"He's been home three days and is settled in. It was a busy weekend." Mitch smiled at Kay. "But he has excellent veterinary care."

Kay studied Mitch. "Did Cody walk some today?"

"Oh yes, he's much more mobile."

Kay squinted at Mitch. "How mobile?"

"We're being careful." She grinned, always happy with the bit of bossy britches that came out when Kay was concerned about an animal.

"As long as he's not training for the Iditarod," Kay said.

Mitch laughed with the rest. "Not this year."

"So, Mitch." Lauren shifted in her seat. "It was nice of you to rescue Cody and adopt him. He's a sweet dog. Good for you." She bent her head and began to poke through her salad.

"Thanks for saying that. Cody is a great dog and I'm glad I could help."

Mitch smiled and Lauren's shoulders relaxed. They still had a way to go, but one day she and Lauren would be friends. Lauren was an honorable person and a caring veterinarian, but most importantly, Callie and Becky loved her. Mitch knew that Lauren's animosity had to do with first impressions, and Mitch's hadn't been great when it came to Lauren and Callie getting together.

Val poked Mitch in the side. "Mitch is an old softy. We're going to call you every time we get stray animals."

"Watch out or Val will have your house full of pets by Christmas," Kay said. "All her relatives have stopped taking her calls because she's filled their homes with everything from gerbils to poodles to orphan lambs."

Val pointed at Kay. "I'm going to find just the right cat for you."

"Cat? Why not a dog?" Kay asked.

"You want an independent pet that can go all day by itself. A pet that doesn't require much attention or effort. Hence, a cat."

Kay forced a laughed. "Is that how you see me? As someone who wouldn't let even a small pet distract her from her path?"

Mitch studied Kay's perplexed expression. But then that was what she'd always said. How was anyone to think differently? Kay glanced at her with an expression of such longing that Mitch suddenly knew Kay wanted more in life. The question was, had Kay realized it yet?

"You've got me pegged as a crazy old hermit with a house full of cats," Kay said.

Mitch winced at the edge of pain in Kay's voice. Was she more perceptive these days or were Kay's barriers dropping? And if an inch of pain had slipped out, how much was still buried?

"You're not old, but you'd make a great hermit. Kay, are you all right? I was just kidding," Val said.

"Sure, Val. I know."

Mitch took Kay's hand under the table. She half expected to be pushed away, but Kay's grip was vise-like.

With another nervous glance at Kay, Val focused on Mitch. "Gwen and I'll be by tonight to check on Cody at about seven thirty."

"I'm working a split shift today." Mitch grimaced. "Another officer is in court, in Saskatoon, and won't be back in time to cover his shift. I'll be home at about five, but I have to head back to work at seven." She'd adopted a dog in need of intensive nursing for four weeks. She'd surprised herself, but Cody's wagging tail and exuberant kisses told her she'd done the right thing.

Kay cleared her throat and released Mitch's hand with a final friendly squeeze. "I'll do it. I'm staying in town tonight." She tilted her head to one side and gave Mitch a slight smile. "If your spare room's available, I'll help with Cody when you get home."

"The room's yours, anytime you want it." If they'd been alone, she'd have reminded Kay that she could have anything she wanted from her. "Go over whenever you're ready."

Lauren glanced at her watch. "It's twelve forty-five." She shoved up from her chair awkwardly given the size of her belly, and Val followed. "We'll head back to the clinic now. I've got afternoon appointments." Lauren and Val dropped cash on the table. "Want a ride back, Kay?"

"I'll stay and have another coffee," Kay said. "Call me if an emergency comes in, otherwise I'll be back by one thirty to discharge my patients from this morning."

"Have fun, you two." Val hugged Mitch and winked at Kay before following Lauren from the diner.

Mitch shook her head when the waitress approached their table with a pot of coffee. "No, thank you." She turned to Kay, who looked pale and sad now that the others had gone. "I'm headed home to check on Cody. Do you want to come?" Mitch frowned. "Or is that work for you? At lunch, I carry him outside to pee."

"I'd like that," Kay whispered. "Please, get me out of here."

Twenty minutes later, they sat on the floor of Mitch's spare room and petted Cody. Mitch kept an enormous pair of coveralls at home to keep dog hair off her uniform. She'd removed her utility belt and vest before slipping on the coveralls. They'd taken Cody outside and brought him in again. All the while, Kay was quiet, her shoulders slumped and her eyes watery.

Now that she was alone with Kay, Mitch had become tongue-tied. She had strong feelings for Kay, and the overwhelming emotions made it more difficult for her to communicate. And something had happened to Kay at the diner, and she needed to ask her about it, but her throat tightened.

"You're quiet," Kay said.

Mitch shrugged. She couldn't push words past the emotion in her chest. They'd planned to sit outside, but Cody had whined when they tried to put him back. He was bored and clingy and wanted more attention, but his eyes kept drifting shut.

"Let's put Cody back. He's ready to sleep," Kay said.

Mitch placed Cody in his kennel and left the room. She stripped off her coveralls and Kay followed her to the living room couch.

"What happened at the diner? Are you all right?" Mitch asked.

Kay scootched closer until their thighs touched. She picked up Mitch's hand and traced her fingers while she spoke. "I didn't like what Val said."

"She wasn't trying to be mean."

"Oh, I know. Val's the best, it's just…she was right, wasn't she? Hearing my words and attitudes from her perspective, I sounded like a closed off automaton. Am I?"

Mitch lifted Kay's hand to her lips and kissed it. Kay looked up. Mitch flinched at the insecurity no longer buried. A woman who could love and wanted to be loved looked back at her. "Once, you might have given that impression, but I never thought you were. Flirting and flippancy is your armor, not your true self."

"How do you know?"

Mitch smiled. "Because I wormed my way in under your armor and got you to talk to me."

Kay laughed quietly. "Very sneaky, Corporal. I'm going to kiss you now."

Mitch gently lifted Kay into her lap. She slid her arms around Kay as their lips came together. They kissed, exploring each other's mouths and lips. After a minute, they paused for breath and held each other. Kay rested her cheek against Mitch's shoulder.

Mitch kissed Kay on the top of the head. "I have to go. Sorry. Do you need a lift?"

"I'll call a taxi." Kay caressed Mitch's face with both hands, then slipped from her lap and fetched her utility belt.

Mitch slid into her gear with great reluctance. "I wish I could stay, but I'll see you tonight, right?"

Kay hesitated as she looked at the floor. "Are you sure I need to sleep in the spare room tonight? I don't want to—to be alone."

"You don't have to. You can bunk with me." Mitch swallowed before she spoke. Finally, it had happened. Kay was asking for more than sex this time. "Make yourself comfortable wherever you like. I'll be home for dinner and then I have to head back for seven." With another kiss, she slipped out the front door. She jogged to her cruiser and sped away.

Mitch drove to the detachment office and pictured Kay in the doorway of her house. She'd invited Kay to stay, and Kay had asked to sleep in her bed. She had all evening to imagine what would happen when she got home. Was it too soon? Not anymore. But it was more than lust, it was a desire to hold Kay closer. A desire for that final connection that only making love could give them.

Mitch parked the cruiser and stared at her fingers curled around the steering wheel. She doubted she had a future with Kay, but she was ready to try for more, and if she was lucky, Kay would stay and make Thresherton her home. That was probably too much to hope, but they had now. She exited the cruiser, and her heart did a happy dance as she strode into the detachment office.

When she left work shortly after five, Mitch picked up some groceries and headed home. She was unloading the bags when Kay pulled in behind her. "Perfect timing."

"No emergencies so here I am," Kay said. She pulled luggage from her car and followed Mitch inside. "I'll put my bags in the spare room."

Mitch put the groceries on the kitchen table and slipped a frozen pizza in the oven.

"What can I do?" Kay said.

Mitch turned and scooped Kay into her arms. Never had it felt more natural to hold a woman and kiss her. "Dinner will be forty minutes. I want to get out of my uniform and check on Cody." She changed into jeans and a T-shirt and met up with Kay in Cody's room. They took care of Cody and left him to sleep.

Kay looked around. "I like your little house, but I've never had an official tour."

"Well then, follow me." Mitch led the way to the living room.

Kay shook her head. "How about showing me your bedroom? It'll help me get to know you."

"If I didn't know better, I'd think that was a line." Mitch entered her bedroom. "Nothing special here." She scanned her room. The bed was made, the floor was clear, and only one shirt hung over a chair.

"You're very tidy."

"The RCMP basic training at the Depot in Regina is like being in the military. I learned ordered habits and kept them."

"I was in the military, remember? Those ordered habits didn't stick with me." Kay opened the closet. "Just how I imagined it. Pressed uniforms to one side, casual clothes in the middle, and several classy suits on the other side. Several still in the plastic from the Thresherton Dry Cleaners." Kay rolled the sleeve of a suit jacket between her thumb and fingers.

"I wore that one to the wedding." Mitch leaned against the doorjamb and watched Kay. That had been a beautiful evening and a sexy homecoming. But back then they'd agreed friendship was as far as they'd go. Where they stood now, she had no clue.

Kay let go of the suit and closed the closet. "I like the color of your walls."

"I painted it to complement my landscapes."

"There're beautiful." Kay turned to a stack of magazines resting on the bedside table. She smirked as she scooped them up. "Now I'll learn your real secrets. A woman's magazine collection is a window to her mind." She spread them on the bed. "Let's see. Magazines on fixing motorcycles, buying motorcycles, and touring on motorcycles. This is interesting." Kay held up a magazine on kayaking. "This month's issue."

"I was curious about kayaking because you love it."

"I do. On a lake with nobody around, it's incredibly peaceful." Kay replaced the magazines and ran her hand across Mitch's abdomen as she passed by her to leave the room.

Mitch sucked in her breath at the unexpected heat and arousal the casual caress provoked.

When dinner was ready, they sat to eat and chatted amicably about Saskatchewan and Thresherton. Twenty minutes before her shift, Mitch put on a fresh uniform. "I should go now. Help yourself to anything you want."

Kay went up on her tiptoes and placed a lingering kiss on Mitch's lips. "Hurry home."

"I'll do my best." Mitch grinned and headed back to work. It was a busy evening at work, and at nine p.m. she phoned Kay. "I'm stuck at work for a few more hours. I was looking forward to spending the evening with you, but it'll be late when I get in."

"Darn. I wanted to spend more time with you too."

"What will you do?"

"I have my computer set up on your kitchen table and I've been working on my research. After I check on Cody, I'll go to bed. I have to be in Saskatoon for eight a.m. tomorrow."

Mitch sighed. "Where're you sleeping?"

"In your bed, and, honey?"

Mitch swallowed and croaked her reply. "Yes?"

"I expect you to wake me no matter how late you arrive home."

"It's a deal. Sorry, I've got to go now." They hung up and Mitch headed out on another call. This night was never going to end, and life was messing with her. She had Kay waiting at home and she couldn't get to her. But she had work to do.

Jacks and some of her friends were getting together to watch the game and she was going to grab some bags of chips and casually show up. Well, as casual as she could in full uniform. Jacks didn't get a good look at the woman who'd sold the ketamine at the party, but Jacks hoped maybe one of her friends had.

Mitch scowled. Jacks was moving around fine on crutches, but it could have been fatal. The bike and Jacks had been hidden from view from the road. If Kay hadn't been there, Jacks could have lain in the field for days until the search parties found her. She slammed the steering wheel with the palm of her hand. Somebody was going to pay for selling her kids drugs.

Mitch finally arrived home at four a.m., none the wiser regarding who was selling the ketamine, since none of Jacks friends had been approached by the dealer. She was yawning so much she thought her jaw would dislocate. She quietly stripped off her clothes, showered, and fetched clean shorts and a top from her laundry room. Kay wasn't in the spare room. She grinned and slipped into her room.

Kay was asleep curled around a pillow. Moonlight flowed in the window and caught her blond curls. Had there ever been anyone so beautiful? She lifted the covers and slid into bed. Kay moaned and skootched back until her back connected with Mitch's front. She kissed her shoulders, but this provoked another yawn. She gave in and closed her eyes.

Mitch raised her head when the unfamiliar alarm went off.

"Sorry, that was my phone," Kay said. "It's six. I need to get up."

Kay tried to get up and Mitch tightened her arm around Kay's middle and dropped kisses on her shoulders. She basked in the contentment of spooning Kay even if only for a couple of hours. She didn't want her to go, but Kay had to be in Saskatoon.

"I have just enough time to drive home, change, and get to school."

Kay was wearing a tank top and Mitch pushed a strap aside to drop more kisses on Kay's bare shoulders and nape. "Morning."

"I like your kisses and my commitment to work is wavering."

"Then stay."

"I wish I could." Kay rolled to face Mitch. "Why didn't you wake me when you got home?"

"I only crawled into bed two hours ago. You're so beautiful and I almost woke you. But I worked sixteen hours yesterday and I'm still beat."

Kay kissed Mitch and when Mitch deepened the kiss, Kay rolled away and jumped off the bed. "You're dangerous and I have to go." Fifteen minutes later, she returned washed and dressed. Mitch was sitting on the side of the bed, struggling to wake up.

Kay bent down and kissed her. "Go back to sleep. I've already taken care of Cody." She pushed Mitch back into bed and tucked her in with a kiss. "I'll be back in four days. I'm on call Friday evening at the college, but I'll be at PVS on Saturday." Kay caressed her cheek. "Can we pick this up again after work on Saturday? Maybe a clothes-off edition?"

"I'd like that."

"Good." Kay kissed her again. "Now sleep."

Mitch woke hours later. She hardly remembered Kay leaving. Waking with Kay in her arms was heaven, and she'd reveled in the sense of well-being as strong as anything she'd experienced before. Mitch sighed. It would've been much nicer if she'd arrived home sooner and less tired, but she had hopes for the weekend. She was ready to make love, and Kay had gone full circle from flirting to friends and had arrived at the same spot as her. Mitch bounced out of bed grinning and whistled as she made a snack for Cody. She would be well rested the next time Kay stayed over, and she promised herself she'd enjoy whatever happened between them, no matter what the future held.

Chapter Twenty-five

K ay, Mitch is here," Val said.

"Coming." Kay hurried to the PVS waiting room and smiled at Mitch. "Perfect timing. The last client just left."

Mitch raised a white paper bag with one hand and a baking tin with the other. "Excellent. I brought lunch for everyone."

Kay popped up on her toes and kissed Mitch on the lips, surprised by how much she'd missed her. "I like a woman bearing gifts." They'd been blowing up each other's phones with texts for the last four days, but words couldn't compare to being with Mitch in person.

Val jumped off a stool at reception and headed toward the lunchroom. "It's just us. Janice has gone home."

Kay locked the front door and followed Mitch and Val to the lunchroom. Mitch unpacked the bag and passed out the usual salads and sandwiches.

Kay pointed to the baking tin. "What's in there?"

Mitch gave a half-smile and shrugged. "Not sure. Callie dropped it off and I'm afraid to open it."

"Corporal Mitchell, are you afraid of a baking tin?" Kay grinned and bit into her grilled cheese.

Mitch pointed to Kay's grilled cheese sandwich with her chin. "Is it still warm? They prepared it last and wrapped it in double foil, just the way I asked."

"It's perfect, thanks. Still warm and gooey." Just the way she'd liked them since she was a kid. Grilled cheese was her comfort food and about the only other thing she could make. She was nervous about the weekend. Not about sex with Mitch, which they'd both agreed was on the agenda. She was more worried about what she'd revealed about herself. She'd let Mitch in and that was scary. In the two months since she'd met her, Mitch had learned more about her than any other woman had.

Mitch took a bite from her sandwich and studied the tin as she chewed. "I'm terrified of Callie's baking tins. There's not enough give in my uniforms."

Kay laughed and drew the tin close. She lifted the lid an inch and peered in. "Oh yuck. It's not fit to eat. I'll take it home and dispose of it."

"Nice try," Mitch said.

Kay attempted to push the tin out of Mitch's reach, but Mitch's hand shot out and she laid it on top of the tin. She curled her fingers over the edge and pressed the tin to the table as Kay struggled to extract it.

"Come on. Let go." Kay wrapped both arms around the tin and yanked on it. When it didn't budge, she sat back and fake-frowned at Mitch. "Do I have to fetch a kitten?"

Mitch raised her hand and returned to her lunch. "Please, have mercy. Not the kitten weapon."

"More effective than pepper spray or rubber bullets," Kay said.

"What's in it?" Val asked.

Kay winked. "Guess."

Mitch and Val responded in unison. "Brownies."

Twenty minutes later, Val forked the last bite of her brownie into her mouth and rose. She waved Kay back into her chair. "You stay, I'll check on the puppy."

"Thanks," Kay said.

Val dropped her trash in the pail. "Thanks for lunch, Mitch. Have a good weekend, you two."

Kay waved as Val left. "You too."

"Will you be done in time to have dinner with me and Cody tonight? Nothing fancy, just a barbecue," Mitch said.

"I want to, but I have a few more hours before I can escape."

"Aren't the clients all gone?"

Kay rolled her eyes. "It's the pets they leave behind that's the work. We've got a puppy in the quarantine room on fluids, and I need to check on him regularly this weekend. Puppies tend to tangle themselves in the IV lines."

Mitch leaned forward and carried Kay's hand to her lips. "Tuesday night was against us, but I'm ready to try again."

Kay cupped Mitch's face and pulled her in for a deep kiss. "I'd like that."

"No jokes?"

"None, but are you sure you're ready?"

"Positive."

"Well, this weekend belongs to us." She was so nervous she doubted she'd be able to finish her brownie. Tonight, they were having sex. No, it was more than sex. There was a closeness with Mitch that was growing. When she let her final guard down in bed, escape would be impossible. She was going to be consumed. And what the hell did that mean for her carefully laid plans?

❖

After lunch Mitch called Callie for help with the menu for the evening. With recipe in hand, she headed to the grocery store. When she got home, she started on dinner and then cleaned her house.

Late in the afternoon, Mitch glanced at her watch as she opened the refrigerator. She rotated the shish kebabs in the pan of marinade, which smelled delicious, then returned to preparing the vegetables. She painstakingly chopped the peppers and alternated green with red and yellow on the veggie skewers the way Callie had told her. She rotated a skewer and admired her work. "Cool." When she'd finished the veggies, she slid them into a container and placed it on the shelf above the marinating meat.

"Well done. You did that without cutting a finger off." Mitch's idea of a barbecue was a giant steak on the grill and a potato in the oven. For Kay, for tonight, she'd branched out.

When the dryer beeped, Mitch fetched her summer comforter. She buried her nose in the fresh scent and carried it upstairs. She'd dusted, vacuumed, and tidied the house. Mitch spread the comforter over the sheets she'd already washed and scanned her bedroom with pleasure. The window was open and fresh air flowed in. She sniffed the air and sighed. Luckily for her nobody had spread manure upwind, a risk of country living. Sometimes the odor of manure wafted through the entire town.

Two hours later, Mitch was rotating the meat in the marinade when somebody knocked on the front door. She glanced at her watch. Four fifteen, even later than Kay expected. Mitch strode to the door and opened it. "Hello." She bent for a kiss and snagged Kay's overnight bag and computer from her hands.

"Hi, you. Sorry, I'm so late. I had an emergency after you left. A cat with a gunky eye that turned out to be a corneal ulcer. It couldn't wait."

"No problem. Better than arriving home at four a.m. the way I did when you were last here."

"Oh, that could happen. In fact, three a.m. is when I need to leave to check on the puppy. Val's dropping in this evening and at midnight, and I'm covering until after church on Sunday."

Mitch walked toward her bedroom, then turned to face Kay. "Where should I put your bags?" It was a simple question, but a loaded one. Putting her bags in the guest room didn't mean they wouldn't be having sex. But putting them in her room made it more intimate, more...certain.

Kay seemed to understand the underlying question and patted Mitch's cheek. "Your room, please. I'll shower and change, then join you outside."

Mitch set the bags inside the door to her room and headed away. "Do you want a drink?"

"A cold diet soda would be perfect, thanks."

Mitch's bedroom door closed behind Kay as Mitch resumed her trip to the kitchen. She extracted a diet soda from the refrigerator and opened it. "Oh, that will be nice and flat by the time she's done with her shower." Mitch shook her head and poured the soda down the drain. When Kay appeared, she'd fetch her a drink. Mitch grabbed a beer, popped the top, and retreated to the patio. She tried not to picture Kay naked in her shower, with shampoo and hot water streaming down her back, but she grinned at the breathtaking image.

Twenty minutes later, Kay appeared in a blue sundress. "It was in my suitcase and got all wrinkled." Kay attempted to brush creases from the dress.

Mitch rose and stepped toward Kay. She lifted her chin with two fingers, slipped an arm around her waist, and kissed her. "You look beautiful."

"You too." Kay wrapped her arms around Mitch's neck.

Mitch's blood pressure shot up a notch and she struggled to tamp down her desire. How hungry was Kay for food? "Have a seat. I'll get your drink." Mitch bolted into the house, splashed cold water on her face, and returned with a soda. She skidded to a stop and admired the sight before her. Kay was leaning on the patio railing with her arms spread wide as she scanned the horizon. Her wet blond ringlets and the blue dress drifted in the slight breeze. The word beautiful was inadequate. Mitch's mind searched for better words, but even if she'd found them her tongue couldn't have formed them.

Kay glanced over her shoulder at Mitch and returned to her view. "I once thought Saskatchewan was barren because it's so flat, but it's full of life." Beyond Mitch's backyard stretched a thousand acres of fields that had held ripening wheat a week ago. Now that the wheat straw had been harvested, they could see clearly for miles. Kay pointed. "Are those deer? Way in the distance."

Mitch squinted at the brown animals as she placed the soda and a glass with ice on the table. She ducked into the house and returned with binoculars she trained on the objects in the distance. "Pronghorn antelope." Mitch handed the binoculars to Kay.

"Antelope? Canada has antelope?" Kay raised the binoculars to her eyes and focused on the distant object.

"They're called antelope, but there's no other species like them. They're not deer and don't drop their horns like antlers. Pronghorns only shed the outer part of their horn."

When the creatures ran away, Kay handed back the binoculars and leaned against the rail.

Mitch lifted the lid off the barbecue, rearranged the vegetable kebabs, and placed the beef ones on. "It's cool they're this far north. They usually stick to the grasslands close to the US-Canada border. This area has more mule deer and white-tailed deer." She popped the top on the soda, filled the glass without creating foam, and handed it to Kay. "I sound like a tourist brochure. Would you believe I'm nervous?"

"Yes, and would it help if I said don't be?"

Mitch smiled. It wasn't sex that scared her, it was the intensity of her feelings for Kay. She was on thin ice and had to be sure not to overwhelm her. "Casual conversation will help me. What animals do you have in Prince Edward Island?"

"If you insist." Kay laughed. "No wild deer and no big predators in PEI. Amazing that four hundred years ago the island was old-growth forest full of bear, lynx, and caribou. Back home, the biggest wild mammals are in the ocean."

"I've seen orcas in British Columbia."

Kay's eyes sparkled with a child's excitement. "Awesome. Someday I'm going to kayak with them."

"Sounds cool." Mitch sipped her beer. "I want to learn to kayak."

"You can take the Paddle Canada training like I did, or I can teach you."

"I'd like that."

They chatted until Mitch lifted the food from the barbecue and placed it on platters. Kay chose the chair across from her and they ate.

"Dinner is delicious. I'm spoiled. You've been feeding me all day," Kay said.

"You're in charge of breakfast."

Kay smirked. "French toast?"

"I bought all the ingredients." Mitch grinned and forked beef and pepper into her mouth. After several bites, she registered the perfectly cooked beef and zing of the spice. Callie would be proud of her and she was proud of herself. It had been a long time since she'd invited a woman home other than Sonny or Maggie. She could learn more recipes and learn to kayak. Kay made her want to branch out and grasp life again and try new things. She was tired of rebuilding motorcycles.

After dinner, Kay helped carry the dishes and leftovers into the kitchen. As they washed the dishes, accidental brushes of skin became casual touches and kisses. She and Kay had been working up to it for days and now they had their chance.

Kay declined the offer of dessert, so Mitch carried Cody to the backyard and Kay examined him before Mitch tucked him into bed.

Mitch set candles on the patio railing and turned the lights off so she and Kay could watch the sunset. "Do you want a jacket?"

Kay shook her head. "Just you."

Mitch wrapped her arms around Kay and Kay snuggled into her. "What a nice day." Kay popped up on her toes to kiss Mitch.

"What would happen if I picked you up?"

Kay sucked in a breath. "You have my permission."

Mitch pushed the candles to the side, encircled Kay's slight waist with her hands and lifted her to the top of the patio railing.

Kay clutched Mitch's shoulders. "Hang on tight. I'm not balanced up here." She kissed Mitch's forehead, eyes, and the corners of her mouth. "I am enjoying the access I have though."

"What next?"

"Take me to bed."

Mitch contemplated carrying Kay to the bed, but she wanted her to feel one hundred percent safe. There would be no repeat of that night in Kay's apartment. She set Kay on her feet, took her hand, and led her to the bedroom.

In the bedroom, Kay started to unbutton Mitch's shirt. "Do you remember my rules? The ones I told you that time at Poplarcreek?"

"I do and you're safe with me."

Kay's hands stilled, and she dropped her head and a second later, she raised it and searched Mitch's face. "Yes, I think I am." She removed Mitch's shirt and hung it over the back of a chair. Kay splayed her hands over Mitch's abdomen. "You're so beautiful."

Mitch slid the straps of the dress off Kay's shoulders. When it pooled around her feet, she snagged it off the floor and draped it over her shirt. She unzipped her shorts and added them to the pile. She caressed Kay's arms and scanned her body. Kay had removed her bra and panties and they lay on the floor in a pile. Mitch had glimpsed Kay's abdominal muscles, legs, thighs, and bare breasts courtesy of Dover, but she'd never seen them all at the same time. Kay was exquisite right down to the small Celtic tattoo on her right hip.

"Are you nervous?" Kay pushed Mitch's boxers down her hips.

"Not anymore. I'm just mesmerized. You're gorgeous." Mitch yanked her sports bra off and rested her hands on Kay's hips. She captured Kay's lips for a quick kiss. She scanned Kay's body from soft blond ringlets, to blue eyes dark with desire, to a tiny nose, and full, kissable lips. She admired her delicate collarbone and full breasts with delectable pink nipples that were now erect.

Kay slipped from her grasp and crooked her finger as she slid into bed. "Come here."

Mitch smiled. She could spend every evening like this and never get tired. But that wasn't in the cards for Kay. Mitch pushed the future from her mind. Anything could happen and nobody had a crystal ball to see the future. She would enjoy the night, the weekend, and whatever time they had left.

CHAPTER TWENTY-SIX

Kay had seen Mitch in uniforms, work clothes, and dress clothes. She could tell Mitch was fit, but nothing had prepared her for how sculpted and beautiful she was. A painting of her in traditional Indigenous dress would have been the centerpiece of any gallery. Kay moved over in the bed to make room for Mitch. "Come here."

Mitch got into bed and leaned against the headboard. Kay straddled her and slipped her arms around Mitch's neck. She dropped light kisses on Mitch's face and lips. "You're gorgeous and this is going to be beautiful. Trust me."

"I do." Mitch dipped her head to a nipple.

Kay tugged gently on Mitch's hair. "Careful, please. They're tender."

Mitch softly sucked and kissed Kay's breasts while she cupped and squeezed her ass. Her excitement grew and her fantasies merged with reality as Mitch's hands claimed her.

Kay rolled Mitch's nipples between her fingers and gasped for breath. "I want you inside me." She moaned the words against Mitch's lips as she rose on her knees and lowered herself on Mitch's fingers. "Mitch, so nice, baby."

She couldn't hold on and came in a long shuddering burst far too soon. She'd been holding back for weeks and didn't have to anymore. She rested her forehead against Mitch's, enjoying the aftershocks and the sensation of Mitch's fingers sliding gently up and down her spine.

She kissed Mitch on the mouth. "That was greedy of me."

"I loved it."

Kay shook her head and slid down Mitch's body. "Spread your legs."

Mitch complied and Kay settled between them. She found Mitch's center and took her time as she explored with her tongue. She breathed in Mitch's scent as it filled her nostrils and brain with sex. She concentrated all her energy on finding what would please Mitch most.

"Please," Mitch said. "Now."

Kay smiled against Mitch's thigh. Usually, she had ten jokes ready for a lover, but not this time. This wasn't like her usual nights of casual sex, full of fun and lust. Tonight was one of real intimacy of mind and spirit. It was not the time for jokes and mockery.

She turned her attention to Mitch's clit, and in a minute had her writhing and then quaking in pleasure.

Kay crawled up Mitch's body and into her arms. She kissed her face and eyelids. The look of naked vulnerability reaffirmed the seriousness of this night of sex. Not sex...for Mitch, this was making love. The thought that it might be for her as well brought with it a shiver of fear.

"You're exquisite. And you better recover quickly, because I want more of you," Kay said.

Mitch grinned. "Fair's fair." She slid down the bed until Kay was straddling her face.

Kay lowered herself until she was impaled on the hot wet tongue waiting for her. She rocked against Mitch's tongue and soft wet lips. She sucked in her breath and grasped the headboard for support as Mitch's tongue entered her. "Mitch, oh, yes." Mitch was an exquisite lover, and Kay had never felt so comfortable, safe, and cherished. The fear of what she was feeling was smothered under the blanket of serenity she found in Mitch's arms.

Kay woke when her phone alarm buzzed. She carefully slid from under Mitch's arm and swallowed back her laughter as she nearly did the limbo to get out of bed without disturbing Mitch.

"You're leaving?"

She bent and kissed her. "I've got to check on the puppy. Back soon."

"I'm coming."

"No, you stay and rest." Kay winked. "You'll need it."

Mitch snapped on her light, stood, and pulled her jeans on, not bothering with boxers. She glanced at the clock. "It's three a.m. and you're not going there alone."

Kay was surprised by the wave of protectiveness from Mitch, but more surprised at how much she liked it. "I can take care of myself, but put on a shirt if you're coming. You topless would definitely distract me from what I need to do."

They climbed into Kay's car and she drove to PVS. Kay unlocked the door, entered, and keyed off the alarm. Mitch followed her into the treatment room and Kay pointed to a stool. "The puppy's in the quarantine room. Best if you stay here."

She put on a lab coat, disposable booties and gloves, and entered the quarantine room. "Hello, Batman. You've got yourself tangled up nicely." She unwound the puppy from his IV line and noted his brighter demeanor. "I like the name Batman, but I can tell some kid named you. When he's older he's going to be embarrassed to have a dog called Batman." She petted the puppy and accepted his kisses. "Maybe he'll just call you Bat? That's cool, eh?"

Her examination done and the puppy set up with a new bag of IV fluids and a snack, she slipped from the room. She hung her lab coat on the door, left her booties, and washed up in the bathroom before returning to the treatment room.

Mitch was perched on a stool staring intently at the surgery cupboard with its array of surgical instruments.

"He's doing better. They recover so quickly on fluids." She kissed Mitch. "Time to get you home and back to bed."

Mitch pointed to the cupboard. "Do you know how to use all of those?"

Kay nodded and a ready joke about not being into BDSM rose unbidden to her lips, but she bit it back. The look of awe on Mitch's face didn't invite jokes.

"I do. I'm still learning, but yes, I've used all of those."

"It must be amazing to be able to help animals." Mitch turned and gathered Kay into her. "I'm impressed."

Usually never at a loss for words or a quip, she was left speechless. The respect spilling from Mitch's voice made her stand a little straighter. She was proud of her work and abilities but enjoyed hearing it from another person, especially someone so important to her. Her brothers kidded her, with love, about being the only doctor in the family. If only her parents thought what she had accomplished was important.

"Thanks. I've worked hard. It means a lot to me that you would say that." She kissed Mitch. "I think you're kind of amazing too. The way the kids look up to you and you help them. I'm in awe."

"Thanks, Kay. It's the right thing to do what I can."

Kay stepped back and turned away from Mitch to brush at her eyes. She busied herself tidying the counters in the treatment room. Val usually left the place immaculate, and it had been when she went home. She frowned. Some of the drawers were partly open and their contents messed up and pulled out as if somebody had been searching for something. She automatically rearranged the contents the way Val liked it and closed them. Maybe someone had been in a hurry during an emergency and had simply failed to clean up.

She took a deep breath. What was happening to her around Mitchell? Was she turning into a weepy sentimental woman? She'd have to watch that. It was her toughness and armor, as Mitch called it, that had protected her from emotion and hurt. But did she still want or need that?

She shook her head to try to dispel the unaccustomed feelings and tugged Mitch to her feet. "Let's go, you. I have to be back here in three hours."

It had been a romantic dinner, and the first time their lovemaking had been gentle, but when they got back to Mitch's house Kay pulled Mitch into the bedroom and yanked off her clothes. Mitch followed suit and they fell into bed. Their lovemaking was fierce and intense, taking their connection to yet another level.

The next morning, Kay woke as Mitch rained soft kisses down her bare back. "Hmm, that's nice," she murmured. "Is it time to get up?"

"Your alarm went off."

Kay rolled onto her back and stretched her arms above her head as she looked up at Mitch. "I'm still on puppy duty." She reveled in a perfect night. It was morning and she was still in bed with a lover. Usually, one of them left after sex, and even if they didn't, it wasn't like there were protestations of love and desire to have breakfast together. But Mitch wasn't just a lover. Kay winced. And Mitch wasn't a "fuck toy" as she'd called herself all those weeks back, she was more. More than a friend or companion? Kay couldn't be sure, but she had an overwhelming sense of safety with Mitch snuggled against her. She caressed Mitch's face and stared into her content hazel eyes.

It was so hard to leave. Kay slipped from bed. At some point they needed to figure out where they were, but right now the puppy needed her. "Puppy duty."

"I'll come too," Mitch said.

"It's only six and too early for Cody. Stay in bed." She rested a finger against Mitch's lips. "I'll be back in thirty minutes."

Mitch settled back into the pillows. "I'll be here."

Kay shot over to the clinic and checked on Batman. While she made him a snack, she scanned the treatment room. Odd that the drawers had been open and messy, and she couldn't let go of the feeling something was wrong. She set the bowl of dog food in Batman's kennel then returned and opened all the cabinets in the treatment room and surgery. The cabinets were fine and the drawers she'd tidied were how she'd left them. The doors to PVS had been locked and the alarm on, so how could somebody have gotten in? No, it had to be that someone had been in a hurry…

"The damn ketamine." She retrieved the key from the new hiding place that only the vets and Val knew about. The last two bottles of ketamine were still there. Of course, they were there.

Nobody was taking their ketamine, PVS was just messed up on their orders.

She focused on the key in her palm. It was strange though. She put the key back and felt a shiver skitter down her back. She glanced into the dark corners of the too quiet treatment room and suddenly wished she'd let Mitch come with her. She turned on all the lights in the clinic and with heart pounding, and a reflex hammer in her hand, forced herself to check all the rooms. Everything looked the way she and Val had left it that afternoon. Still, she gave in to her nerves and ran to the back door.

Kay quickly turned off the lights and locked up. She shook off the unsettling feeling that PVS had been invaded and smiled as she drove back to Mitch. She tried hard to watch her speed. It wouldn't do to get a ticket. But it was her first break from Mitch since dinner and all she wanted was to rush back to her. Funny how the space she usually craved for herself was so much smaller now. She was back in twenty-five minutes, dropped her clothes on the floor, and slid in beside Mitch.

Mitch sighed and, in her sleep, gathered Kay against her. Kay set her alarm for nine. She longed to touch her, not sexually but just for the physical connection. She carefully moved in as close as possible and sighed in unaccustomed contentment. A successful surgery, especially a complicated one, filled her with a sense of triumph, but never contentment. What did all that mean? Was her career no longer important?

The next time her alarm buzzed she found Mitch awake and staring down at her.

"You watching me sleep?"

"I am and you're lovely."

"And that's not creepy at all." Kay laughed and got out of bed. "Last puppy trip and I'd better go now. Val takes over after church. I'll make you breakfast when I come back."

"I'll take care of Cody and we'll see you soon."

Kay kissed Mitch. "It's so hard to leave you." The words slipped out without permission and she didn't want them back, though they made her heart beat a little faster. "It's so hard to go."

"Me too." Mitch rested her hands on Kay's hips. "See you soon."

She arrived at PVS and drove around the building before parking and opening the door. She almost called Mitch to join her, but how could she explain? She unlocked the door, coded off the alarm and listened. There was nothing but the quiet hum of the drug refrigerator and the overhead lights warming up. She checked on Batman and removed his IV. "You're doing much better. Let's try without this nasty thing." She ducked her head to protect her face from his overly effusive kisses as she bandaged his leg where the IV had been. After feeding him breakfast, she phoned Val.

"Morning, Kay, how's Batman?"

"I just took his IV off. It was half-chewed anyway. Val…"

"Something wrong?"

"I don't know. We cleaned up before we left yesterday, right?"

"Always. Why?"

"I was back a couple of times through the night, and there were drawers opened and messed up. No signs of anybody breaking in and I checked the ketamine and it's all there."

"That's weird. But Ian was on call. Maybe he came back and was looking for something. Have you seen his office? It's a little messy."

Kay looked around. The dark shadows in the clinic were gone but she couldn't escape the chill. "Okay if you say so, but maybe have a look around when you come in. And maybe bring Ronnie with you?"

There was talking in the background. "Sorry, a bit of chaos here. Sure, Kay, I'll have a look around. Talk to you later."

"Bye." Kay hung up and rolled her shoulders. A rushed Ian rummaging for something made sense, but only a little sense.

Kay arrived home just as Mitch was heading into Cody's room with a bowl of food.

Mitch showed her the bowl. "I cut him back as directed."

"It's for the best." Kay followed her in. Cody rose and wagged as Kay approached. "Hi, Cody, you're looking better, tough guy."

"Is he, really?" Mitch asked.

"Absolutely. It's going to be a struggle to keep him still long enough to heal. He's still such a puppy. He's ready to have his sutures out. How about Tuesday, after work?"

"Thanks." Mitch nodded. "And then will you stay, for the night?"

Kay kissed her cheek. "Just try to get me to leave." She tickled her playfully, to avoid eye contact. She wanted to stay with Mitch, and that was a little scary.

Mitch set the bowl down and Cody ate. When he'd finished eating, he scanned the room as if searching for more food. "Sorry, Cody. Your doc put you on a diet."

Kay petted him on the head. "I'm the bad guy, but too much weight is hard on your healing pelvis."

Mitch propelled Cody into his kennel. "She's always got a good reason and we listen to her." She kissed him on the top of the head and closed his kennel door.

Kay followed Mitch to the kitchen.

"How's your other puppy?" Mitch asked.

"Much better. I removed his IV. He's so bouncy he almost had it out anyway."

"That's good news." Mitch bent and kissed Kay on the lips. "I'll make coffee and then I need food."

"And I'm on breakfast duty." Kay saluted. "Yes, Corporal." She prepared the French toast. They were halfway through breakfast when Kay looked up. Mitch was no longer eating. Her gaze was locked on Kay and the hazel of her eyes had darkened to a hunter green.

Kay winked. "Race you."

Mitch leaped to her feet, scooped Kay up in her arms, and ran with her to the bedroom. They made love and Mitch fell asleep curled around her.

Kay held Mitch's palm to her lips and kissed it. Her heart pounded in her chest and her mind spun with possibilities. Had she ever been this content before? Had she ever been this connected to another woman or another person before? She caressed Mitch's cheek. Was this what love felt like? Love wasn't meant for *her*, though. Love meant staying in one place and dividing her energies between her career goals and a relationship. Didn't it? Hell, but she loved it here. Why couldn't her mind shut off? Did she need to examine her every feeling and motivation?

She tucked her head under Mitch's chin and drank in her strong, delicious scent. She risked a couple of kisses along Mitch's collarbone and then sighed as a curtain of peace draped around them and shut out the world.

Chapter Twenty-seven

Sunday night, Kay finally dragged herself from Thresherton at ten p.m. She wasn't sure if she or Mitch was more reluctant to see her go. She convinced herself that the time apart would do them good. Her emotions were all over the place, and some away time would help her sort things out.

She had a busy day at the college on Monday and was on call Monday evening. When she did have a second to think about her life, it was only to wish she was back in bed with Mitch.

On Tuesday morning, she woke with the birds, tossed a pile of random clothes in a bag, grabbed her computer, and headed back to Thresherton and Mitch.

"Morning." Kay hugged Val. "How're you this fine Tuesday morning?"

Val sighed. "Tired. I was up half the night trying to get my homework done. Why're you so bouncy? You have a tough surgery today that's got you pumped?"

"Not that I'm aware of. I just had a good weekend and Mitch is bringing Cody in this afternoon to have his stitches out." She and Mitch had spent as much time as possible in bed. They'd only gotten up to take care of the dogs and make some food.

"A visit from Mitch. Explains your happy state." She squeezed Kay's hand. "I'm happy for you both."

Given that she had no idea what was going to happen between them, she wasn't sure what to say in response. "Now what else do we have today?"

"Guess?"

"Spays and neuters."

"Got it in one."

Kay helped Val sedate and prepare the first animal, and then she started on the surgery. By twelve thirty, they had all the scheduled surgeries finished and Kay called a break for lunch. "Do you want to get something from the diner?" Kay asked.

"Ronnie sent me with lunch, for the both of us."

"Thanks." Kay followed Val to the lunchroom. Val put the container in the microwave, split the contents onto two plates and passed one to Kay. She dug in and moaned in approval. "It's not fair that both you and Ronnie can cook. People who can cook should be obliged to pair up with those of us who are culinarily challenged."

Val laughed. "Ronnie didn't realize she was so good. She cooked about twice a week when me met, and the rest of the time, she lived on pizza. Anyway, she says she has more time now, but when school starts, we'll be back to my hash casseroles."

"Mitch barbecues all summer and fall, and when the snow flies, she switches to frozen meals. If we weren't sponging off Callie so much, we'd never get a home-cooked meal."

"You and Mitch are pretty tight these days? What're you—"

Val never got to finish her sentence because Janice barged into the room and dropped a box on the table narrowly missing Val's lunch. "I'm delivering this personally and I have Kay as a witness, so you won't be accusing me of misplacing it again."

"What is it?" Val asked.

Janice sneered. "I'm not the expert, but looks like ketamine." She whirled and stomped from the room.

"I ordered it last week. Why'd it take so long to get here?" Val dug in the box. "And there's three bottles, I only ordered two."

Kay plucked the invoice out of the box. "It's the ketamine I ordered. Yours can't have been filled."

"It wasn't? I'm so sorry, I didn't realize that."

Kay gave her a one-armed hug. "It's okay, you've got Gwen and school keeping you busy. And Ronnie." Kay forked some food into her mouth. "Do you want me to take over tracking the drugs?"

"The whole pharmacy?"

Kay raised her hands. "No, please no. Just the controlled drugs and anesthetics. I'm the one using them the most."

"No, thanks. It's my job. I'll talk to Ian and see what he wants to do. If I can't handle it, he'll want me to train Minnie." Val pushed her half-eaten lunch away.

"I didn't tell Ian about the missing order. I just ordered more."

"I get that and you're very kind. But it's not a drug we can run out of. An animal's life might depend on it. I'll see if Ian's in now. Thanks, Kay."

"Wait. Remember I told you about stuff being moved around on the weekend. Did you look? What did you think? I'm still weirded out by it. Was it Ian?"

Val shrugged. "It looked okay to me, but you said you cleaned up. I'll ask Ian if it was him."

"Thanks." Kay dug into her excellent lunch. Poor Val. She wouldn't want to have to admit she couldn't do her job. How humiliating.

Val returned ten minutes later and dropped into her chair.

"How'd it go?" Kay asked.

"Ian wants me to stay in charge of the controlled drugs for now and start Minnie on learning to order the other drugs. In January, I'd be full-time at university and Minnie will be head tech and be in charge of all of it." Val laughed. "Ian said I was entitled to make a mistake and he's not sure it is my mistake. I'm to call our supplier and find out where my order went."

"Maybe the courier lost it, or the drug company lost your order. It's not your fault. You're very organized and don't miss details like this." Kay smiled thinking of the wedding and Colonel Connor and her clipboard with all the minutiae. "It's the drug company that needs to smarten up. We need a steady supply. We're using more since I started."

"More complex surgeries." Val shrugged. "But not a huge amount more. I'm not washing many more instruments for you than I was for Lauren."

"Then what's the answer? I use the same dose of ketamine as she does." Kay patted Val's shoulder. "I'm sure it's just a gap in delivery and will correct itself. Maybe it's backordered."

"But I'd know that. This is at least the second time we've gotten so low. I'll go through the surgery logs and find out how much we're really using."

"I've got an hour before Mitch comes in. Let me do it."

"No, it's okay, I'll go get started."

"But it's lunchtime. Come on, help me finish this lovely lunch Ronnie made. After we eat, I'll take the surgery logs and you take the inventory. Then we'll compare notes later."

Val shook her head. "I can't relax until I know."

"There's still some ice cream in the freezer," Kay said in a teasing voice.

Val laughed. "You win. Thanks." She picked up her fork and started eating again.

"Did you ask Ian? Was he in on the weekend messing up drawers in the treatment room?" Kay asked.

"Not him or Fiona, and Lauren wasn't working either. Only you and me were in on the weekend. Fiona did a couple of farm calls, but she left from home because she had all the gear she needed in her work tuck."

Kay shook her head. Was she imagining the messy drawers? She was the only one who'd seen them. She should've shown them to Mitch, but she was afraid she'd go into cop mode and ruin their sexy weekend with work or worrying about Kay.

After lunch, Kay took the surgery log to her office and went back three months to check surgeries. She'd been a lot busier than she remembered. She typed the pet, their weight, and the amount of ketamine used into a Microsoft Excel spreadsheet and then based on the pet's weight, she had the spreadsheet calculate the ketamine dose. Everything matched and then she tallied up the total amount of ketamine used and compared it to the bottles delivered as per Val's records. They were off by five cc, but it wasn't enough to explain the frequent shortages.

Kay returned the surgery log to the treatment room. "All done," she said to Val.

"That was fast. What's the verdict?"

"The ketamine used matches the amount delivered, if we don't count the two bottles that never showed up. There's five cc unaccounted for, but that's nothing. Just one procedure we forgot to record."

"Thanks for checking, but it's still strange."

Janice entered the treatment room. "That cop's back."

Kay frowned. "Do you mean Officer Mitchell?"

Janice shrugged.

"Officer Mitchell is a client. Could you please send her into exam one?"

"Sure." Janice shrugged again and left.

"What's up with her?" Kay asked.

"Boyfriend trouble. Her new guy thinks he's Mr. Gorgeous and keeps looking at other women."

"Spare us." Kay laughed. "You want to see Cody? He's put on too much weight, but don't say anything to Mitch. She's already had the lecture from me."

"I'll bet."

Kay grabbed the suture scissors and she and Val walked to the exam room. "Hello," she said and smiled.

"Hi, Kay, Val." Mitch grinned back, but didn't move a muscle.

Val looked from Mitch to Kay and back. "Did I just walk into a romance novel or not? Kiss already." Val bent and petted Cody. "Don't look, Cody. It's not for little boy puppies to see."

Kay shrugged. "Val's orders." She stepped up to Mitch and kissed her quickly on the lips. "Can you please put Cody on the table?"

"I'll take that kiss as a down payment," Mitch whispered. She scooped Cody up and set him on the table.

When Kay approached Cody, he stretched his neck out to kiss her. She scuffled his ears and kissed the top of his head. "You're such a good boy. Look at how well you're healing."

Val and Kay removed the skin sutures, Mitch put Cody back on the floor, and Val left with a wave.

"He's looking good. The incision is healing well." Kay petted Cody. "You might be up and around sooner than I anticipated."

"That's good because he's getting bored. I moved an old television into his room last night and we watched the game together, just so he'd have company."

Kay kissed Mitch on the lips again. "And you are *great* company."

"Are you free for dinner? I'm making another one of Callie's recipes."

"I'd like that. Is this a bed and breakfast deal?"

Mitch caressed Kay's cheek. "I was hoping you could stay the night."

Kay kissed Mitch until Val knocked on the exam room door to tell her the first patient was ready to be discharged. She kissed Mitch again, then Cody, and sent them home.

It was a busy afternoon of discharges and other patients. At five she texted Mitch. *Forgot to ask, what do I bring?*

Just yourself.

Lauren brought in a fresh tin of brownies this morning.

Two please.

Kay grinned and headed to the lunchroom to pack up some of Callie's homemade brownies. She changed out of her scrubs into the old capris and T-shirt she'd worn to work. She wished she worn something prettier, but it couldn't be helped. Finding time to do laundry was difficult.

Kay drove across town, and when Mitch didn't answer her door, she went inside and made her way to the back patio. "You didn't lock—" She skidded to a stop and stared. "Geez, Mitchell, you could warn a girl when you plan to dress like that. My brain just shorted out." Kay put the brownies down and made a show of checking her pulse. "Pulse through the roof too."

"It's just shorts and a top. I was gardening."

"Shorts and skimpy bikini top, under an apron. If you were a barbecue ad, people would be lined up from here to Saskatoon to buy one."

"Just a second." Mitch slipped off the apron and pulled on the T-shirt that was draped over the patio railing. "Better? I don't want you to get a heart attack."

Kay put her hand over her heart. "Too late." She forced a smile, but she was freaking out. She settled in a patio chair, never taking her eyes off Mitch. Where would she find the self-control to keep her hands off her? Did she have to anymore? They'd spent the whole weekend making love and she was ready for more, but she wanted kissing and cuddling first. Who was she?

Mitch scooped her up into a tight hug and kissed her. "I didn't have all the ingredients for Callie's meal, so it's only hamburgers I'm afraid. Nothing fancy."

"Suits me and smells awesome. Anything I can do?"

"When they're ready I'll bring them in and we can dress them up. There's a tomato on the counter and lettuce in the fridge if you want to get that ready."

"Will do." Kay leaped to her feet and walked inside.

A few minutes later, Mitch came in with the burgers. They dressed them with toppings and headed back to the patio with burgers and cold sodas in hand.

Kay took a huge bite. "Delicious."

"Can you taste it through all the toppings you put on?"

"My brothers say I put so many toppings on, that one day I'll forget the burger and just be eating a bun full of toppings." Kay waggled her eyebrows and took another huge bite, chewed, and swallowed. "I like my burgers fully dressed and my women undressed."

"You do indeed."

Kay paused and then laughed when she caught the smile on Mitch's face. "It's a beautiful sunny day and I'm having a tasty meal with a tastier woman. Life is good." Kay took another huge bite.

"For now, anyway."

What did Mitch mean by that? She almost asked and then changed her mind. *Don't ask questions you don't want the answers to.* She wasn't in any way prepared to talk about the future. "How would you like to go kayaking this weekend? You told me you had three days off and I can swing it if I stay at the WCVM the rest of the week."

"All week? When would I see you again?"

"Very late Friday night. It's only four days away. What do you say?"

"All I know about kayaking is what I read in that one magazine, but I want to spend the weekend away, with you."

"I'll teach you to kayak and it'll be fun." Kay wiped her mouth and put her napkin on the plate. "That was delicious. Want the brownies now?"

Mitch stood and held her hand out to Kay. "Later. When we need the energy."

Kay grinned and leaped to her feet. She didn't need a second invitation to accompany Mitch to bed. Mitch was an attentive, considerate lover with a sense of adventure. The sex was amazing, as were the gentle caresses afterward. Funny that her nightmare from Afghanistan hadn't plagued her since she'd made love to Mitch that first time. It seemed like she wasn't the same person she'd been when she'd arrived in Thresherton. She wasn't sure who she was anymore, but as she lay in Mitch's arms, she decided she didn't need to know right now.

Chapter Twenty-eight

The four days apart dragged past for Kay, even though she was concentrating on her research and teaching. She missed Mitch, but she found she also missed her friends at the clinic and the camaraderie they'd developed. The knowledge that she was developing roots was worrisome, but she couldn't bring herself to fill out the applications to the places in the States she'd planned on applying to. They remained buried in her desk, and she didn't fish them out.

After breakfast on Saturday, they took their kayaks down to the water. Kay had booked a cabin on a lake an hour north of Saskatoon and they'd brought her camouflage kayak and rented one for Mitch. They each had a fifteen-foot sit-in day-tripping kayak with two watertight compartments. The cabin rental had taken half the money she'd earned at PVS, but it was worth it.

"Before we head out you get a lesson."

Mitch winked. "I'm in if you're teaching."

"I'll ignore that look. Here are the basics of paddling a kayak. Amateurs paddle by moving their shoulders. Proper paddling involves a subtle side-to-side motion using your waist, back, and abdominal muscles. Your hands should not be wind milling. Twist at the waist." Kay stood at the edge of the lake and demonstrated proper paddling technique. When Mitch had it down, they climbed into the boats and paddled off.

"I found something else you're serious about," Mitch said.

"Kayaking? Because it's your safety and I'm responsible for you."

"Ah, you want to protect me."

"I do, now shut up and listen." Kay pulled up beside her and they discussed the safety equipment on Mitch's boat. When Mitch was sufficiently trained, they headed out following the edge of a calm lake. She sent Mitch out first so she could watch her. "Remember, steady gentle strokes." She studied Mitch and admired the way her muscles danced in her arms and shoulders. Mitch powered through the lake like an expert for the next thirty minutes and then dropped back behind Kay.

The large splash had Kay looking over her shoulder at Mitch.

"Well, that wasn't supposed to happen." Mitch treaded water beside her boat, water streaming from her hair and into her eyes. Her kayak was upside down. "I was trying to look at a fish going under my kayak and I leaned too far over."

"I'll have you out of there in a minute. But you must do what I say."

"Always and especially when you use your command voice." Mitch winked.

"How are you joking? You must be freezing."

"Water's warmish."

"Okay, newbie, now we'll practice assisted rescue. Hand me your paddle and hang on to the nose of my boat so you're safe."

Kay carefully hauled Mitch's kayak out of the water pulling it on top of her kayak in front of her. She rolled Mitch's kayak to drain the water, and then slid it back into the lake. She leaned over the bow of Mitch's boat and hung on. "Go to the stern, haul yourself up on your stomach and slide in."

Mitch lifted herself with ease and slid into her boat. "I'm sitting in two inches of cold water."

Kay grinned. "Use your pump, woman."

Mitch grabbed the pump tucked under the bungee cords on the front of her kayak and placed one end of it in the water between her thighs.

"*Wait!* Point it away from me," Kay said.

Mitch rotated the tool and pumped. "Wow, it sprays far." When her boat was empty, she tucked the pump in place and accepted her paddle from Kay. "Thanks."

"That was an assisted rescue. I hope you paid attention in case I capsize. So, how cold are you?"

"Not too bad."

"Your shirt will dry quickly but your lifejacket will be cold and wet for a while. Why don't we stop for lunch and dry off on that island?" They paddled toward the little island in the middle of the large lake. Kay climbed out of her boat and pulled it up the bank to a flat, grassy area protected on three sides by trees and vegetation and Mitch followed.

"Spread your wet shirt on your kayak. It'll dry soon enough," Kay said.

"You're always trying to get me out of my clothes." Mitch slipped off her shirt and draped it and her lifejacket over the top of the kayak.

Mitch wore a sports bra of light material, designed to dry in fifteen minutes or less. Her bare torso was hard and muscular, and Kay marveled as always at the width of her shoulders. She enjoyed sex with Mitch, but in the last week it had edged past the just physical to real intimacy each time they made love. She'd never felt like this before with anyone and it was amazing, but still a little scary. If she let herself fall further, would she give up her goals? Would she end up as just another country vet like Lauren? But then Lauren was in love and very happy. It couldn't be all bad. She wanted to stick her head in the cold lake until life made sense again. Instead, she tossed aside her worries and looked at Mitch.

Mitch surveyed the lake. "I'm enjoying the sun on my skin. I'm also enjoying your expression, and if you keep ogling me as if I'm lunch, I'll get ideas."

"Don't I always approve of your ideas?" Kay grinned wickedly as she slid her hands over Mitch's strong back and circled her waist. Further wisecracks died on her lips. With her cheek resting on Mitch's bare back, the moment was too special for her usual flippancy. She inhaled the scent of her skin and placed a row of gentle kisses down her spine.

"Hmm, I'm enjoying this, but I'm feeling left out," Mitch said.

Kay stepped back to allow Mitch to pivot in her arms. She slipped in against Mitch's body and placed a kiss on the tops of Mitch's breasts peeking out of her sports bra.

"How private is this area? You picked a secluded spot." Mitch held Kay by the hips and scanned the bushes and the lake.

"We've been alone all morning." Kay kissed her and slipped out of her arms. She opened a watertight compartment on her kayak, removed a dry bag and drew out a thick blanket she spread on the ground. "What did you have in mind?"

"I want to take my shorts off."

"Don't let me stop you."

Mitch removed her quick-dry shorts and spread them on the branches of a shrub.

Kay sucked in her breath. "You're commando?"

"Yup. Are you shocked? I have another pair of shorts with me."

"Come here," Kay said.

"Oh, Dr. Gallant, what is that look for?" Exaggerating the swing of her hips, Mitch sashayed away from Kay and stripped off her sports bra.

Kay caught the bra Mitch tossed at her as she dove into the water. Mitch broke the surface with hardly a splash and traveled a long way under water before surfacing. She marveled at the beauty and elegance of the maneuver. "You've got great style."

"Join me. The water's cool and clean and it's deliciously sinful to be naked in here."

"I won't be as elegant." She scanned the lake and the forest, and she removed her top and bra and slid off her shorts and panties.

Mitch walked out of the water and slipped her arms around Kay's waist. Kay shivered. Was it the cool water coating Mitch's arms or the skin-to-skin contact? Most probably it was the strong feelings she couldn't ignore yet wasn't ready to examine.

In one fluid motion, Mitch scooped her up and leaped into the lake. Kay surfaced sputtering. "A warning would've been nice, you big goof. Oh my God, the water's freezing. I won't last long." As she spoke, Mitch swam closer to her and stood, but Kay couldn't touch the bottom.

"You're so lovely," Mitch whispered.

Kay's lips parted a little at the desire on Mitch's face and the heat in her hazel eyes. She caressed the tops of Mitch's breasts loving the way they floated in the water with erect nipples pointing at her.

When Mitch drew closer, Kay looped her arms and legs around Mitch's body and kissed her. They didn't need conversation. They both knew what they wanted.

Mitch cupped Kay's ass and drew her in for a deep kiss. Kay spread her legs to give Mitch access and gasped as Mitch's cold fingers met her warm inner flesh.

Mitch brushed the hair from Kay's forehead. "You're so beautiful. Just like this. With your hair framing your face in blond ringlets."

Kay muttered and slid against Mitch as Mitch thrust. She'd never made love in the water and she enjoyed the buoyancy. Her arms tightened and her breath emerged in little gasps as she became more aroused with each deep thrust. When she was close, Mitch emerged from the water carrying her and laid her on the blanket. Mitch resumed her thrusting and lowered her mouth to cover Kay's center.

Kay was overwhelmed by the sensations of Mitch between her legs, the hot sun on her body, and a whisper of a breath of wind caressing her wet skin and making her already hard nipples even harder. Naked and exposed to nature should feel dangerous, but she was safe and cared about with Mitch. Kay closed her eyes as electricity pulsed up her body. She moaned as she crashed over the edge. Mitch's tongue was lethal.

"Did you hear something?" a stranger spoke close to their location.

Kay gasped. Somebody was on the other side of their small island.

"What?" another person answered.

Kay lunged for her top and tossed Mitch hers. They yanked their tops on and used the blanket to cover their bottom halves. Five seconds later, four women paddled into view and spotted Mitch and

Kay. One of them winked. "Afternoon, ladies." Another woman grinned at them and two more exchanged looks and laughed.

Mitch waved. "Nice day for a paddle. Have fun."

"We're alone on this lake all morning, until we take off our clothes," Kay whispered.

"Bad luck, but they were family."

"Family is worse. A straight group might not have been as quick to figure out what we were doing."

"You worry too much." Mitch lifted Kay and plopped her in her lap.

"And you don't worry enough. Aren't cops supposed to be against public nudity and skinny-dipping?" Kay slid her hand under the blanket. "Your turn."

Mitch's eyes grew wide with desire and she arched to give Kay access. She slid two fingers inside Mitch and moaned when she encountered the signs of Mitch's excitement. She withdrew her fingers, bringing Mitch's wetness with her and circled and tugged on Mitch's clit. Mitch sighed and lay on her back with Kay on top.

Kay shifted position without stopping her motion. She pulled the blanket over their bottoms and after a tender kiss, she slid up Mitch's top and sucked a nipple between her teeth and then moved to lavish attention on the other breast. She rubbed harder until Mitch jerked several times beneath her and let go with one long sigh.

When Mitch had relaxed, Kay pulled her shirt down and rested her head and body on top of Mitch's. Mitch draped her arms over her, and they remained under the blanket in the sun for several minutes. "We better move before we fall asleep," Mitch said.

Kay didn't want to move. There was no safer, happier place than curled up with Mitch in this little bubble of paradise. Maybe they could build a house on the island and never leave. "Longer."

Mitch laughed. "What if the next group to come by are schoolchildren?" Mitch clutched at Kay and embraced her for a second more before releasing her.

Kay stood and reluctantly flung on the rest of her clothes. She pulled out the food, and surrounded by the smells of sex and nature, they ate their lunch interspersed with kisses and gentle caresses.

Kay sighed as she brushed Mitch's hair from her face. When Mitch looked at her, she saw genuine warmth and caring. Could this be true? Could it be real? Had anyone looked at her like that? Plenty of women had satisfied her sexually, but that had been all they did, or perhaps all she'd allowed them to do. Mitch was a beautiful lover. Perhaps *the* best, and every inch of tall leanness said she could be more. Could she let her be more? She kissed Mitch on her bare shoulder. When Mitch smiled it felt like another bit of her resolve to remain remote just drained away.

Two days later, Mitch and Kay left the lakeside cabin they'd stayed at. Kay watched out the window of the truck as the resort faded into the distance. With a sigh, she turned and faced forward. An examination of what she wanted from life was in the cards when she got back. She yawned and rested her head on Mitch's shoulder with the strongest sensation of well-being and contentment. Figuring out the future could wait.

❖

On Wednesday, Kay slipped into PVS and put her bag in her locker. She rolled her shoulders and stretched muscles still sore from three days of kayaking.

"Morning, Kay."

"Hey, Val. What's on for today? Spays and neuters?" Kay laughed.

Val shook her head, her brow furrowed as she failed to return Kay's laugh and only looked away. "Only two were booked, so Fiona moved them to next week. We're all in the lunchroom."

"This sounds serious." Kay followed Val and took the last empty chair in the room. Ian, Fiona, Lauren, Val, Minnie, even the receptionists, Janice and Vicki, were there.

"Good, we're all here." Ian leaned on the table and looked at each of his staff in turn. "We have a serious situation, which I'm sure will turn out to be a mistake. We're missing the equivalent of five bottles of ketamine."

Kay surged forward in her chair. "Five? How did it become five? I thought we were only missing the two that didn't arrive."

"Go ahead, Val," Ian said.

Val cleared her throat. "The two we thought didn't arrive, actually did arrive. I have the confirmation from the courier, but the signature of the person who signed for it is only an illegible scribble…"

"Go on," Ian said.

Val shuffled her papers nervously and continued to look only at Ian. "I also checked the surgery logs to see what we'd used and—"

"I did that already. It all added up," Kay said.

Val shook her head. "We only did three-quarters of the surgeries listed in the log for the last three months. I didn't recognize their writing, but somebody entered a bunch of fake owners and fake pets. It started in mid-May."

"Fake? I didn't know that." Nobody was stating the obvious, but Kay had started at PVS in mid-May. Was everyone looking at her and wondering if she were a thief? Nobody really knew her. She was friends with Val and Lauren, but not at a very deep confiding level, and PVS would come first with them. Only Mitch knew her best and would have her back.

Val continued to focus on Ian as she answered Kay. "It's because you're still new and you don't remember names. I do and I didn't recognize a bunch of the people and pets listed, so I compared them to the client log."

"I did notice that I'd been busier than I thought." Kay laughed nervously and scanned the table. Everyone *was* looking at her and she wanted to crawl under the table and hide her humiliation. She'd made a foolish mistake not cross-referencing the surgeries to PVS patient records. She'd been so sure it was an inventory error. Shame flowed through her in a wave. She hadn't done her job and there was no excuse for that.

"So, we've got five unaccounted for bottles," Fiona said. "We're closing the clinic for two hours this morning. Lauren will answer the phone and let us know if there are urgent issues. The rest of us will split up and search PVS from the front door to the trash bins out back. Open every drawer and every cupboard, check everything. Some of you will be assigned to a vet's office. Don't hold back. We've got nothing to hide. Open every drawer. Are we clear?"

Kay nodded with the others.

"Good," Fiona said and started to assign people to areas of PVS to check. Fiona asked Kay to search Ian's office, so she started there. She started on the shelves and then reluctantly opened the first desk drawer. Ian was her boss. How weird was it to be going through his stuff?

If it hadn't been so serious, she'd have laughed. His drawers were full of junk he'd clearly pulled out of his pockets and dropped there. He had a stack of magazines to rival a museum's collection, and there must have been twenty pictures of Fiona at various ages scattered around the office. This was the kind of mess you got when you stayed in one place too long. She'd never have that problem. The stab of regret startled her, but she packed the emotion away with a lifetime of practice and continued to search.

Kay met everyone back in the lunchroom two hours later. Lauren had donuts and fresh coffee waiting. Kay poured a coffee, but her stomach was in knots and she couldn't eat. She glanced around the table and took in the tired, dejected faces.

"We checked everywhere," Fiona said. "Val even went through the trucks. We found nothing. No sign of the missing bottles."

Val started to cry. "I'm sorry. It's all my fault."

"*You* didn't take them," Ian said.

Kay was only shocked for a moment at how adamant he was. Val was clearly above suspicion and why wouldn't she be? She'd started working at PVS when she was a kid fourteen years ago.

Val sniffled and accepted a tissue and a hug from Fiona. "But I should've realized it was missing. It's my job." She hiccupped and sipped the glass of water Kay fetched for her until she was quiet again. "Sorry, Ian and Fiona."

Ian patted Val's hand. "It's okay. The point is we know now. We've looked for the drug and can't account for its use. It's time to call the RCMP."

"There's also that teenager, Jacks." Val looked around the table. "The gossip mill says she was high on ketamine when she crashed her bike three weeks ago. You know her, right?"

Kay flinched. This was the first time Val had made eye contact with her since she'd arrived at PVS. Val's eyes were a steely blue and missing their usual warmth. Kay cleared her throat. "Yes, Jacks. She's a friend of Mitch's. She bought ketamine at a party from some…" She squared her shoulders and looked hard at Val. "From some woman. There's no way it could be PVS ketamine, or at least I thought so. But now…"

"I didn't hear about that," Ian said.

Kay glanced at Ian. His shoulders were slumped, and he looked like he'd aged ten years in ten seconds.

"It's past time to call the police." Ian stood. "Thanks, everyone. Let's go back to work." He held out his hand to Fiona. "Honey, can you come with me, please?"

A pain stabbed Kay in the chest. There were tears in Fiona's eyes as she nodded and left the room with Ian. Even though they were father and daughter, at work Ian and Fiona always used each other's first names. Never pet names. Val had told them about Kay's sense that the drawers in the treatment room had been searched, but nobody else had seen it. But now there was ketamine missing? What should she do?

Kay sat at the table alone and sipped her now cold coffee. This was serious. Five bottles of ketamine were missing. If they couldn't find them, Ian, and Fiona, as the practice owners, were in big trouble with the RCMP. They might even be sanctioned by the veterinary association. There would be nothing more humiliating to a veterinarian than having their professional credibility questioned. A viral YouTube video of them running naked through Thresherton would be easier to handle.

CHAPTER TWENTY-NINE

"Mitch, do you have a minute?"

Mitch stood and followed her detachment commander into his office.

"Prairie Veterinary Services has lost control of some bottles of ketamine. I know you've been trying to track down where your friend Jacks got her ketamine. Any luck?"

Mitch shook her head. "I've talked to a lot of kids. They just think it was a woman. Nobody got a good look at her face."

"I don't like the coincidence. I want you to go to PVS and investigate. Ian Wilson is a good guy, so I'm sure you'll find the ketamine the kids got came from somewhere else. I'm hoping it's some clerical error at PVS."

"Sir, I'd prefer not to go there officially. Most of the PVS staff are my friends. Can Jo or Phil do it?" She'd back Jo and Phil up. She jammed her fists into her pockets. She wanted that ketamine found as much as everyone else, even if it was leaking out of PVS, and it was too much of a coincidence for that not to be the case. But please, please, she didn't want to be the lead in the investigation.

"There's nobody else available."

Mitch squared her shoulders and locked eyes with her commander. "I'm in a relationship with Dr. Kay Gallant, a PVS veterinarian." Kay and she had never used the word relationship, but they were, weren't they? This feeling, this connection between them, was more than the sex. They hung out together, had meals together, planned their schedules together and spent every night they could in each other's arms. Not always having sex, but often curled together and chatting peacefully until one or both of them fell asleep. It was an idyllic life and one she hoped they could find a way to make last.

"Unfortunate, Mitchell, but the job's yours. Thresherton is a small town. You'd better learn to police your friends and be prepared to lose them. I've known Ian Wilson for twenty years. Hell, two years ago we took our wives on a cruise together. I trust you to be professional and do your duty. We're talking about ketamine."

"Yes, sir." Mitch loathed ketamine. It didn't make people high. It caused the user to disassociate and act crazy. Jacks had survived her motorcycle crash, but she was stuck on crutches for the rest of the summer, and it could have been so much worse.

"I recall hearing that PVS was struggling with their ketamine inventory, but they assured me it was a clerical error." She'd been so sure Kay and Val would sort it out. Had she let her friendships and infatuation for Kay cloud her judgment? She straightened as determination took over. It had been her job to find the ketamine and protect those kids. And this time she'd do it, no matter the consequences.

"I see. Well, all the more reason for you to go. I'll help you with the investigation, if you can't handle it. And I'm available to talk, if you have trouble being impartial."

"Thank you." She turned and left his office. As usual, she did her due diligence research on every employee, and the only one with a file was Kay. It made her stomach turn. Reluctant to investigate her friends, but determined to solve the mystery, she cursed as she drove to PVS. Along with Callie and Becky, the staff at PVS were more like her family. She groaned. Was there an easy way to question your ex-addict girlfriend about drug thefts? This would be a crappy ride. She parked at PVS and ran into Kay at the front counter.

Kay wore scrubs with puppies on them and a white lab coat. Her blue eyes twinkled with mischief and she smiled at her with unguarded warmth. Mitch's heart ached. She'd been waiting for months for Kay to look at her that way. It had been an awesome kayaking adventure with a ton of sex. But it was more than sex. They'd made love. Neither of them had used the word, but she'd come close. What she'd wanted for so long was nearly in her grasp. Was there any chance that Kay would understand she was just doing her job? Kay understood the seriousness of the situation. Maybe it would be okay.

"Hi, Janice. Is Dr. Ian Wilson available?" She used her cop tone instead of the one she usually used when she showed up there with lunch or coffees.

Janice glanced toward her and dropped the papers she held.

Mitch winced. Even innocent people acted guilty when a cop talked to them.

"I'll get him."

As Janice scurried off, Mitch glanced at Kay. "Hi, Kay." *Oh, shit here we go.* Kay squinted at her. She'd clearly figured out why Mitch was at PVS. *Let the games begin.*

"Corporal Mitchell?"

Mitch turned quickly when Ian Wilson spoke. She'd met him several times at parties at Poplarcreek and had run into him at the clinic here and there over the years. He appeared to be an honest man and had an excellent reputation in the community. She couldn't picture him selling ketamine out the back door of his clinic.

"Are you here about the ketamine?" Ian asked.

Mitch nodded. She was there to talk, but her throat had dried up. She wasn't afraid of doing her job, but she hated that she had to investigate Kay and the rest of them. She glanced to her left, but Kay had vanished.

"Janice, please ask Val and Kay to come to my office. This way, Corporal."

Mitch followed him to his office, dropped into a chair, and removed her notebook from her pocket.

"Val and Kay brought the thefts to my attention," Ian said.

Val stepped into Ian's office. "You wanted to see me?"

"Yes, you and Kay, please."

"She said she can't leave her patient."

"Okay then, come in and close the door," Ian said.

Val dropped into the chair beside Mitch. "Hey, Mitch."

"Hey, Val." Mitch glanced at the door. Did she want Kay here or not? She didn't need a PhD to know Kay was avoiding her. She refocused on Val. "I'm here about the ketamine."

"Figured that."

"I wish someone else was available, but I'm under orders. Can you please start at the beginning?"

"Go ahead, Val," Ian said.

"I inventory our controlled drugs every two weeks, and we were going through it awfully fast. We always seemed to be almost out. I kept ordering, but still we were short and then Kay and I did some checking and discovered ketamine missing."

Ian nodded. "Tell her what we did, in detail."

Val relayed all the activities and conclusions of the day before and earlier.

Mitch sat back and reviewed her notes. "So, you and Kay both reviewed the surgery log and only *you* discovered the fake entries? And you discovered that they started about the time Kay began working at PVS? And Kay told you someone was searching drawers in the treatment room, but you never saw it?"

"Nobody else saw the mess and nobody was in that weekend but Val and Kay. Is that right, Val?" Ian asked.

Val nodded as she worried a loose thread on her lab coat.

Why hadn't Kay told her about the messy drawers? She'd been right there at PVS with her. She didn't want to consider it, but pretending the clinic had been searched while you were with a cop would be an excellent alibi. But how could it be Kay? She shook her head. Professionalism was her priority. She wouldn't be swayed by her feelings for Kay, not again. She'd be impartial if it killed her, and it might just. "Tell me again about what goes into a surgery log."

"We have to record the amount of controlled drug used and every surgery we do. The amount used corresponds to the animal, the animal's weight, the owner, and the date of the surgery."

"So, what made you check the logs when Kay said they were okay? Why did you change your mind and decide the ketamine hadn't just been used?"

"It didn't make sense. I couldn't believe we'd done that much surgery. I also thought I'd forgotten to order, but then I discovered one of the orders had arrived at PVS. But I never saw it."

"So how much is missing?"

"Sometime in the last three months, five bottles," Ian said.

Mitch's head snapped up, and she squinted at Ian. "Five?"

"Corporal Mitchell, I didn't report the first two bottles because I assumed it was a mistake." Ian looked at Val. "Sorry, Val. There's no way after all these years you became sloppy with the inventory of our controlled drugs. I should've called the RCMP sooner. I apologize."

"And you didn't find it?" Mitch asked.

"We looked everywhere."

"Anything more?" Mitch asked. "Could you have sold the missing bottles?"

Val shook her head. "We never dispense ketamine, but Fiona double-checked just in case and found no sales."

"They didn't break in. The criminal must have had the alarm code for the door and figured out where we keep the key to the drug lock box," Ian said.

"Who has the code?"

"Everyone, but only the veterinarians and technicians know where we keep the key," Ian said.

"You need to install a hidden video camera over the drug lock box, but use somebody from Saskatoon, when PVS is closed. If you use someone local the whole town will know. Gossip spreads quickly here."

"Good idea. Dammit, this thievery is annoying. Let's hope this hasn't been too costly a lesson. Val, don't tell anyone about the hidden cameras. I trust everyone working for us, but somebody has been fooling me."

Mitch winced as she wrote. When Kay found out she'd been covertly videoed she would quit. She'd feel betrayed by Ian and Fiona and her humiliation would send her running. She'd take that job in the USA and they'd never see her again. But if Mitch told her, she'd be going against her duty as an officer, compromising the investigation. She didn't even consider for a second telling Kay.

Mitch's hand shook and she studied the illegible scribble on the last page in her notebook. She flipped to the next page and started again, forcing her mind to concentrate and stay professional.

"What next?" Ian asked.

Mitch stood. "Time to talk to your staff." She followed Val and Ian out of the office.

"I'll gather everyone," Val said.

Mitch scanned the people gathered in the treatment room. "I'm in charge of the investigation into the missing ketamine. PVS is missing five bottles. Is there any chance you put them in a drawer or a pocket?" Most of the staff of the clinic had been her friends for years, except Kay. None of them was devious enough to steal drugs from PVS, including Kay. "I understand how it can happen. You have a bottle in your hand and stick it in your pocket. You plan to lock it up but forget."

Mitch lounged against the treatment-room counter, to appear less threatening and smiled at the assembled group. "No problem if you have it. If you took it home by accident, bring it back tomorrow." She watched the group for guilty faces, awkward shuffles, or people who didn't make eye contact with her. She only found expressions of boredom, curiosity, and anger. Mitch shifted to stand straight. "Sorry to offend anyone, but I need to do my job. Ketamine is a dangerous drug." Several staff nodded in agreement but with no change in expression.

"I've posted my phone number on your bulletin board. If you have anything to report, please approach me in person or call." She scanned the PVS employees as they fidgeted with impatience. "Do you have any questions?" They were silent. "Thanks for your cooperation. Can the veterinarians please stay for a minute."

Lauren, Kay, Ian, and Fiona remained in the room.

"Ian, I'll start by searching the vet vehicles and offices," Mitch said.

"Wouldn't the criminal have moved it by now?" he asked.

"You'd be surprised."

Ian focused on Lauren and shrugged. "Would you like to go first so you can head back home?" He turned to Mitch. "Lauren had the day off, but I asked her to come in to meet with you."

"Thanks, Ian." Mitch stretched her shoulders, focused on the ceiling, and groaned inwardly. Wonderful, now Lauren would be annoyed with her, just when they were becoming friends. With resignation, she followed Lauren to her office to get her truck keys and begin the search.

"Satisfied?" Lauren said as she frowned at Mitch an hour later. "You've gone through my bag, my truck, my desk, and now my locker and found nothing."

"Thanks, Lauren. Sorry, but I have to be thorough."

Lauren pressed her hands to the middle of her back and leaned back with a groan. "I know, I know. It's just that I would never *sell ketamine*. Nobody here would."

Mitch shifted nervously and debated getting Val. She didn't like to see Lauren so upset. They'd been getting along better since the wedding and she was sorry to have damaged that. And was Lauren about to cry?

"Stop staring at me." Lauren dropped into her office chair, grabbed a tissue, and blew her nose. "Just find it, okay? Ian and Fiona are my friends. They took a chance on me when I was a grouchy mess and gave me a job. Without PVS I'd never have met Callie." She blew her nose again and smiled slightly. "And apparently, I'm still a grouchy mess."

"Can I do anything? Get Val or call Callie?"

Lauren shook her head. "Just tell me I can go home now, please."

Mitch nodded so hard her neck hurt. "Yes, thanks. That's all I need. You can go home." She watched Lauren for a few seconds and then slipped out and gently closed the office door.

If investigating Lauren resembled a forest fire, then investigating Kay would be a volcanic explosion. At lunch, Mitch fortified herself by cuddling with Cody and eating half a tin of brownies. She'd have to confiscate Callie's key if she kept dropping off baked goods.

After lunch, Mitch followed Kay into her office and closed the door. Kay's back was straight, her chin was high and there was a coldness in her eyes. "I'm sorry this upsets you, but I'm only doing my job. We have to find the ketamine. You know how serious this is."

"Of course, Officer Mitchell."

Mitch almost shivered in the cold wafting off Kay. Kay was being polite and calm. Almost too calm. "Val explained the confusion over the surgery log book. Do you want to add anything?"

"I didn't do a thorough job of checking. Do you think I was hiding something?"

Mitch was going to let that go. "How come you didn't mention your suspicion that somebody had been searching for something in the treatment room?"

Kay shrugged. "I wasn't sure. Then I talked to Val and became convinced that I was wrong." Kay looked away. "Besides, that was our first night together and I was thinking about other stuff."

Mitch jotted some notes in her book to cover her emotion. She sighed. She couldn't wait any longer and presented Kay with the file from the RCMP investigation of her in Charlottetown. She showed Kay reports of drug dependency, buying drugs on the street, stealing drugs from family friends, and a list of items Kay stole from her parents and sold to buy more drugs. The detailed reports also contained several pictures of Kay as an emaciated, scared girl with dying eyes.

Kay snatched the pictures from Mitch's hand and collapsed into a chair. "I've never seen these. I looked terrible, half-dead."

Mitch leaned forward, wanting to pull her into an embrace, to tell her everything was okay. She hated the pain she was causing Kay. It was as if she'd shredded Kay's armor of protection with love and then exposed her vulnerable center to attack.

Kay winced. "When you come back from war at twenty-three with no hope, a crushed knee, and constant pain, you have a pity party for yourself. That's what I did. But I overcame it."

The pain in Kay's voice sliced into Mitch and she regretted her next question, but as an officer, she had to ask the logical questions, not avoid them for fear of personal repercussions. "Are you using ketamine to ease the pain in your knee?"

"What? Why would you say that?"

Kay's devastated expression almost broke Mitch's heart. A second later, Kay's face shuttered closed and a layer of armor seemed to grow around her. "Kay, I—"

"If I stole drugs from the clinic, for pain relief, it wouldn't be ketamine. There are a dozen better products and before you ask, we aren't missing any."

Each of Kay's words hit harder than a physical blow. Mitch held Kay's eyes and struggled to keep her posture neutral. "I'm sorry it was a painful conversation, but I had to ask. I believe you." She refused to apologize any longer for her questions. She'd done enough apologizing already in this investigation. It was her job, and they knew it. "It's ketamine and we have to find it before it's sold. Or any more is sold, as the case may be."

Kay sneered. "Did you dig into everybody's past as much as mine? Oh wait, I told you all about it. Made it easy for you to find your suspect. I trusted you."

"And you still can, but I couldn't ignore the information, now that some ketamine is missing. And I would've found the details anyway. You're in the police system."

"You're going to ruin my life." Kay carefully set the pictures on her desk. "What a fool I am. I trusted you, but you're a cop first and you don't trust me. Once an addict, always an addict. Right, Mitchell? Anything else you want to check? My bag?"

Mitch picked up the pictures as Kay's anger knifed into her. Kay upended her bag on the top of her desk and Mitch half-heartedly searched the contents. "Nothing here. Thank you for your cooperation." She exited Kay's office and escaped from PVS after inspecting and searching the rest of the offices, vehicles, lockers, and bags.

When she arrived back at the detachment office, Mitch rested her forehead against her steering wheel and breathed slowly. Had Kay ever been so furious with her? Mitch shuddered. At times the icy anger surging from Kay had bordered on hate.

This was one of the rare times she loathed her job. She stepped out of the cruiser, squared her shoulders, and headed inside to report to her commander that she'd alienated everyone at PVS and still found nothing. Her only accomplishment was to upset all her friends and destroy any chance she might have had with Kay. Today, she'd ruined both their lives. And how deep was the hole they were in? Was there something that could pull them out, or was this investigation going to heap shit on top of them until everything they'd been building was obliterated? Would Kay eventually understand?

CHAPTER THIRTY

Mitch pulled into the parking lot at PVS. It was a beautiful sunny Wednesday, and the air was sweet with the smell of fresh cut hay, but the lead in her soul made it difficult for her to care.

Kay's car was parked at the side door. "Kay's here today, Cody." It had been a week since she'd last seen her. She'd texted Kay a few times with no replies except one where Kay had asked Mitch to leave her alone. Today was the appointment she'd made with Kay for Cody's follow-up X-rays.

Cody sat up and wagged his tail. He gave her a kiss and then looked out the windshield as he searched for Kay.

She caressed his head and sifted his ears through her fingers. "You miss her too, don't you, boy?" She rubbed her palm over her heart. Would losing a limb hurt less than losing Kay? Likely not, but she hadn't wanted to experience either. There'd always been the risk Kay would leave for the US, but this was worse. Today the pain was a sharp stab with each breath.

Mitch kissed Cody on the tip of the nose, lifted him from the truck and carried him inside with difficulty. He wriggled in her arms and whined as he looked around for Kay. "Poor Cody." She'd screwed up and lost Kay for them both.

"Hey, guys. You're in exam room one," Val said. "I'll tell Kay."

Kay entered the exam room. "Morning, you." She immediately bent to pet Cody who tried to jump up and cover her with kisses.

"Settle down, mister. You're not healed yet." She grabbed hold of his collar. "I'll take him for X-rays."

Mitch didn't let go of Cody's leash, even when Kay tugged. Eventually, Kay looked up at her. Mitch schooled her expression to serious, swallowing her shock. Kay's face was pale and puffy, and she had dark circles under her eyes. She wanted to hold her and comfort her. Was Kay hurting too? Was her PTSD acting up? "How are you?"

"Fine." Kay smiled but it didn't reach her eyes.

"Freaked-out, insecure—"

Kay cleared her throat. "He's gained more weight. Cody needs to be on a diet kibble."

Mitch smiled, trying again. "You calling my dog fat?"

"When he's healed and running around you can switch him back to regular kibble."

Mitch sighed. She'd given Kay the perfect opening, but there was no joke and no answering smile for her or Cody. "He misses you."

"And I miss him."

Mitch took a tentative step closer to Kay, but she stepped back. "What about me?" Mitch asked.

Kay shrugged and turned her head to stare at the wall. "I miss you too."

Mitch had to strain to hear Kay's words. "I'm sorry for everything, but I have to—"

"Get the ketamine off the street. I remember. How's that going?"

"We have a few leads. Jacks, Jules, and Bobby have been helpful."

"And you can't tell me anything more since I'm a suspect."

"I can't tell *anyone* anything more, but I wish I could. Wish I could tell you everything."

"Me too." Kay tugged on the leash.

Mitch released Cody, but she laid a restraining hand on Kay's arm. "Can we ever get past this?"

"You let me down. Told everyone my secrets." Kay shook her head. "It was humiliating and hurtful."

Mitch wanted to scream in frustration. She'd heard the rumors about Kay circulating in Thresherton. "I didn't tell anyone outside the detachment."

Kay shrugged. "Let's just get Cody's X-rays done." She left with Cody walking slowly behind her.

Mitch punched her palm. When would this be over? When would the criminal hurry up and steal more ketamine from the lock box? They'd be scared right now, but in two or three weeks, they'd get the nerve to try again and then she'd catch them and clear Kay, and everyone else, of all suspicion. But would what she and Kay had built survive two more weeks? Could they get back to where they were once the thefts were solved? What if she never caught the thief?

Kay returned with Cody. He hobbled over to Mitch and sat at her feet. She petted him and waited.

"His X-rays look good and he's healing well. Do you want to see?"

Mitch shook her head. "No, I trust your judgment."

"But do you trust me?"

"What?"

"Never mind. Continue to keep him quiet and come back in another—"

"I do trust you, more than anyone on this planet. I don't think you're the one responsible, Kay."

"But you had to print the file, didn't you? You had to ask if I was using it, and you can't tell me there wasn't at least some part of you that thought it might be true. I let you really know me, and now you'll never see beyond what I was." She took a shaky breath and swiped at her eyes. "In another month, Ian will see him. Keep Cody quiet until then. Bye, big guy." Kay kissed Cody on the top of the head and left.

Ian will see him. Kay was leaving, just like she'd always planned to. Mitch's chest tightened and she needed to be outside in the fresh air. Inside, it felt as if she were dragging air into her lungs through a sea of glass. She'd been inches from Kay, but it felt like miles. They were further apart than when they'd met two and a half months ago. The ketamine investigation had broken them and the most wonderful woman she'd met in years would soon be gone from her life forever. She paid her bill and made it home with Cody before she lost it.

She lifted weights until her arms ached, but she wanted to punch something. Kay cared about her work and her reputation and the latter was in shreds. The story about PEI had gotten out, and the gossips had spread it around town. The tale had grown from Kay, the poor wounded kid with an addiction to painkillers, to Kay being some drug dealing kingpin. Somebody at the RCMP office had a big mouth and when Mitch found them, she'd show them what she thought of such assholes. It was their fault Kay was leaving, not to mention it was information that was part of an investigation and there was no excuse for revealing it outside the detachment. She couldn't imagine how Kay felt at the personal intrusion.

The hours and days dragged. She wouldn't give up though and limited herself to one text a day to remind Kay that she was still thinking of her and wanted to see her. She stopped short of going to her apartment as that was too intrusive, but she sent flowers twice. Could she find her at the college? Probably, but Kay was sensitive to humiliation and having some woman chase her around wouldn't help with that. Showing up at PVS for no reason was out too.

Instead, Mitch moved through town with her head held high and did her job. She worked constantly, trying to track down any and every lead she could. Her evenings and days off were different. She spent them shuffling through her house eating and drinking too much. Was being a cop worth it if she lost Kay? Was anything worth losing Kay? Cody kept her company, but he moped too. But if Kay wanted space, she would respect that.

Even when Callie told her she was taking lunch to PVS again, Mitch found a reason not to be in town. The next day, she dropped in at Poplarcreek on her own and had a quiet chat with Callie, who hugged her and reminded her that she had only done her job and wasn't responsible for the leak.

It was a relief, after two weeks of waiting, to get the call from Val that they had something on video and were all meeting at PVS after closing.

Val let her in. "Hey, Mitch, you're early. Come with me."

Mitch followed Val into the treatment room.

"It's been a busy day and I need to get the surgical instruments washed, packed, and into the autoclave. I'm not here tomorrow to do it and I try to leave your girlfriend ready to do any surgeries."

"Kay's not my girlfriend, or not anymore. Maybe she never was. I don't know."

Val stopped moving and focused on Mitch. "Don't give up. She's just hurting. She'll come around. She's too sensible not to see that you had to check her office and locker. You checked everyone's."

Mitch nodded.

"And the rumors flying around town are only embarrassing. They'll die down."

"I didn't tell anyone."

Val patted Mitch's arm. "I believe you, but there was a leak. People know now that she had drug problems in PEI, but they'll get over it. Nobody will judge a wounded veteran, especially one who was only a kid at the time."

"She wasn't much younger than you are now, but thanks for the support." At twenty-four, Val had been a mom with a seven-year-old child and a steady job. At the same age, Kay was out of work, wounded, suffering from PTSD, and drifting on a sea of drugs. They couldn't be more different, and public perception could be a hard thing to battle against.

When Ian and Fiona arrived, they all crowded around the video. Janice, the constantly rude and recalcitrant receptionist, looked furtively around and then rummaged through a storage cupboard and emerged with the key to the drug lock box. She opened the lock box, quickly took two bottles from it, then stuffed them in her pocket and relocked the cabinet. With another furtive look around, she returned the key and darted from the office. The clock read three a.m.

Ian thumped the desk with his fist. "Dammit. One of my own people. I didn't want to believe it. How did she find the new hiding spot for the damn key?"

"Janice has worked at PVS for three years, but it's only been the last few months there has been any drug thefts," Val said.

"That you know of," Mitch said. "She may have been at it before but took smaller amounts that didn't get missed. The next steps are mine. I'll keep you informed."

Mitch left PVS and strode to her cruiser. The weight fell off her shoulders and her heart did a happy dance. Soon, Kay would be vindicated and there would be nothing to keep them apart. She'd always known it couldn't be Kay stealing the ketamine, and now the world would have its proof. But would it be enough to keep Kay around? Or had the damage been done?

Before dawn the next day, Mitch and her colleagues raided Janice's house. She found two bottles of ketamine and thousands of dollars in cash. Val had a list of the lot numbers stamped on the bottles of stolen ketamine and she'd put a distinctive small red mark on the labels. The ketamine Mitch found matched Val's information. Once in handcuffs, Janice confessed to stealing from PVS and selling some of the ketamine to local teenagers. The interviews and paperwork moved quickly, and Janice was charged with theft, drug possession, and drug trafficking. She'd be looking at jail time, and Mitch was glad the kids she worked with would be safe. For a while, anyway. There was always another dealer to be on the lookout for. As happens in small towns, the details circulated at the speed of light.

As soon as she could, Mitch texted Kay with an update and waited for a response. One never came. Mitch spent a lonely evening at home. She played with Cody, washed down a half a box of chocolate cookies with beer for dinner, and crawled into bed. She and Kay were letting the criminal win. How weak of them to let a drug thief and rumors come between them. She was sorry Kay was hurting and humiliated by the rumors, but that wasn't Mitch's fault. It made sense that a younger, wounded Kay had turned to drugs. Hadn't she said as much to Kay?

Mitch punched her pillows and rearranged them. Her priority had been finding the drugs and if Kay couldn't understand that, they had no future together and maybe Kay *should* leave Thresherton.

Mitch rolled over and wished she could fall into the abyss of a deep sleep. She didn't want Kay to leave.

She wasn't a woman who cried easily, but the tears slipped down her cheeks and she didn't care. Her life was imploding, and her heart was breaking.

She sat up. A midnight run would help, but she had no energy. So what if she got fat and had to get a larger sized uniform?

Mitch collapsed back on her bed and pulled Kay's pillow to her face. She'd washed the pillowcase, but the pillow held the scent of Kay's skin and favorite shampoo. She tossed the pillow off the bed in frustration and before it had even hit the floor, she dove for it, and pulled it back into her arms like it was precious. She gave in and let it absorb her tears. She cried like she hadn't in years.

After a middle of the night trip to the backyard with Cody, she crawled into bed. Exhaustion filled her, but her tears were done. Sleep was what she needed. Mitch started to dismantle her motorcycle in her mind, but it didn't work its usual magic. Her job and her responsibilities had lost her an amazing woman. Kay was the first woman to touch her heart in years. She'd fallen in love with Kay and lost her already. She wanted Kay to stay and make a life with her. But there was zero chance of that happening now.

Chapter Thirty-one

The heat of summer burned off with the arrival of the first of September. On Kay's trips between Saskatoon and Thresherton, she watched the giant tractors remove the last of the bails of wheat straw from the fields. The air around town was filled with dust and small particles of wheat that settled in the air with a golden glow, but she took no pleasure in the sight.

Kay kept her head down and did her work at PVS, but all the fun was gone. She and Val had purchased some funny scrub tops with animals that made people laugh, but she couldn't wear them these days. She stuck to plain dull green as it suited her mood. She didn't accept the invitations to Callie's for dinner, or to Val's for game night. She didn't want to sleep in Thresherton anymore.

Janice had been caught and Kay wanted to enjoy being vindicated, but she was too humiliated. How could Mitch have ever thought she would steal from PVS when it would mean jail, or at the very least the loss of her veterinary license? How could she have trusted her so little? Veterinary medicine and being a surgeon were all she had. She'd devoted all her money and energy to her education. She was thousands of dollars in debt and had worked too hard to throw away her career.

Kay shook her head. How could they have spent so much time together and Mitch not know her? She'd shown Mitch her soul, had confided in her, told her about her past and her hopes for the future. She cared about her like she'd never cared about another woman.

She'd known better than to get involved with someone. She'd known she wasn't built for a relationship, that people always let you down and held you back. But she'd been unable to keep her shields up in the face of Mitch's relentless optimism, humor, and kindness. And look where it had gotten her.

Kay dug through her desk for a tissue. How could she be crying again? She never cried, but Mitch's accusations had destroyed everything loving they'd built between them. Mitch had cut them apart, forever. Beside the tissues were her applications to Davis and Cornell. She would mail them today. When she finished her residency, she would quit PVS. Perhaps sooner if it didn't inconvenience Ian and Fiona. She cared about PVS and her bosses. She cared about Lauren and Val and their families and would miss them, but she was finished in Thresherton. She could never forgive Mitch's betrayal. It was hard enough holding her head up to speak to clients. It was time to leave.

On her way out of Thresherton, Kay stopped for groceries. She wasn't hungry but needed to eat and couldn't wait until she got to Saskatoon. She instantly regretted her decision as whispers followed her down the aisles. She straightened her shoulders and filled her cart. Once again, she was the outsider in a town that had just started to feel like home. Putting down roots in Thresherton might once have been possible, but not anymore.

Kay placed four bags of potato chips in her cart and glanced at the two women ten feet from her. They had their heads together and were looking at her. Everyone in town had heard her story. Kay Gallant, veteran, and drug addict. Damn Mitch and her big mouth. She promised she hadn't told anyone and maybe she hadn't, but surely it was still her fault that Kay's secrets from PEI were out.

Kay rested her forehead against a shelf and fought back a new wave of tears. She couldn't escape the humiliation.

"Dr. Gallant. Are you okay?"

Kay straightened and stepped back from the shelves. "I'm fine." She almost laughed. Freaked-out, insecure, needy, and emotional was her these days.

"You poor kid."

A woman of about sixty pulled Kay into a hug. The hug startled Kay and she wracked her mind for the woman's name. "Thank you, Mrs. Hammond." She'd spayed her cat. Kay surprised herself by hugging Mrs. Hammond back. She hadn't realized how much she missed physical comfort.

"Don't you worry about what the others say. My son was in Afghanistan and he told me how bad it was."

"It was terrible." An understatement. "What's your son doing now?"

She shook her head. "My boy died over there."

"I'm so sorry."

"Yes, me too. You take care of yourself and ignore all the busybodies in this town. You deserve our compassion, not mean gossip." She glared at the two women huddled together until they scurried off.

If Kay hadn't been so sad, she'd have laughed. "Thank you."

"You're a good one. Smart people will understand. You were a veteran, and you were hurting. Everyone has a story, but most prefer to judge rather than look in the mirror." Mrs. Hammond patted her shoulder, abandoned her cart full of groceries, and left the store.

Kay headed over to a cashier who looked about sixteen. "Mrs. Hammond forgot her groceries."

"Why was she crying?"

"She was telling me about her son."

The girl nodded. "Billy Hammond died in Afghanistan. He was a friend of my brother's."

"Help me pack up her groceries, please. I'll pay for them and drop them off."

"You're a nice lady. My dad said..."

"What did he say?"

The girl looked down and fiddled with her name tag. "That you were into drugs and bad stuff."

Kay took a deep breath. It was her personal business, but if her mistakes could help this young woman become more compassionate, she'd tell her. That's what Mitch would do. With her sweet soul and big heart, Mitch would tell this girl. "It's true, but that was seven years ago when I was a kid, and I was in a really bad place. I don't do that anymore."

"Mom said people can change."

"She's right, they can, and I have." She paused and waited for the cashier to smile at her. Kay smiled back. "I'll fetch Mrs. Hammond's cart." Kay pushed the two carts through the checkout and paid for both sets of groceries. After loading the groceries in her car, she called Val.

"Aren't you on your way home?" Val asked.

"I just picked up a few groceries. Do you know a Mrs. Hammond whose son Billy was killed in Afghanistan?"

"I sure do. He was a nice guy."

Kay got the address from Val and delivered the groceries. Mrs. Hammond invited her in for tea, but Kay needed to get home. She promised to call back another day and knew she would. Once, before she moved away.

Kay opened a bag of chips and munched as she drove to Saskatoon. She could never settle in an area where the whispers started behind her as she walked through the grocery store. It was clear from Mrs. Hammond and the cashier that her history with drugs was now town gossip. Maybe some people understood, but she'd bet there were more who didn't.

Mitch had betrayed her. Mitch hadn't protected her and kept her past a secret. Was it the truth or was she harping on something because of her own insecurities? "True all right." She slapped the steering wheel of her car for emphasis and shoved the chips in her mouth as she drove. Since the wedding, she'd returned with reluctance to the city. She'd preferred to stay with Mitch or at Poplarcreek. But not anymore.

Kay sighed. Why was the thoughtful, gentle, and careful Mitch her enemy? "Because she blabbed my secrets to everyone." It was possible one of the teens had told people, but she'd never told the teens the part about stealing stuff to buy drugs on the street. No, it all came back to Mitch collecting the details from Kay's past and telling the world. But then…other people worked at the detachment. Plenty of other people, who would have had access to the investigation files. The fact remained that in a small town there was no escape from the rumor mill. At least in a city she could get lost among the multitudes, and she'd never risk her heart this way again.

Kay talked herself in circles and sniffled as she looked at the bare wheat fields, cleared now of their summer harvest. "Get me out of here." She dug out a tissue and blew her nose as she drove.

"What the hell?" Kay's car swerved hard. It didn't wobble like a flat tire. The gust of wind had pushed her to the other side of the road.

The next gust slammed into her car and it sputtered but kept going. Her heart raced and her hands shook. If there'd been a car in the other lane, she'd be smashed toast now. She slowed to pull off at a small picnic area on the highway where she often stopped on her way home to watch the sunset. Today a solid ceiling of dark clouds hid the sun, and it suited her mood perfectly.

Kay strolled through the small park, absently eating chips as she walked. She enjoyed watching the prairie dogs that the locals called gophers. She smiled as they popped in and out of their holes. She perched on top of a picnic table and dropped chips to the gophers as they scurried around the table legs.

She glanced up as the sky darkened and the wind picked up announcing that it might rain at any minute. An RCMP cruiser flew by her location. Kay scowled. Cops could speed whenever they liked. She smiled as another gopher poked its head out of a hole. The animal studied the dark clouds and ducked back into its hole, ignoring the chip she dropped to him.

An instant later, Kay turned as a car skidded into the rest area. Mitch leaped from an RCMP cruiser and raced toward her.

"Are you crazy?" Mitch yelled.

Why did Mitch have to intrude on her special spot? Why couldn't she leave her alone? Kay squared her shoulders and turned her back on Mitch. "Go away." All she wanted was for the day to be over and the drama to end. She was leaving Thresherton, PVS, and Mitch and she didn't want to think about it anymore. It was a hard decision to make, but it was the right one if she was going to save herself from more hurt. These days she was struggling to find the armor and detachment she'd moved there with, but she couldn't, and that was Mitch's fault too.

CHAPTER THIRTY-TWO

Mitch would go away, happily, just as soon as she could. Kay was still angry about the investigation and refused to budge on the feeling of betrayal. Mitch scowled. She was fed up and angry too.

She glanced up at the darkening clouds and braced herself as the wind whipped at her uniform. She gritted her teeth and stepped in front of Kay. "I repeat, are you crazy?"

"Well, I was, Corporal Mitchell, but not any longer."

Kay's sharp words stabbed at her and Mitch staggered back a step. "Do you mean you were crazy to become involved with me?"

Kay pointed at Mitch with a potato chip and opened her mouth to speak.

"Forget it. Have you seen the sky? Do you know what that means?" Squabbling with Kay would have to wait.

Kay retrieved her phone and fiddled with it. "Nothing on my weather App."

"*Look at the sky!* Forget your phone. There's no cell signal out here. We're under a tornado warning. That greenish dark sky and the high wind are a prelude to tornados. One has already touched down west of Thresherton and one is north of us now. Everyone needs to find shelter, immediately."

Kay focused on Mitch. "Are you kidding?"

Mitch almost screamed but bit back her frustration. "No, I'm serious. Why would I make that up?"

Kay started to climb down. "What should I do?"

Mitch snatched Kay off the picnic table, sprinted through the rest area, and set her beside her car. "That way, two miles, is Kingsway Farm. Maggie's house is white, and it has a large vegetable garden in front. Go to the basement. Don't bother to knock."

Kay spread her arms wide. "I can't do that. Maggie's your friend, not mine."

Mitch peered across the fields in every direction.

"You're really scared, aren't you?"

"You would be too, if you had any sense." She opened the door of Kay's car. "Stop fighting me or I'll toss you into the back seat of the cruiser and drag you there." Mitch shouted as she scanned the horizon. "Please, Kay, please go. I need you safe. I'm headed there too."

"Okay, okay." Kay jumped into her car. "I guess every second I argue puts you at risk."

Mitch closed the door and waved Kay out. She sighed with relief as Kay turned her car around and shot along the highway in the direction of Kingsway.

Mitch jumped in her cruiser just as the hail started. She grabbed the radio and struggled to hear over the pounding of the ice balls as they rained down on the cruiser. "I missed that, please repeat."

The dispatcher came on again, his voice crackling with static as he spoke. "Mrs. Cornish says Dr. Cornish was at Kingsway checking on some chickens, but she left ten minutes ago. She can't reach her by phone to tell her about the tornadoes."

"I'm near Kingsway. I'll look for her." Mitch cursed as she drove. Why was Lauren driving around during a tornado warning? The baby was due in two months. She should've been home with Callie, with her feet up.

The cruiser swerved as a gust hit her broadside. She was ready and held the car on the road, but she couldn't keep in her lane. A second later, a large recycling bin blew by as if it were a leaf in autumn. She had to find cover or die. She couldn't see Kay anymore and hoped she'd reached Kingsway.

Mitch followed Kay's route, glancing over her shoulder for the status of the tornado, thankful that the brief burst of hail had stopped.

"What the hell?" On a side road Lauren's truck was parked crookedly, stuck in a ditch. "Shit." She stomped on the brake, spun the steering wheel, and roared down the side road. She skidded to a stop and jumped out beside the truck. The driver's door was open, but she didn't see Lauren.

"Lauren. Lauren," she yelled. The wind whipped through the fields carrying a thick cloud of dust with particles of wheat debris mixed in. She covered her nose and mouth with the collar of her shirt and struggled to breathe. It sounded like a freight train was about to barrel over them.

She looked up and down the road and checked the ditches until she found Lauren huddled in the mud with her arms wrapped around her large pregnant belly.

Mitch slid down into the ditch and grabbed Lauren's arm. "Get up. We have to run. There's still time to find cover."

"I'm fine here." She huddled around her belly, her eyes wide with fear.

"Get up, *now!* There's flying debris and it'll only get worse. You're not safe." An entire fence panel sailed past and then broke into lethal pieces midair. "Oh shit." They were out of time already. She dropped on top of Lauren, covering her body with her own and wrapped her arms around her. She closed her eyes against the dust and grunted as the debris rained down on her.

"Get off me. Get the heck off me, Mitchell."

When the wind died down for a minute, Mitch rolled off with a groan and shifted until she lay on her stomach.

"You're bleeding. Something hit you in the head. You're right. We have to run," Lauren said.

If she hadn't been in so much pain, Mitch would've laughed. Lauren had said she was right. Callie would laugh until she cried. Lauren never agreed with Mitch. "Too late."

"Your ass has a stick in it."

"Screw off, Cornish."

"You screw off, Mitchell. Not a stick up your ass, genius. A stick in it. Wood has slammed into your left butt cheek and your leg."

"Pull it out." Mitch groaned and tried to look but couldn't angle right.

"Not the best decision. You leave imbedded items for the hospital to remove."

Mitch tried to reach the stick, but couldn't. "Aren't you a doctor?"

"For animals. That's close for you, but we still need to leave it."

Mitch made a shooing motion. "Go back to Kingsway. The back door will be unlocked. Get to the basement." It was a risk. Lauren couldn't walk fast right now, but she had a hell of a better chance of making it to Kingsway, which wasn't far, than she did if she stayed here. She just had to pray the tornado held off long enough.

"You're coming with me."

Mitch shifted and pain shot from her butt to her ankle, and she felt the trickle of blood slide over her thigh. Her leg was all but useless. "I can't walk. You go. I order you to go."

"Come with me."

"We're not in a heroic war movie where you can support me. I'm too big and you shouldn't lift heavy items."

"Then we stay here and find cover. I'm not abandoning you, and besides, I'm not sure I can run that far by myself," Lauren said as she looked across the field.

"Run while the wind has dropped and before it picks up again. The ditch is poor cover. Go, please, Lauren. I won't have anything to do with your losing the baby or getting hurt, please."

"What about you?"

"Why won't anybody listen?" Mitch shouted. *"Are all veterinarians as pigheaded as you and Kay?"*

Lauren looked around them. "The tornado is over. No more debris."

"Over? Look at the sky! The clouds are already circling," Mitch yelled, *"Go, go, go you stupid, stubborn, frustrating woman!"*

"Okay, okay." Lauren helped Mitch drag herself under a bridge that spanned the ditch and hurried away as quickly as her large belly would allow.

Mitch lay in the mud under the bridge with her eyes closed and thought of Kay and of happier days making love and kayaking at the lake. Kay was so tender with her and Cody. She smiled at the memory of Kay's jokes and the endless plates of French toast she'd made Kay make.

Kay's eyes were a brilliant intelligent blue, but when she was happy, they turned a shade violet. Today they'd been a dull blue, filled with resignation and sadness. It cut into her to see them that way.

Mitch shaded her eyes from flying dirt and looked up at the inky sky. With any luck the tornado would shift and fail to touch down, but if it did, she'd be in trouble when debris really started to fly again. The bridge offered some semblance of safety, but a big enough twister could rip the bridge away too. If only she'd been able to tell Kay she loved her. But nature wasn't going to give her a chance.

CHAPTER THIRTY-THREE

Kay cowered on the couch in the basement of Kingsway and listened to the wind roar overhead. She stood when it died down. "I don't understand where Mitch is. She was right behind me."

"She's okay," Maggie said. "She knows what she's doing."

"Hello, Mrs. King? It's Lauren Cornish."

Kay and Maggie ran to the base of the stairs and met Lauren. Lauren slipped near the bottom and might have fallen but Maggie caught her.

"Are you okay, dear?" asked Mrs. King.

Lauren looked exhausted and unsteady on her feet. "My truck went into a ditch. Mitch found me and told me where to go, but she's injured, and she's hiding under the bridge over your ditch. She can't walk."

"I'll get her," Maggie said.

Mrs. King clasped Maggie's arm. "No, it's too dangerous."

"Gran, I've got to go. She's my friend. We can't just leave her out there."

Kay stepped beside Maggie. "I'm coming too." She followed Maggie upstairs, her pulse hammering in her neck. The thought of Mitch being alone and injured made her want to vomit. When they exited the house, Maggie started to run toward the bridge. Kay followed as fast as she could and reached them as Maggie emerged from the ditch half carrying Mitch. She had blood dripping from her head and leg.

"We have to hurry," Maggie said. "It looks bad."

Kay slung her arm around Mitch's waist and helped propel her to the house. In an attempt to keep from panicking, she mentally ran through how she could help Mitch, if only she had her medical gear. When blood dripped from Mitch's head and onto her shirt, she walked faster and prayed they'd make it in time. The wind howled and the sky grew pitch-black.

Ten minutes later, Kay and Maggie staggered downstairs with Mitch almost limp between them. Blood oozed from Mitch's head and the outer cloth of her bulletproof vest was torn where debris had bounced off her back. Her leg dragged, leaving a bloody smear behind her. Maggie and Kay lowered Mitch onto a sleeping bag on the floor.

"Thank goodness," Lauren said. "Mitch protected me from the debris. I think she's cut up pretty bad. That stick in her leg looked serious."

"Maggie, do you have anything to drink?" Mitch mumbled. "This hurts like a f—hurts painfully. Hurts painfully."

"Bad idea. Don't give her any alcohol," Kay said.

"I agree with Kay," Lauren said.

"Quit pushing into my business, Cornish."

"You are my business, Mitchell. You're part of my family and as soon as we get out of here, you'll need surgery to remove that stick from your—butt."

"Both of you, quit yelling," Kay said. "Mitch, honey, alcohol doesn't mix with anesthetic." Kay concentrated and just managed to keep the worry from her voice.

"What anesthetic?" Mitch asked. "Do you vets carry it in little vials around your necks? Feel free to use it, if you do."

Maggie shrugged. "Kay, is there anything to do for her pain? What if we remove the sticks?"

Kay drew Maggie closer to Mitch. "See this chunk of wood in her leg? The wound is bleeding and it could be near a major artery. If we pull the stick out, we might tear the artery and cause her to bleed to death." Kay's eyes welled with tears at the idea, but she fought them down. Mitch needed her help, not her tears.

"We'll leave it for the hospital to remove," Kay said. "Our job is to keep her comfortable and keep her from moving. Give her only a few sips of water at a time. She'll need emergency surgery and her stomach needs to be empty."

"Where're your first aid supplies?" Lauren asked.

Maggie pointed and Lauren strode to the storage shelves, returning a few minutes later with medical supplies. Kay bandaged Mitch's leg, stabilizing the chunk of wood to prevent it from moving. She felt bad when Mitch sucked in air at the pain, but once it was stable, she settled a little. Kay turned to the head wound next, which looked superficial, but was still oozing blood.

"You must remain still," Kay said. "If you move you could tear an artery."

"Vets are such bullies," Mitch mumbled.

Kay ignored the remark. Mitch was in pain and thus entitled to be crabby.

Maggie squatted beside Mitch. "Including yours, Mitch?" Maggie chuckled. "Is Kay the boss of you?"

Mitch squeezed her eyes shut. "I don't have Kay anymore. I messed up, and I lost her."

Kay wrapped her arms around herself. The agony in Mitch's voice showed more pain than when she complained about the sticks lodged in her body. Had she caused this? Was this her fault?

Kay lay beside Mitch. She placed a pad on the cut on Mitch's head and applied pressure. Mitch grunted softly. "Val has been reminding me for days you were only doing your job. I get it and I'm sorry for being a bitch. It was my baggage, not anything you did." The truth of it stung, but when she saw it for what it was, all the anger fell away. Now she just needed to make things right.

Mitch mumbled something.

"I can't hear you."

"I miss you. I'm so sorry I hurt you, but I swear I didn't tell anyone about your past. I know you felt betrayed, and I know you hate me. But I just want you back."

"I don't hate you." Kay caressed Mitch's cheek. "I'm miserable without you, you great, brave goof."

Mitch laughed slightly and Kay joined her.

"How is this funny?" Lauren asked.

Kay glanced up at Lauren who stood over them with a bottle of water and a straw. "Private joke." She took the bottle and fed Mitch a few sips.

"How is it you're here?" Lauren asked when Kay got more comfortable with Mitch's head on her lap.

"Mitch chased me from a picnic area on the highway. She found me staring at the clouds and watching the wind as if I were a newbie to the area and had never heard of tornados."

"Well, you are new, aren't you?" Lauren pulled a chair over and sat down.

"I don't remember any tornados in Prince Edward Island, but we have hurricanes. It shouldn't have been such a leap for me to register the wind and the dark sky and go for cover. But I was distracted." Kay shrugged. "She ordered me to drive here and hide in the basement."

"I thought I'd lost her." Kay's voice caught on the last word. "I could still lose her if she bleeds out." She caressed Mitch's check and brushed away some dirt.

"Looks like you did a great job with the bandages." Lauren lifted her chin to point toward Mitch, who seemed to be dozing. "If she stays still, she'll be okay."

"I'm such a fool."

"You're not a fool." Lauren's face creased in confusion as she peered at the bandages. "You did an amazing job."

Kay grimaced. "I'm a fool for pushing Mitch away. I love her. I love how she's tough and gentle and how she cares about her chosen family. Mitch cares about the community and I love how she cares about her kids."

"Her kids? Mitchell doesn't have children."

"Does too," Maggie said from her place against the wall. She hadn't taken her eyes off Mitch.

Kay smiled at her. "She has a whole slew of kids. A bunch of LGBT kids have gravitated to her. She's a good listener." Kay fished a tissue from her pocket and blew her nose.

"So much about her I never understood." Lauren stared at Mitch with respect in her eyes.

"What can I do?" Kay said. "Mitch could never love an addict."

"But you're in recovery." Lauren sighed. "I suck at this. Callie's the smart one about relationships and she'd say to tell Mitch what's in your heart so you'd know you'd tried. She'd say you're only holding yourself back by identifying with a label instead of the person you are. You were hurt and scared."

How had Lauren figured it out? She'd hoped everyone thought she was just angry at Mitch. Being hurt sounded too much like being humiliated. But she was wrong. She'd *allowed* herself to be humiliated.

"Somebody, please shoot me or drug me. My leg is killing me." Mitch rolled onto her side as she searched for a more comfortable position.

"Stop moving!" Kay gripped her arm to stop her moving. "If you tear an artery and bleed to death, I'll—I'll kill you."

Mitch settled on her side. "Come here."

Kay remained still and took deep breaths. How much blood had Mitch lost? Was she pale from blood loss or pain?

"Please, come here. I need to kiss you. But I'm forbidden to move."

Kay shifted carefully from under Mitch's head and Maggie was quickly there with a pillow. Kay lay beside Mitch and took the proffered kiss. "I wouldn't really kill you, but I'd make you watch four straight hours of ice dancing as a punishment."

Lauren got up and motioned for Maggie to follow her, and they moved to the couch beside Mrs. King to give Mitch and Kay some semblance of privacy.

Mitch managed a half-smile. "A fate worse than death." Mitch's expression turned serious. "Are you still angry at me for the investigation?"

"No. I've been sensitive and stubborn and foolish. It was your job to find the drugs, but you revealed private information about me."

"I didn't. Someone else did, and I'll find out who it was one day. But the important thing is who you are now. Not who you were. You're the strong, capable, kind vet we all know and love. Nothing changes that."

"Having the whole town know is still embarrassing."

"I expect it will be for a while, but nobody in this town will turn on a veteran because she had problems when she got home. And isn't it freeing to have your secret exposed and to discover people still love you?"

She'd never thought of it that way. "Maybe the gossip will die once everybody knows, which should be in about two more days." Kay laughed. Mitch had used the word love and she wasn't sure if she was excited or terrified or both.

Mitch squeezed Kay's hand. "Being an ex-addict doesn't make you less of a person, Kay. If anything, it shows how strong you are to overcome it and build a life."

"I planned to run away from Thresherton. But I have so many reasons to stay. I like my job, my friends, and…"

"And?"

"You, you big goof." She pressed her finger to Mitch's lips. "No more talking. Try to rest."

"Will you stay with me?"

She kissed Mitch again. "I'll be right here when you wake up." She stroked Mitch's cheek until her eyes closed. She lay beside her, uncomfortable as hell on the cold cement floor, but shards of ice could grow up from the floor and she wouldn't move. Wouldn't leave Mitch. Not now when she needed her. Maybe not ever. The thought warmed her. Now they just had to make sure Mitch got medical help.

They could hear the wind raging outside, along with hammering of debris as it hit the house, and conversation was sparse. When the storm ended and it grew quiet once again, Maggie ran outside, and returned a few minutes later. "The power is out, and the house phone and my cell are dead."

"Can you drive us to the hospital?" Lauren asked.

"Sure. The road's a mess but I'll clean it off as we go."

Lauren and Kay followed Maggie outside. Maggie disappeared and ten minutes later, arrived in her rusty old farm truck. Kay frowned. "This?"

"Mitch needs to lie down, and my farm truck is all she'll fit in so she can stretch out. I put a foot of fresh straw in the back to cushion it a little."

"If it's good enough for the animals…" Lauren said.

They couldn't carry Mitch, so they helped her to her feet and supported her while she staggered upstairs.

Mitch chuckled when she saw the truck. "Funny, kid. I'm not a cow."

"We need a hospital and soon. Don't be a pain, Mitchell. Maggie's smart. The straw's clean and you'll appreciate padding between you and the floor. I know I do."

Kay winced at the sharp tone of Lauren's voice that was laced with fear. She pointed to the cab of the truck. "You ride inside, Lauren."

"It hurts less to lie down. I banged up my hip and I have blood spotting. Gross, sorry."

Mitch's expression turned to horrified as she registered Lauren's comment. "Blood? The baby?"

"Don't know. I'm trying to stay calm, so help me out, everyone, and don't fuss. Let's go to the hospital. Nice and slow, Maggie. Stick to forty and avoid the bumps. Mitch and I are stable, but the jarring over rough surfaces will be bad for us."

It took an hour of slow driving to get to the Thresherton hospital and Maggie had to stop a few times so she and Kay could move debris from their path. When they arrived, Kay ran to the back of the truck, while Maggie ran inside.

A minute later, a doctor jumped in beside Mitch. "Forget me," Mitch said. "Take Lauren first. She's pregnant and took a pounding in the storm."

Hospital staff helped Lauren down from the truck onto a stretcher and wheeled her into the hospital. Kay stayed with Mitch.

"Will the baby be okay?" Mitch asked a nurse.

"I don't know, but we need to take care of you." The nurse looked at the debris and head wound and started giving orders.

Hospital staff loaded Mitch on a second stretcher, and it looked like she might have passed out with the pain. Fresh blood slid from the head wound and seeped through the bandage on her leg. They moved quickly as they rolled her inside. Kay found a phone and took a deep breath before she called Callie, and then Val. And then there was nothing she could do but wait. Maggie found a deck of cards and they played whatever they could think of to keep them distracted, but the minutes seemed to drag past.

Eventually, Val arrived in the hospital waiting room, dropped into a chair beside Kay, and hugged her. "How's Mitch?"

"Surgery to remove the wood from her leg. It seems like it's taking ages, but they were waiting for a vascular surgeon. How's Lauren?" Kay asked.

"Stable, but scared. She has a few scrapes and bruises. The doctors want to keep her here for a few days. Callie's with her."

"The RCMP detachment commander was here to take charge of Mitch's weapon. He said he'd call her mom, but I doubt she'll come."

Val fished out her phone. "That reminds me, Callie asked me to call her mom." Val punched numbers and hung up after a brief conversation. "She's on her way."

Kay sat quietly with Val as they worried for their friends and waited for information.

"Maggie, it just occurred to me that Cody, Mitch's dog, is home alone. He's probably terrified. Can you swing by her place and check on him? There's a key under a rock by the back door."

Maggie practically leapt from her seat, clearly relieved not to have to sit in limbo. "Totally. Want me to bring anything back? Like, clothes or whatever?"

Kay shook her head, hoping she was doing the right thing by allowing Maggie into Mitch's house without her there. "No, thanks. Just make sure Cody is okay. Maybe take him out, give him some love. I'll go to her place and get her things once we know how long she'll be here."

Maggie waved as she practically ran from the waiting room.

Kay had worked on one of the nurse's beloved dogs, and through her got regular updates on Mitch, who'd made it out of surgery. The branch had missed her main artery by millimeters, but she'd be okay. Eventually, Callie joined them, and Kay moved so Callie could sit between her and Val.

Callie took Kay's hand. "How's Mitch?"

"Doing well and in recovery," Kay said.

"Thank God," Callie said. "My wife and my best friend at the same time. It's a wonder I could drive I was shaking so hard."

"How's Lauren?"

"Asleep." Callie pulled a worn tissue from her pocket and blew her nose. "I hid in the basement with Becky and our pets and listened to the wind howl. I closed the shutters over the windows in the horse barn and opened the cattle barn so my cows could shelter inside. What more could I do?" Callie sobbed. "I couldn't do anything for Lauren. I couldn't protect her. I was afraid I'd be a widow again. And then Mitch was hurt too." Callie croaked out her words as painful sobs stole her voice.

Val took Callie in her arms. "Ah, Callie, shush. You mom is on her way. Ronnie will pick her up at the Saskatoon airport tonight. Lauren and Mitch will be okay."

"Thanks." Callie cried some more.

Kay rubbed Callie's back. "Val's right. They'll both be okay." She was happy Callie's mom was coming. Sometimes you still needed your mom, even when you were in your thirties.

Kay blew her nose and focused on the door to the surgical wing. She would be there when the nurses said she could sit with Mitch. They were severe wounds, but Mitch was strong. She would be fine. She had to be, because it would take more than a tornado to tear them apart. Mitch was the only woman who had captured her heart and soul. She'd never walk away again.

Chapter Thirty-four

F ive days after the tornado, Kay looked out the windows of Mitch's house, contentment filling her. The trash and other debris that the storm had brought had been cleaned up by Mitch's neighbors. It was a warm sunny day and the sky was a brilliant clear blue. If it weren't for half of Mitch's fence being blown away, she'd never have known the tornado had passed so close.

She picked up the phone when it rang. It was Callie again. They'd spoken every day since the storm. "How's Lauren doing today?" Kay asked.

"She's sore, but the huge bruise on her hip isn't as painful. She's just happy to be home. She's still on bed rest and she's not going back to PVS. The baby's due in two months, and she was supposed to work for another month, but I told her she couldn't go back to work until after her maternity leave. She's worried about dumping all her work on you."

"You tell her we'll cope with the work and to stay in bed. We're so glad she's okay and that Little Corny is safe."

Callie chuckled. "Has the name Little Corny caught on everywhere? Aren't you and Val just teasing Lauren?"

"We are, but we promise to drop it when the baby's born or until one of you is pregnant with the next Little Corny."

Callie laughed. "You never know."

"Your mom dropped by yesterday to visit Mitch. I forgot you all knew each other back in British Columbia."

"It was a lifetime ago. Ronnie drove my mom into Saskatoon this morning. She's headed home, but I liked having her here. How's Mitch?"

"She's happy to be home, but she's hurting."

"Is she as good a patient as Lauren?"

"Is Lauren a good patient?"

"Lauren does what I tell her."

"Then no, Mitchell is not a good patient. Mitchell is stubborn, and after breakfast I threatened to sit on her head if she didn't stop walking around the house."

"She's not used to it. Nobody's ever looked after her. She needs time to adjust. Do you want me to drop off more food?"

"Come for another visit, but no more food, *please*. Half of Thresherton has brought food for her. I persuaded Maggie and the other kids to stay and help us eat it. They didn't need much coaxing. They're watching the game."

"What game?"

"Isn't there always some kind of game on?" Kay didn't try to hide the sarcasm in her voice. "Don't you watch? Aren't you into sports?"

"I play sports. I don't watch them. The only games we watch are Becky's, the Grey Cup, and sometimes the Olympics. Don't tell anyone or we'll lose our Canadian citizenship, but none of us follows hockey."

Kay laughed. "I'll keep your secret." She glanced into the living room. Mitch was lying on the couch with one large hand resting on Cody's head as he lay in his bed on the floor beside her. "I'm running a hospital with two patients."

"How's Cody?"

"Moving better and insists on being with Mitch every second. Mitch is lying on the couch drinking beer through a straw. She's only allowed one a day because of her medications. I offered to buy her a Wonder Woman sippy cup. I thought it was practical, but she forbade me. She's fed up with being teased. Jo Scott kidded her about getting shot in the ass by a tornado. I mean, how is that funny?"

Kay grinned as she listened to Callie laugh. There'd been little laughter from Poplarcreek since the tornado. It was a hopeful sound. "Time to go and feed everyone again. Talk to you tomorrow?"

"Yes, see you," Callie said.

Kay warmed up one of the donated casseroles for lunch. She carried a plate to Mitch while Maggie and the others served themselves. "Try to eat all of this."

"Thanks." Mitch nodded and ate dutifully, if not with an abundance of appetite.

Kay sat on the floor beside the couch and fed Cody a handful of carrots as a snack. He was walking better, but not anywhere near fully healed. She kissed Cody on the top of the head. "You're a good boy, Cody."

After the game, Maggie and the others left after giving Mitch plenty of teasing. The kids loved her, it was obvious, and their hero being down for the count had scared them. Mitch was tired and hurting and moaned as she tried to get comfortable on the couch. Cody whined in sympathy.

"Why not take your meds and go to bed?" Kay asked.

Mitch scrutinized the pill bottle Kay handed her. "I'm all right. I don't want those here. I wish you hadn't filled the prescription."

Kay frowned. "You can bring painkillers into your house. I won't take any."

Mitch looked surprised. "I know you won't take my painkillers, but you told me how addictive they are. I don't want them for the same reason, and I know you'd never start up again."

Kay felt bad for her gut defensive reaction and reined herself in. "But they're safe for you, as long as you know when to quit. I hide Cody's pain pill in a piece of hotdog. If you're scared, I could do the same for you."

"Okay, one, but hidden in a piece of brownie."

Kay laughed and helped Mitch to bed. She fetched the pill, settled Cody on the floor of the bedroom, and left them both with a kiss on the forehead. She collected the dishes and carried them to the kitchen.

With reluctance, she sat at the table in front of her computer. She was working, but not accomplishing as much as she hoped. Every time she started to type, her mind wandered, and she pictured Mitch. Her wide mischievous grin and the way the skin beside her eyes crinkled with delight when she smiled. In her mind, Kay kissed the wrinkles and ran a finger over them, admiring how they framed Mitch's smiling hazel eyes. "Focus, Gallant." She scrolled through her computer files and became enveloped by science.

Later in the evening, shuffling steps filtered from the bathroom. Kay knocked on the door. "Do you need any help?"

"I've got this covered. Been doing it for many years."

Kay smiled at the wisecrack. It was a good sign and meant Mitch felt better. "Are you hungry?"

"Starving."

Another good sign. "Come to the kitchen when you're ready." Kay heated a bowl of stew and put it on the counter with a large glass of milk. Mitch could eat standing or lying down.

Kay took Cody outside and returned ten minutes later. She caught Mitch with her mouth full and a guilty expression on her face. "You look like a chipmunk."

Mitch chewed a few more times and swallowed. "I'm sorry. I should've waited for you, but I was starving."

"Go ahead. I didn't wait for you. I ate a bowl earlier."

"This stew is awesome, as delicious as anything Callie ever made."

Kay straightened and crossed her arms over her chest. "Oh? As delicious as Callie's?"

Mitch froze with her mouth full and looked wide-eyed at Kay for a few seconds before chewing and swallowing. "I meant that as a compliment."

"I see. And Callie Cornish's cooking is the benchmark from which we're all measured?"

Mitch hung her head in apology. "Sorry."

"I'm the one who should be sorry. Confession time." Kay busied herself pouring Mitch another glass of milk while Mitch regarded her with a worried expression. "You're eating Callie's stew. She dropped it off yesterday with a few other meals to freeze for later."

Kay opened the refrigerator and pointed to the shelves full of bowls and plastic containers. "The entire community is donating food. I turned two women away this morning. I explained to them we couldn't eat all the food already delivered." Mitch blushed, and Kay caressed her cheek. "This help is a credit to you and shows how well you're thought of in Thresherton."

Mitch stirred her stew.

Kay squeezed Mitch's arm. "You're shocked, aren't you?" She slipped her arms around Mitch from the side, being careful not to touch her wounds. "The community has rallied around you. I've done no yardwork. Sonny, Ronnie, and Val have dropped by with food. Your kids helped me with Cody and cleaned the house before you came home from the hospital. Everyone loves you."

Mitch looked at her but didn't say anything.

Kay saw the unasked question floating in a bubble above Mitch's head, but the time didn't feel exactly right. They still had things to discuss.

When dinner was over, she settled Mitch on the couch with the sports channel. Cody curled up in his bed beside the couch.

She returned to her computer, but she couldn't concentrate. What could she say? What did she want? What could be better than having a family like Lauren did? Surely not another degree, or another twenty casual sexual encounters. Thresherton was a great town and she loved working at PVS, but more importantly she had Mitch. Solid, steady, Mitch with her big heart and protective spirit.

She tried to concentrate on her work, but the words melted away as if of no significance, and perhaps they *were* irrelevant compared to love and having a family. She had her career, but it wasn't enough anymore. A career couldn't fill the empty room in her heart. Only love could do that.

Kay glanced at Mitch stretched out on the couch and shut her computer with decision. She walked over and sat on the floor by Mitch's head.

Mitch clicked off the television.

"Do you like having me here?"

Mitch nodded. "Very much."

"I want to be with you. I don't want to be anywhere else."

"You're not moving to the US?" Mitch searched her face, her eyes hopeful.

"Not anymore. Once my residency's done, I'll have no job in Saskatoon, but I'll still be working at PVS." Kay scooted closer to Mitch and pressed Mitch's hand to her lips for a second before tugging Mitch's arm around her body. "What if I stayed?" she asked.

"Yes. Yes, and yes. Stay." Mitch squeezed Kay and kissed the side of her head.

"Ian and Fiona offered me a full-time job and expect me to expand the small animal surgery client base at PVS and take referrals from other clinics."

"And what did you tell them?"

She bit her lip as she dove into the deep end of the emotion pool. "It depends on you. I'll stay at PVS if I can be with you. I never thought I'd say this, but I don't want Davis or Cornell. All I want is to move to Thresherton and be with you."

"What about the gossip?"

"To hell with the gossip. It'll die down or it won't. It doesn't matter. I get it now."

"Will you live with Cody and me?"

Kay cupped Cody's head and kissed him on the nose. "Cody's a good dog. He's quiet, well-trained, and does what he's told. You, not so much." She shifted onto one hip and cupped Mitch's face in her hands. "I'd love to live with you and Cody." Kay kissed her and rested her forehead against Mitch's. "I love you," Kay said.

"I'm so happy I can hardly speak." Mitch grabbed Kay's hand. "I love you too, and yes, I'd love for you to live with us. I'd ask you to move in tomorrow if I thought you would."

Kay hugged Mitch. "How about several nights a week and weekends while I finish my residency? Then every night starting at Christmas. Every minute I can, I'll be with you." She kissed Mitch to seal the pact.

"Will you regret not going to the US? Will you regret not following the plans you laid out?"

"Never. It would've been an adventure, but you and Cody are all the adventure I want. And there's lots of professional fulfillment waiting for me at PVS." She took a deep breath. "The chaos made me see that I've been running. I was worried that if I set down roots anywhere, I'd fail again. If I kept moving, my past wouldn't catch up with me. But it did, and you know? It sucked, but it isn't the end of the world. I don't want to run anymore."

Mitch's eyes were filled with unshed tears. "I love you, Kay."

"I love you too, Sergeant. And don't blush. You deserve the promotion for saving an unborn baby and rescuing two foolish veterinarians from a tornado." Kay shook her head. "Several months ago, I was planning to live alone and concentrate on my career. Now I'm in love and planning to stay with you. I'm so lucky. All I want is to be with you, forever."

Mitch pulled Kay in close and kissed her. "I'm never going to let you go. I'll look after you and you can look after me."

"Together, we'll build a new life and that will be enough adventure, for now." They sealed the proclamation with another kiss and laughed when Cody pushed between them for his share of the love.

"I love you too, Cody," Kay said.

Epilogue

Mitch stepped down and leaned against the wall. Just a few seconds of rest and she'd do another set. "Okay, Cody. Watch me." She smiled down at her dog and stretched out on the floor where he could watch her. He always watched her and would've followed her into bed if she let him. But he was sixty pounds of dalmatian and nothing was getting between her and Kay. She and Cody did their snuggling on the couch.

It didn't matter that it was Christmas Day. She did her physio every day, as often as possible, until she couldn't stand anymore. Nearly two months of inaction was driving her crazy. Mitch took a breath and lifted her foot to the top of the workout step and with a grunt pulled herself up. She paused for a second and stepped down.

"How many of those have you done?" Kay asked.

Mitch glanced over her shoulder. "Are you spying?"

"Yes. I came through ten minutes ago and you were doing steps. You're not supposed to overdo it."

Mitch stepped up with a grunt and spoke between gritted teeth. "I'm tired of being injured. Time to get stronger." She stepped down and gasped as pain shot from her waist down to her foot.

Kay scooted in and looped an arm around her waist. "And you are getting stronger, but if you overdo it, you'll have a setback."

Mitch allowed Kay to help her to the couch. At least she could sit like a normal human again. She didn't have to always be standing or lying down. "I know, I know. But look at Cody. He's running around just fine. I watched you guys from the window, and he was leaping in the snow." Cody had been cute, but watching a carefree Kay leap around and play with him, had been the best part of her day.

"His accident was six weeks before yours. He had a head start on the healing process." Kay held up a hand. "I know, and you'd have been up and around faster if there hadn't been an infection."

"I can't believe they missed some slivers."

"It's not like they could X-ray for the wood that was stuck in your leg. It wouldn't show up and your surgeons did their best."

"I guess." Mitch scowled. She didn't feel like a cop these days. She just answered the phone and helped walk-ins. And then there were endless hours on the computer doing research for other officers. They appreciated the help, but she was bored. "I'm so tired of sitting behind a desk. I want to be out in a cruiser again."

"And you will, eventually. Now quit grumbling and go get dressed." Kay glanced at her watch. "We're expected at Poplarcreek in an hour."

Mitch started to get up but overbalanced and fell back into the couch. Kay didn't reach to help her up. They'd had that argument already. Kay stood patiently and chewed her bottom lip while she waited.

Mitch tried again and as she stood, accepted her cane from Kay. She was a little sore, but wouldn't admit it. She needed to do lots of physio until she was strong enough to pass the physical at work and get let out of the office.

"I'll be quick," Mitch said as she walked to the bedroom. She concentrated on walking evenly but couldn't hide her limp. Okay, so doubling up on physio wasn't smart. She slowly turned as pivoting was out, for now. "You look lovely, by the way. I love that sweater." She waggled her eyebrows.

"Flirt. Now go get dressed."

Mitch headed to the bedroom.

"And thanks, I love my new sweater," Kay said.

Mitch laughed. Callie had picked it out for her to give to Kay for Christmas. There was no way she'd have managed the shopping mall and she didn't know what to buy anyway. The sweater was a perfect blue and made Kay's eyes pop, and bonus, it was just tight enough to show off her trim figure with a hint of cleavage.

When Mitch was dressed, Kay collected the dessert they were bringing and drove them to Poplarcreek. That was another thing she was tired of. Call her old-fashioned, but Mitch liked to be the one behind the wheel.

Becky opened the front door. "Mom, they're here. Hiya, Mitch." Becky and Bobby leaped down the two steps. They each slung an arm around Mitch's waist and propelled her toward the stairs.

"I can walk."

"Callie said to make sure you didn't slip. I shoveled, but it's still slippery," Bobby said.

Mitch didn't argue as there would be no point. They were doing what Callie said and everyone did that.

Kay followed them in and gave the cake box to Jules. "Are we late?"

Jules shook her head. "Right on time."

Callie kissed Mitch on the cheek and then Kay. "Merry Christmas. Dinner's almost ready. Becky and Bobby, please finish setting the table." Callie tipped her head toward the living room door. "Lauren's in front of the fire. You have just enough time to say hi before we eat."

Mitch looked around and took in the table laden with dishes of food. Callie didn't need her help and never had. Kay wouldn't be allowed to wash dishes either, not with Jules and Bobby around. She loved how Callie had taken to the teens Mitch mentored. Callie had been a bit miffed that Mitch hadn't involved her before, but she'd forgiven her. Jules had a knack for working with animals, and Callie had hired her on weekends to help at Poplarcreek, with the promise of a full-time job in the summer. PVS had taken Bobby on for Saturday mornings and some days after school. Jacks wasn't fully mobile yet, but she and Kay were helping at the veterans center a couple of nights a month. One of the veterans had been a schoolteacher and was helping Jacks catch up on her reading.

"Hi, kid." Mitch gave Jacks a one-armed hug. Jacks was sitting at the table folding Callie's good cloth napkins for the dinner table. "How's your physio going?"

"It's going. Doing lots of walking and stairs. I'll be playing ball again by spring."

"Good for you. I'm proud of you." Mitch smiled when Jacks sat a little straighter. Jacks was a young woman who would do important things in life. All she needed was some support and love.

"Come on, Mitch," Kay said after giving each of the teens a motherly hug and a kiss on the cheek. "Let's go see the baby."

Mitch started to walk to the living room door and stopped. "Is it safe?"

Kay sighed in exasperation. She opened the living room door and looked in. "Hi, Lauren." Kay returned and smirked at Mitch. "It's safe."

Mitch followed Kay into the living room. She didn't care what anyone said, she didn't want to see Lauren breastfeeding the baby. Natural or not, she wasn't having it. They were solid friends now and the past was in the past, but there were some things she wasn't ready for.

"There they are." Lauren gave Kay and then Mitch a hug. "Merry Christmas. Sit here, Mitch. Softest seat in the room."

Mitch sat on the couch and Kay slid a stool under her leg when she raised it.

"Who wants to hold her first?"

"Me, me." Kay held out her arms and accepted the baby from Lauren. "Hello, little Abby Sue. How are you, tiny one? Happy six weeks birthday." She kissed the baby on the forehead and nuzzled her nose into her neck.

Lauren glanced at Mitch's leg. "How're you doing?"

"Still on desk duty, but working full shifts and getting stronger."

"How was the drive over?"

Mitch waited for a beat for Kay to answer, but she was only interested in the baby. "The roads were clear. We made good time. We only had to stop for a couple of minutes to let a small herd of deer cross."

Lauren laughed. "How're the new super-safe wheels?"

Kay looked up. "Super safe. I love driving my new SUV. Although my car—"

"Was junk and wouldn't have lasted another winter," Mitch said. "You've been going back and forth to the college two or three times a week for the last few months. Your car wasn't safe." She scowled at Kay and dared her to argue. She'd insisted on the new vehicle, especially once the snow had come.

"You win, Mitch. She wins, doesn't she, Abby Sue? Mitch always wins." Kay kissed the baby and cuddled her.

Mitch snorted. She and Cody rarely won in their house. Not with Kay around. "So has Abby Sue stuck then?" Mitch asked Lauren.

"As a baby name. Abigail Suzanne Lee Cornish is quite a mouthful. She can decide when she's older if we drop the Sue bit."

"You didn't have to name her after me."

Lauren squeezed Mitch's forearm. "You saved our lives." She glanced at her baby. "Thanks for saving us." She cleared her throat in a vain attempt to disguise her emotion and then leaped to her feet. "How about a beer? You allowed to drink yet?"

"I am and Kay's driving. I'd love a beer."

"Kay, soda?"

"Thanks."

Lauren left the room and Kay carried Abby over and sat beside Mitch. "You want to hold her?"

"She's so tiny."

"She's not going to break. Here."

"Okay, but stay right there." Mitch took the baby and cradled her against her chest. She took a deep breath and forced herself to relax. She'd learned the hard way that if she was scared and her muscles tensed, that it scared Abby and made her cry. "There you go, little Abby. Aunty Kay says you're not going to break, but you are so tiny."

Kay leaned against Mitch's shoulder and caressed the side of Abby's face. "She's so beautiful. So perfect."

Mitch looked at Kay. Her face was soft and her eyes wide with wonder. "We could do this," she whispered. She held her breath to see if Kay would pull back and dismiss the idea as she had before. Kay was just getting used to living with her full-time. She hadn't heard a word about Cornell or Davis since Kay had moved in. Kay was focused on developing a surgery practice at PVS and finishing up her research articles. She should've been done with her research by now, but had gotten behind because she'd spent so much time in Thresherton looking after Mitch. "We could, you know. Have a baby."

Kay leaned back and looked up at her. "I'd like to have a baby with you, but a little later." She kissed her. "I love you, Mitch."

"I love you too." She kissed her back and listened to Abby make happy cooing noises. They would do this, someday. Maybe marriage and a couple of kids, when they were both ready. In the spring she'd get Kay to help her look for a bigger house. One with more space, so Kay could have a home office and there'd still be a couple of extra bedrooms. The adventure for them was just beginning.

About the Author

Nancy Wheelton graduated over twenty years ago from the Ontario Veterinary College in Guelph, Ontario, Canada. She spent the first few years after graduation working in a mixed animal practice in a small town in the province of Saskatchewan. Then she settled in the Great Lakes region of Ontario, where she is a practicing veterinarian.

When Nancy's not kayaking, photographing wildlife, or working on her beach house, she enjoys the crashing waves and sunsets while writing. Please visit her at Nancywheelton.com.

Books Available from Bold Strokes Books

Bury Me in Shadows by Greg Herren. College student Jake Chapman is forced to spend the summer at his dying grandmother's home and soon finds danger from long-buried family secrets. (978-1-63555-993-4)

Can't Leave Love by Kimberly Cooper Griffin. Sophia and Pru have no intention of falling in love, but sometimes love happens when and where you least expect it. (978-1-636790041-1)

Free Fall at Angel Creek by Julie Tizard. Detective Dee Rawlings and aircraft accident investigator Dr. River Dawson use conflicting methods to find answers when a plane goes missing, while overcoming surprising threats, and discovering an unlikely chance at love. (978-1-63555-884-5)

Love's Compromise by Cass Sellars. For Piper Holthaus and Brook Myers, will professional dreams and past baggage stop two hearts from realizing they are meant for each other? (978-1-63555-942-2)

Not All a Dream by Sophia Kell Hagin. Hester has lost the woman she loved and the world has descended into relentless dark and cold. But giving up will have to wait when she stumbles upon people who help her survive. (978-1-63679-067-1)

Protecting the Lady by Amanda Radley. If Eve Webb had known she'd be protecting royalty, she'd never have taken the job as bodyguard, but as the threat to Lady Katherine's life draws closer, she'll do whatever it takes to save her, and may just lose her heart in the process. (978-1-63679-003-9)

The Secrets of Willowra by Kadyan. A family saga of three women, their homestead called Willowra in the Australian outback, and the secrets that link them all. (978-1-63679-064-0)

Trial by Fire by Carsen Taite. When prosecutor Lennox Roy and public defender Wren Bishop become fierce adversaries in a headline-grabbing arson case, their attraction ignites a passion that leads them both to question their assumptions about the law, the truth, and each other. (978-1-63555-860-9)

Turbulent Waves by Ali Vali. Kai Merlin and Vivien Palmer plan their future together as hostile forces make their own plans to destroy what they have, as well as all those they love. (978-1-63679-011-4)

Unbreakable by Cari Hunter. When Dr. Grace Kendal is forced at gunpoint to help an injured woman, she is dragged into a nightmare where nothing is quite as it seems, and their lives aren't the only ones on the line. (978-1-63555-961-3)

Veterinary Surgeon by Nancy Wheelton. When dangerous drugs are stolen from the veterinary clinic, Mitch investigates and Kay becomes a suspect. As pride and professions clash, love seems impossible. (978-1-63679-043-5)

A Different Man by Andrew L. Huerta. This diverse collection of stories chronicling the challenges of gay life at various ages shines a light on the progress made and the progress still to come. (978-1-63555-977-4)

All That Remains by Sheri Lewis Wohl. Johnnie and Shantel might have to risk their lives—and their love—to stop a werewolf intent on killing. (978-1-63555-949-1)

Beginner's Bet by Fiona Riley. Phenom luxury Realtor Ellison Gamble has everything, except a family to share it with, so when a mix-up brings youthful Katie Crawford into her life, she bets the house on love. (978-1-63555-733-6)

Dangerous Without You by Lexus Grey. Throughout their senior year in high school, Aspen, Remington, Denna, and Raleigh face challenges in life and romance that they never expect. (978-1-63555-947-7)

Desiring More by Raven Sky. In this collection of steamy stories, a rich variety of lovers find themselves desiring more, more from a lover, more from themselves, and more from life. (978-1-63679-037-4)

Jordan's Kiss by Nanisi Barrett D'Arnuck. After losing everything in a fire Jordan Phelps joins a small lounge band and meets pianist Morgan Sparks, who lights another blaze, this time in Jordan's heart. (978-1-63555-980-4)

Late City Summer by Jeanette Bears. Forced together for her wedding, Emily Stanton and Kate Alessi navigate their lingering passion for one another against the backdrop of New York City and World War II, and a summer romance they left behind. (978-1-63555-968-2)

Love and Lotus Blossoms by Anne Shade. On her path to self-acceptance and true passion, Janesse will risk everything—and possibly everyone—she loves. (978-1-63555-985-9)

Love in the Limelight by Ashley Moore. Marion Hargreaves, the finest actress of her generation, and Jessica Carmichael, the world's biggest pop star, rediscover each other twenty years after an ill-fated affair. (978-1-63679-051-0)

Suspecting Her by Mary P. Burns. Complications ensue when Erin O'Connor falls for top real estate saleswoman Catherine Williams while investigating racism in the real estate industry; the fallout could end their chance at happiness. (978-1-63555-960-6)

Two Winters by Lauren Emily Whalen. A modern YA retelling of Shakespeare's *The Winter's Tale* about birth, death, Catholic school, improv comedy, and the healing nature of time. (978-1-63679-019-0)

Busy Ain't the Half of It by Frederick Smith and Chaz Lamar Cruz. Elijah and Justin seek happily-ever-afters in LA, but are they too busy to notice happiness when it's there? (978-1-63555-944-6)

Calumet by Ali Vali. Jaxon Lavigne and Iris Long had a forbidden small-town romance that didn't last, and the consequences of that love will be uncovered fifteen years later at their high school reunion. (978-1-63555-900-2)

Her Countess to Cherish by Jane Walsh. London Society's material girl realizes there is more to life than diamonds when she falls in love with a nonbinary bluestocking. (978-1-63555-902-6)

Hot Days, Heated Nights by Renee Roman. When Cole and Lee meet, instant attraction quickly flares into uncontrollable passion, but their connection might be short lived as Lee's identity is tied to her life in the city. (978-1-63555-888-3)

Never Be the Same by MA Binfield. Casey meets Olivia and sparks fly in this opposites attract romance that proves love can be found in the unlikeliest places. (978-1-63555-938-5)

Quiet Village by Eden Darry. Something not quite human is stalking Collie and her niece, and she'll be forced to work with undercover reporter Emily Lassiter if they want to get out of Hyam alive. (978-1-63555-898-2)

Shaken or Stirred by Georgia Beers. Bar owner Julia Martini and home health aide Savannah McNally attempt to weather the storms brought on by a mysterious blogger trashing the bar, family feuds they knew nothing about, and way too much advice from way too many relatives. (978-1-63555-928-6)

The Fiend in the Fog by Jess Faraday. Can four people on different trajectories work together to save the vulnerable residents of East London from the terrifying fiend in the fog before it's too late? (978-1-63555-514-1)

The Marriage Masquerade by Toni Logan. A no strings attached marriage scheme to inherit a Maui B&B uncovers unexpected attractions and a dark family secret. (978-1-63555-914-9)

Flight SQA016 by Amanda Radley. Fastidious airline passenger Olivia Lewis is used to things being a certain way. When her routine is changed by a new, attractive member of the staff, sparks fly. (978-1-63679-045-9)

Home Is Where the Heart Is by Jenny Frame. Can Archie make the countryside her home and give Ash the fairytale romance she desires? Or will the countryside and small village life all be too much for her? (978-1-63555-922-4)

Moving Forward by PJ Trebelhorn. The last person Shelby Ryan expects to be attracted to is Iris Calhoun, the sister of the man who killed her wife four years and three thousand miles ago. (978-1-63555-953-8)

Poison Pen by Jean Copeland. Debut author Kendra Blake is finally living her best life until a nasty book review and exposed secrets threaten her promising new romance with aspiring journalist Alison Chatterley. (978-1-63555-849-4)

Seasons for Change by KC Richardson. Love, laughter, and trust develop for Shawn and Morgan throughout the changing seasons of Lake Tahoe. (978-1-63555-882-1)

Summer Lovin' by Julie Cannon. Three different women, three exotic locations, one unforgettable summer. What do you think will happen? (978-1-63555-920-0)

Unbridled by D. Jackson Leigh. A visit to a local stable turns into more than riding lessons between a novel writer and an equestrian with a taste for power play. (978-1-63555-847-0)

VIP by Jackie D. In a town where relationships are forged and shattered by perception, sometimes even love can't change who you really are. (978-1-63555-908-8)

Yearning by Gun Brooke. The sleepy town of Dennamore has an irresistible pull on those who've moved away. The mystery Darian Benson and Samantha Pike uncover will change them forever, but the love they find along the way just might be the key to saving themselves. (978-1-63555-757-2)

A Turn of Fate by Ronica Black. Will Nev and Kinsley finally face their painful past and relent to their powerful, forbidden attraction? Or will facing their past be too much to fight through? (978-1-63555-930-9)

Desires After Dark by MJ Williamz. When her human lover falls deathly ill, Alex, a vampire, must decide which is worse, letting her go or condemning her to everlasting life. (978-1-63555-940-8)

Her Consigliere by Carsen Taite. FBI agent Royal Scott swore an oath to uphold the law, and criminal defense attorney Siobhan Collins pledged her loyalty to the only family she's ever known, but will their love be stronger than the bonds they've vowed to others, or will their competing allegiances tear them apart? (978-1-63555-924-8)

In Our Words: Queer Stories from Black, Indigenous, and People of Color Writers. Stories selected by Anne Shade and edited by Victoria Villaseñor. Comprising both the renowned and emerging voices of Black, Indigenous, and People of Color authors, this thoughtfully curated collection of short stories explores the intersection of racial and queer identity. (978-1-63555-936-1)

Measure of Devotion by CF Frizzell. Disguised as her late twin brother, Catherine Samson enters the Civil War to defend the Constitution as a Union soldier, never expecting her life to be altered by a Gettysburg farmer's daughter. (978-1-63555-951-4)

Not Guilty by Brit Ryder. Claire Weaver and Emery Pearson's day jobs clash, even as their desire for each other burns, and a discreet sex-only arrangement is the only option. (978-1-63555-896-8)

Opposites Attract: Butch/Femme Romances by Meghan O'Brien, Aurora Rey, Angie Williams. Sometimes opposites really do attract. Fall in love with these butch/femme romance novellas. (978-1-63555-784-8)

Swift Vengeance by Jean Copeland, Jackie D, Erin Zak. A journalist becomes the subject of her own investigation when sudden strange, violent visions summon her to a summer retreat and into the arms of a killer's possible next victim. (978-1-63555-880-7)

Under Her Influence by Amanda Radley. On their path to #truelove, will Beth and Jemma discover that reality is even better than illusion? (978-1-63555-963-7)

Wasteland by Kristin Keppler & Allisa Bahney. Danielle Clark is fighting against the National Armed Forces and finds peace as a scavenger, until the NAF general's daughter, Katelyn Turner, shows up on her doorstep and brings the fight right back to her. (978-1-63555-935-4)

When in Doubt by VK Powell. Police officer Jeri Wylder thinks she committed a crime in the line of duty but can't remember, until details emerge pointing to a cover-up by those close to her. (978-1-63555-955-2)